Praise for Jack Campbell's
LOST FLEET Series

"An excellent blend of real science and space action. I enjoyed myself thoroughly from first to last page."—Brandon Sanderson, #1 *New York Times* bestselling author of the Mistborn series

"Strong characters, complex politics on multiple worlds, battles against impossible odds, this book has the whole package."—Elizabeth Moon, Nebula Award–winning author

"Jack Campbell is one of the absolute masters of military science fiction."—Michael Mammay, author of *Generation Ship*

"Nobody brings the military to life like Campbell."—Myke Cole, author of *The Armored Saint*

"Combines the best parts of military SF and grand space opera."—*Publishers Weekly*

"Campbell has a sure hand with military SF balanced with political intrigue and heroic protagonists."—*Library Journal*

"Top-notch space opera."—*Booklist*

"Riveting battles, knotty dilemmas, desperate actions, and lower-deck humor."—*Kirkus Reviews*

"Campbell's genius is action in space."—Tor.com

RENDEZVOUS WITH
CORSAIR

A LOST FLEET COLLECTION

JACK CAMPBELL

JA**B**

Published by JABberwocky Literary Agency, Inc.

JABberwocky Literary Agency, Inc.
49 W. 45th Street, Suite #5N
New York, NY 10036
awfulagent.com/ebooks

ISBN 978-1-625676-54-2 (ebook)
ISBN 978-1-625676-55-9 (print)

CONTENTS

To Katherine Law and William Law
Because the kids are alright.

"Look within; do not allow the special quality or worth of anything
pass you by." (Marcus Aurelius, Meditations*)*

For S, as always.

CORSAIR

1

"HOLD them off as long as you can…"

The fleet commander's grim expression matched his tone of voice. He hated giving that order, Michael Geary realized. And not just because he was giving the order to his grandnephew. This wasn't the Black Jack that Michael had been told all his life he had to revere, a flawless officer focused solely on victory regardless of the cost. Instead of launching a grand, heroic assault which would have surely wiped out the rest of the Alliance fleet, Black Jack had tried to save every surviving ship. But the plan wasn't working exactly as it should and now a ship, Michael's ship, and her crew would have to be sacrificed to try to save the rest. This was a commander with only one right choice—and who hated making that choice.

Maybe Michael had been wrong about Black Jack. Maybe everyone had been wrong about him.

Michael had spent his whole life fighting against Black Jack's legacy. Being born a Geary, the endless war with the Syndicate Worlds devouring Alliance citizens and warships, meant your path was laid out for you. Join the fleet. Fight the Syndics. Try to act, try to fight, try to die, in a way that honored your great ancestor. Michael and his sister Jane had seen their aunts and uncles perish in battle, had lost their own parents the same way, and had known when the time came they would face similar fates.

Now it was Michael's turn. His turn not just to be the "hero," but to be the rear guard, making a last stand in the hope of saving others. Chance, or fate, had left *Repulse* not only closer to the Syndics, but also close to the fastest intercept trajectories for the nearest Syndic warships if they aimed for the slowest, most vulnerable, and critically important unit in the Alliance Fleet, the auxiliary *Titan*. To reach *Titan* as quickly as possible, those Syndics would have to pass through space close to *Repulse*.

Which meant, finally, with probably little time left to live, a few moments to grasp some of the reality of what his granduncle had faced a century ago.

"This isn't easy, is it?" he said to the fleet commander, Black Jack, the mythical hero back from the dead. His great-uncle. "I understand a bit now. I truly didn't want this. You do what you have to do, though, and it's up to your ancestors how it all turns out."

He exchanged only a few more words with his granduncle before he had to end the call. The enemy was too close, everyone else on the bridge of the battle cruiser *Repulse* waiting for him to tell them their fate.

"Engineering status," Michael called out.

"Main propulsion is still at thirty percent, Captain," Chief Petty Officer Sabit Taman replied.

"Any word on Lieutenant Nadu?"

"Still unconscious from injuries, Captain."

Since Commander Boiko had died in the initial ambush, that made Chief Taman the senior engineering officer aboard. "What are our chances of getting more out of main propulsion, Chief?"

Taman shook his head. "We're at maximum available for now. Estimated time for repairs is at least six hours."

"We're not even going to have one hour," Michael said. The crew needed to know what was happening. "All hands, this is the captain. *Repulse* has been ordered to screen the rest of the fleet as it repositions." The Alliance Fleet never retreated. It repositioned. "We will hold off the Syndics for as long as possible. To the honor of our ancestors!"

He looked at Chief Taman again. "Cut propulsion to zero. Make it look like our remaining main propulsion units failed under stress."

"Yes, Captain."

He made another call, to his executive officer, Commander Estrada. "I'm going to need every weapon back on line. Do whatever it takes."

Thecla Estrada replied in a steady voice. "You'll have them, Captain. We'll override safeties where we have to. May the living stars light your path."

She didn't expect any of them to live through this. Neither did he.

Several Syndic Hunter-Killers, what the Alliance usually called HuKs, a bit smaller and a bit faster than Alliance destroyers, tried to race past the apparently crippled battle cruiser, aiming to intercept the track of the Fast Fleet Auxiliary *Titan*. If *Titan* didn't get away, the Alliance Fleet's already small chances would shrink a lot further. The HuKs could have safely avoided *Repulse* by swinging wider, but that would have increased the distance they needed to cover, and given *Titan* more time to flee.

Suddenly reengaging *Repulse*'s full remaining propulsion and maneuvering capability, Michael swung the ship about and tore apart the first two HuKs with a barrage of hell-lance particle beams and grapeshot. The third came close enough to hit with *Repulse*'s null field, a short-range weapon that dissolved atomic bonds on the target. Most of that HuK, and its crew, vanished into a cloud of loose atoms.

Two more HuKs tried to sweep past *Repulse*, their focus also on the wallowing *Titan*. Michael Geary let his automated weapons controls take them out with another barrage of hell lances and specter missiles, his crew cheering as the enemy ships and their crews were annihilated.

The enemy were Syndics. The people the Alliance had been fighting for a century, while the Syndicate Worlds' rulers ordered atrocity after atrocity in hopes of forcing a victory. After all that, Syndics weren't seen as other humans anymore. They were just Syndics, their deaths cause for celebration.

Another five HuKs tried to accelerate past, but Michael brought *Repulse* about again and managed to kill one of them while crippling three more. Not a clean sweep, but close enough. The last HuK would catch *Titan*, but *Titan's* escorts could easily handle it.

"Well done, *Repulse*," he called out to the crew.

The mass of the Syndic flotilla was beginning to reach *Repulse*. A swarm of more HuKs, augmented by light cruisers, each individually not much of a threat to a battle cruiser, but in numbers able to wear down shields with barrages of hell lances and missiles.

"Forward shields are at twenty percent," Lieutenant Aiko reported from the weapons station. "Spot failures occurring in midships and stern shields."

Syndic heavy cruisers were reaching *Repulse*, followed by battle cruisers.

Repulse trembled as shots started coming through the shields, tearing through the hull and any sailor unfortunate enough to be in their path.

"Forward shields have collapsed. All missiles expended. Hell-lance batteries 1A, 3A, and 4B are out of action. All grapeshot expended."

Michael stared at his display, trying to judge whether the rest of the Alliance Fleet was far enough off to have escaped the

Syndic trap. Not that it mattered as far as *Repulse* was concerned. There was no way out for this ship.

"Multiple hull breaches. Hell-lance batteries 2B and 6B are out of action."

"Multiple hits in engineering," Chief Taman called, his voice still steady. "The power core is becoming unstable."

Enough, Michael thought. He'd done all he could. "All hands, this is Captain Geary. Abandon ship! I say again, abandon ship! Everyone get off!"

Repulse shuddered like a dying animal as more Syndic hits tore into her.

Michael unstrapped and stood up, gesturing at Lieutenant Aiko and Chief Taman and the rest of the crew on the bridge to get going and not wait for him.

He couldn't remember anything after that.

He didn't know how he got off the ship. He didn't know how many of his crew had survived, or even how long he'd been a prisoner of the Syndics here...or even where "here" was.

His cell was as featureless as it could be. No window. He couldn't even tell where the door was when it was closed. There was no way to measure time. Even the meal times and frequencies were deliberately staggered by the Syndics so they couldn't be used to count the days. He knew he'd been shifted to new locations sometimes, drugged and awakening in apparently the same cell but with tiny differences. And, rough as it was, he could count how many times he'd slept, hanging onto that number as one thing he could measure. That number was more than five hundred now. He'd been a prisoner for at least several months. Quite likely more than a year. Maybe years.

He'd been taught techniques, mental and emotional, for surviving prolonged periods of solitary confinement. He had played the mind games and meditated and (so far at least) had held any emotional deterioration at bay.

What had happened to the Alliance Fleet? Had the legendary Black Jack, miraculously returned from the dead, been able to save it? Or had it been destroyed, along with the last hope of the Alliance? Had the Alliance finally lost the war, as his captors claimed?

Hundreds of star systems belonged to the Alliance, and hundreds more to the Syndicate Worlds. With those kinds of resources, a war could go on and on, decade after decade, the Alliance refusing to lose and the Syndics refusing to stop trying to win. But, after nearly a century, the strain had been showing. That was why the insanely risky attack on the Syndic home star system had been approved, out of desperation. Michael had argued against it, for one of the few times in his life trying to use his status as a Geary to make people listen to him. Having been proven right when the Alliance Fleet ran head on into a Syndic ambush didn't bring him any joy.

He'd been interrogated quite a few times. The Syndic security agents always insisted the war was over, the Alliance having lost, but kept asking questions about John Geary. His great-uncle. Black Jack. He told them only things they'd already know. Yes, he was back. Michael didn't tell the Syndics that instead of dying a century ago in Grendel Star System during a last stand against the initial Syndic attack, Black Jack had been frozen in survival sleep, his escape pod damaged and drifting unnoticed amid the wreckage orbiting that star.

The Syndics always demanded more information. What did Black Jack want? What was he going to do? Very odd questions given their claim that Black Jack was dead, the Alliance Fleet destroyed, the Alliance defeated. Michael didn't have to feign ignorance, though. He had no idea what Black Jack would do. After only two brief conversations with the hero from the past, Michael had learned just enough to realize that the "legend" of his great-uncle wasn't the truth. But that didn't tell him what the truth really was.

And so Michael lay on the bunk in his cell, playing games in his mind to keep from going insane as who knew how many days went by, trying not to imagine a rescue that would probably never come.

Remembering growing up. Being told again and again that he had to do better. That a Geary had to be the best. Knowing that his path in life led straight to the fleet, and would end there somewhere in the endless war. Rebelling against that, refusing to serve, would have dishonored not only him, but also his parents, tarnishing them and the sacrifices they had made, and that was unthinkable. He and his sister Jane had promised each other they wouldn't marry anyone, wouldn't have children, so there wouldn't be another generation bound by that curse.

Remembering how he'd broken that promise, keeping it secret from almost everyone, and hating himself for it. Wishing he could have seen Kahoku again, wondering how their children were doing, wondering how they'd react if they ever learned their father's real name. No. He had to protect them from the Geary curse. And that meant never letting them know.

Not that he was likely to ever have the chance to tell them. Not anymore. Odds were he'd die here.

As if triggered by his thoughts, a low hum told Michael the door to the cell was opening, sections of the wall dissolving to reveal a woman. She had on a black skin suit designed to be worn under Syndic battle armor, revealing she was a Syndic soldier. In one hand, she held a pistol that stayed aimed at Michael as she walked into the cell. Her face bore scars from old wounds and a hard expression that held no hint of mercy.

Michael sat up and turned on the bunk, facing her, numb with the weariness of his long confinement. "If your masters have finally decided to get rid of me, go ahead and take your shot."

Her expression didn't change. "You want to die with your precious honor intact? Not this day. A Geary is too valuable."

Michael shrugged. "The Syndics have gotten nothing from me. You'll get nothing from me."

"Are you Black Jack's scion?"

He'd been expecting a shot that would end his life, not a question he couldn't understand. "His what?"

"His heir," she said, her words as hard as her expression. "Are you like Black Jack?"

Why did that question make him want to laugh? "Like him?" Michael shrugged again. "I've walked in his shadow my whole life. You try having a great-uncle with a superhuman legend, and we'll see how your self-confidence fares." He paused, thinking. "But a lot of things change when you get to meet the man behind the legend."

Michael looked at her, thinking that he should be honest with himself for once. "So, yeah, I guess I am like him. More like him than I ever wanted to admit. What does that matter to you?"

She lowered the weapon a bit, her eyes still fixed on him. "Because if you're like Black Jack, I have a deal for you."

Michael shook his head. "I don't make any deals with Syndics."

Her weapon came up again, aimed at his face. "My name is Executive Destina Aragon, commander of the 1233rd Assault Regiment. The Syndicate doesn't know about this deal. I want you to help me capture a mobile forces unit—and help me and my troops to get home."

A revolt? Alliance intelligence had reported on occasional mutinies by Syndic soldiers, always mercilessly crushed. But they happened sometimes when the Syndics demanded too much of their own "workers." "You're revolting against the Syndicate Worlds? And you need me to fly a captured Syndic spaceship?"

She nodded once, her eyes intent. "Decide, now. We've only got a few more minutes before the snake surveillance systems might realize I'm here."

"Snake?"

"Syndicate Internal Security Service. Snakes. My unit wants to get back to Anahuac Star System. No Syndicate. Just us. Will you deal?"

Michael stared at her, trying to judge Aragon's sincerity. "Why would you trust an Alliance officer?"

"I *don't*," Aragon said. "I'm offering a deal. Only because you're a Geary. Black Jack is for the people. Maybe you are, too."

For the people? What did that mean? Did this Syndic soldier think Black Jack was somehow sympathetic or supportive to Syndics? Why? "What's in it for me?"

"You get us home," she said. "Then the mobile unit is yours. You can go anywhere you want." Her eyes narrowed and she stepped closer, the muzzle of her pistol nearly touching his face. "But if you betray us, you'll wish I'd killed you here and now."

Was this some trick by the Syndics? But to what purpose? He wasn't being asked to betray the Alliance. He could stop cooperating at any time. And if the deal being offered was sincere, if these soldiers really were revolting against the Syndicate Worlds, helping them would hurt the Syndics. "All right," Michael said. "Why not?" There was a way to test this woman's sincerity. "But I can't drive a spaceship alone. I'll need help. Are there other Alliance prisoners of war here?"

She nodded, stepping back and lowering her weapon. "Fine. We'll free all of the Alliance Fleet prisoners here as well."

How deliberate was her wording? "*All* of the Alliance prisoners of war here. Ground forces, too."

It was her turn to shrug. "All of them. Agreed. But they don't get weapons. Deal?"

"Deal."

"Done. I'll be back." She turned to leave.

Michael stood up, suddenly realizing how much he wanted to know. "Wait! What happened? At least tell me what happened after my ship was destroyed!"

Aragon paused just outside the door of the cell, looking back at him with a slight, humorless smile. "They didn't tell you? No, of course they wouldn't." She activated the door control, the wall between her and Michael beginning to solidify again. "The Alliance won. The Syndicate lost. And now we want to go home. Stay quiet. Act normal. I'll be back."

Michael stared at the solid wall where the door had been, the image of Aragon's face fixed in his mind. The Alliance had won? The war had finally ended? How?

He finally had some answers, but all they did was create an avalanche of new questions.

Including whether or not Aragon had told him the truth, or simply told the lie she thought was needed to gain his cooperation.

EXECUTIVE Destina Aragon didn't pause before heading down the hall away from Michael Geary's cell. She didn't want to be near it if the snakes' surveillance systems recovered from the special glitches her own hackers had slipped into the mix.

There was an art to walking in the Syndicate. It required a deliberate pace—not too fast, which would attract attention from the snakes or supervisors, and not too slow, which would make it look like someone was dragging their feet, and also draw the eyes of snakes and supervisors. She had seen images of Alliance worlds, seen how crowds of people moved at wildly different rates. It had felt weird and dangerous. In the Syndicate, a crowd of people all moved at the same pace, no one wanting to stand out. An Alliance POW had sneered that the people of the Syndicate Worlds were so regimented they moved in formations, when the truth was they moved that way voluntarily, hiding within a mass of others.

The walls she passed were uniformly drab except for colorful posters urging passersby to obey their superiors, to defeat the Alliance, to defend the homes and the families of Syndicate workers, and to serve in the Syndicate mobile forces or ground forces. The Syndicate had never informed its people that the war was officially over. Everyone knew, but no one was supposed to acknowledge it.

The phrase "for the people" was repeated frequently on the posters. Maybe that had really meant something once, a commitment of the leaders to serve those they led. But no one remembered such a time. "For the people" was a joke at the highest levels, a meaningless phrase the Syndicate repeated as if it still mattered.

But at the lower levels, even among executives, there were more and more who were trying to reclaim the motto, to make "for the people" mean something again. The irony wasn't lost on her that Black Jack, hero of the Alliance, had proven to actually care about the workers the Syndicate's own leaders treated like disposable parts.

Reaching the barracks where the remnants of the 1233rd Assault Regiment were quartered, she paused for just a moment. They'd started out with over two thousand soldiers. Only a little more than three hundred were left.

Supposedly, they were temporarily assigned security duty at this orbital prison that did not officially exist, augmenting the snakes who handled regular guard duties. The Syndicate had promised to send them home, having done their duty and paid an awful price in blood. But no one believed promises made by the Syndicate, and Aragon had found growing evidence that the remnants of her unit were intended for another combat mission against a very formidable opponent.

If they were going to die anyway, they might as well die trying to get home.

Aragon slammed open the hatch to the barracks. "I'm calling a surprise inspection. The workers have been getting slack. Half an hour. Full combat gear. Weapons safed. Everyone had better be ready."

The unit sub-executives and senior workers jumped to their feet, saluting. "Yes, Executive Aragon," they chorused.

Aragon paused to exchange a look with Sub-Executive Alarik Harbin, her second-in-command. He knew the entire plan. The rest of the unit would go along with her orders, but she'd needed Harbin to be a full participant, ready to act in special ways when her orders came in.

Harbin nodded to her. "We'll be ready for the inspection, Executive Aragon."

They were putting on a show for the snakes who monitored everything going on in the facility. Aragon had carefully learned all that she could about a special, sealed room that always held two snakes on watch. Those snakes would be reporting to the snake CEO who ran this place, telling her about the sudden inspection, that the soldiers would be donning their battle armor as if preparing for a fight. CEOs never objected to anything that looked like a crackdown on workers, though, and she'd be told the soldiers' weapons would be inactive. The CEO would surely tell the snakes to keep a close eye on things and leave it at that.

They'd also be noticing that their surveillance systems were acting buggy, however. Aragon had made sure certain signs of someone attempting an apparently futile malware attack would be apparent to the snakes.

Aragon headed down the hallway again, this time aiming for the door to that special sealed room. She had spent the last couple of weeks pretending to clumsily flirt with one of the snakes who stood watches there every day, even though the act left her feeling unclean. But snakes were used to people offering favors in exchange for special deals. This one had been grinning and looking Aragon up and down, making sure she knew he was interested.

"Commander," Harbin called over her comm link. "The unit is ready for inspection."

"Understood, Sub-Executive Harbin," Aragon said. "Two minutes. Bring them to attention now."

Harbin knew what that meant. "Confirm. Two minutes. Bringing to attention now."

The combat systems on the battle armor worn by her soldiers had been set to SAFE, unable to fire. At this moment, in response to her command to "bring them to attention," Harbin would be shifting every set of battle armor to READY, all weapons active.

She reached the door to the sealed room, fixing a false smile on her face. Her pistol was still in one hand, but the surveillance software should still be unable to see it thanks to the malware her hackers had inserted. But more alerts would have appeared by now, warning the snakes that something was wrong. "I need to see you right away," she called in on the intercom.

The image of the snake she'd been flirting with appeared. "Why? What do you want?"

"I may have some problems," Aragon said. "Immediate problems." It wasn't too hard to look nervous as she spoke.

The snake shook his head slowly. "You know someone's been messing with our systems? And you don't want to take the fall for it? Motivate me, Executive. Why do I help you right away?"

"You get what you want from me right away," Aragon said, smiling.

"I'm not alone in here," the snake said.

I know, Aragon thought. "Then I can make you both happy," she said.

The sealed door slid open.

Just before it finished opening, Aragon heard the snake speaking to his partner. "Relax. She's unarmed."

Another voice, that of the other snake, sounding worried. "If we let her in here…Hey, if someone's been messing with the surveillance system, how do we know she's unarmed?"

Her arm was already coming up, centering her aim on the forehead of the second snake, the slug from her pistol punching a hole between his eyes, her aim shifting slightly, putting two more slugs into the first snake while he was still realizing how stupid he'd been.

Stepping to the console, she dropped a data coin into the programming slot. Her hackers had sworn if given full access their malware would freeze all of the snake systems. "Sub-Executive Harbin," Aragon called over her link, "the inspection will begin in thirty seconds. Get everyone in position."

She watched the consoles, seeing the impact of the malware spreading.

"What's going on in there?" someone called over the snake link. "Report!"

She stayed silent.

"Enter status code now!"

Aragon stepped to the door, glancing down the hall.

"Quick reaction force to the central surveillance room! I rep—"

The voice cut off as the malware finished locking out the snakes from their own systems. "Harbin, all snake surveillance and control systems are locked. I want every snake dead before they can unlock them."

"Understood," Harbin replied, his voice slightly rushed. He, and the rest of her soldiers, would be racing to hit the snakes before they realized there was a serious fight on their hands. "Be careful. You're the only one out there without armor."

Aragon spotted figures in light armor running down the hallway toward her and leaned out enough to fire, hitting the snake in the lead. A storm of answering shots came at her, forcing Aragon to duck back. "Yeah. I know."

Slugs and energy bolts flayed the sides of the doorway as Aragon stayed back, extending her hand out far enough to fire blindly twice more down the hall, grateful that her opponents were regular snakes, not trained combat soldiers. If they'd been vipers, the combat branch of internal security, they'd already be charging toward the room while some of their number kept up fire to pin down Aragon.

The incoming fire slackened for just a moment, allowing Aragon to duck out for a moment and fire twice more.

She leaned against the inner wall of the door, seeing the outer frame fragmenting under the snake barrage. Regular snakes or not, they'd charge her soon. "I could use a little help here, Harbin."

"On our way."

"I need you here now!"

The incoming fire slackened.

Aragon risked another quick look. Harbin and twenty soldiers with him had arrived and opened fire on the snakes from the back and sides. "No quarter!" Harbin ordered as the soldiers closed with the snakes, using the power of their battle armor to literally crush the lightly armored snake battle suits. "Finish them!"

Some of the snakes bolted down the hall toward Aragon. She stepped out, firing. One of the snakes dropped, another grappled with her. As she put a shot into that snake's faceplate, Aragon heard an impact behind her. Turning, she saw the last snake had been aiming at her, but was falling, a large hole in their helmet where Harbin's shot had hit.

She turned to face Harbin and the other soldiers as they reached her. "Took you long enough to get here, Sub-Executive Harbin. I expect better work than meeting the bare minimum required."

Harbin's face was hidden behind his face shield, but she could hear his grin. "If the minimum wasn't good enough, it wouldn't be the minimum. No injuries?"

"One second later and you would have been senior executive in this unit," Aragon said, hastily donning the battle armor the soldiers had brought for her.

"That's why I hurried," Harbin said. "I don't want the job. Too many CEOs breathing down your neck." He gestured toward the other soldiers. "You should commend the workers. They were pushing to get here as hard as I was."

One of the soldiers laughed. "We just didn't want Sub-Executive Harbin taking over, Executive Aragon. We're used to you." The other soldiers laughed as well, nervous excitement riding in their voices. They were finally getting to hit back at the snakes who had terrorized them all of their lives. The possible consequences of that were huge, but for the moment the workers were not thinking of the future, only the next few minutes and how many more snakes they might kill.

"That's what happens when you're not hard enough on your workers," Harbin told Aragon. "They get insubordinate."

"And they save your butt when it needs saving," Aragon replied. "To hell with Syndicate management rules." Her battle armor was booting up, the situation display still settling out. "How do things look?"

"Most objectives have been secured," Harbin said. "But the snake vipers managed to armor up before we could neutralize them. They're trying to fight their way in to link up with the security forces protecting the snake CEO."

She could finally see on her display where her soldiers were, and where they were fighting. Aragon took off at a run, Harbin and the others following. "We have to take the snake CEO's office fast, Harbin. They'll be trying to bring all of their systems back online. And make sure there's a unit protecting cellblock 333."

"We need all of our forces against the vipers," Harbin protested. "There are plenty of Alliance prisoners who can—"

"Only one of those prisoners is Black Jack's scion. We need to keep him alive. He's the only one of the Alliance scum who might keep his end of the bargain."

But if they didn't take the CEO's office fast enough, that wouldn't matter. Everyone knew snake CEOs had access to hidden nukes they could use as a final measure to halt a revolt. Technically, that "Armageddon option" was a secret, but the Syndicate had made certain that particular "secret" was widely known so it could serve as another deterrent to revolt. Right now, the control links to detonate the nuclear weapon concealed somewhere in this facility would be frozen. If the snakes got their systems working again…

"I've got a unit heading for the cellblock," Harbin said.

"Good. I need you to be flexible," Aragon told Harbin. "We weren't able to make detailed plans with the snakes watching everywhere." She aimed and fired in one motion, taking out an unarmored snake dashing for safety.

"We could have waited until our hackers could work up a way to permanently fry every snake subsystem," Harbin protested.

A volley of shots told them they'd reached the vipers, who had forted up in a hallway blocking access to the CEO's offices. Aragon returned fire, cursing, mentally tallying up the time being wasted in this fight. "It took us two months to plan this much!"

"Another month—" Harbin began, kneeling beside her to fire at the vipers.

"We didn't have another month! Two days ago I found out that snake reinforcements are due here in less than three weeks."

"Reinforcements? What would happen to us?"

One of her soldiers fell as a viper shot hit home.

"Rebellion suppression," Aragon told Harbin. "Against Midway."

"Going up against Drakon's unit? That's not combat. That's suicide."

"That's why we didn't have another month," Aragon said. "And right now we don't have another minute to waste."

"We're pinned down! They've got too much firepower!"

Sometimes the options were easy to decide, even if they were ugly. "There's only one way in the time we have left to get our workers to charge." She shifted her comms to speak to all of the soldiers with her. "How many of you want to die for the Syndicate? Because the Syndicate is planning to kill us. Anyone who wants a chance at life, or a chance to die fighting against the Syndicate... *follow me!*"

Aragon leapt up and charged toward the vipers despite the

barrage of fire that greeted her, slugs ricocheting off of her armor, energy bolts hitting, damage alerts appearing on her display...

She heard a collective shout from her soldiers. *"Aragon!"* As she staggered from another hit, her soldiers were around her and passing her and in among the vipers, killing without mercy.

This was why she treated her workers as well as she could and still maintain discipline. Because she did that, at times like this they repaid her a thousandfold.

Aragon kept on her feet, staggering to keep up as her soldiers swept through the dead vipers and wiped out the regular snakes defending the CEO's office.

As she came through the door, Aragon saw the CEO pounding her desk controls with one hand while firing a pistol wildly with the other. Then a half-dozen shots flung the CEO away from her desk to sprawl lifeless on the floor.

Aragon reached the desk, seeing a message still displayed. *You are not connected to nuclear termination device detonation authorization. Try again?* "She was trying to detonate the hidden nuke, but our hackers' malware kept her out long enough. Is Michael Geary's cell secure?"

"I sent a squad," Harbin said. "Rispoli's. They should be on site about now."

A sudden worry caused Aragon to turn toward Harbin. "Did you tell them who they were supposed to guard? That it wasn't just some average city-destroying Alliance scum officer?"

"No, Executive," Harbin said, sounding offended. "I didn't tell the workers anything they didn't need to know."

"They need to know he is Black Jack's scion so they don't 'accidentally' revenge kill him! Come on! We have to make sure he lives or we'll be stuck here waiting for the Syndicate to give us traitors' deaths."

She took off at a run again, her injuries and fatigue forgotten. "Squad Supervisor Rispoli, respond!"

MICHAEL Geary stood in the center of his cell, listening. Alarms had been sounding. Did that mean Aragon was taking action? He was used to battles where a warship's sensors could see for millions of kilometers. Now there might be a war going on a few meters away and he could see nothing, do nothing.

Except wait, as a familiar hum warned him the door was opening.

Two Syndics in light armor started to enter, their weapons lining up on him.

Both staggered, twisting under multiple impacts. One slug tore past Michael, embedding in the wall behind him.

More Syndics, these wearing full battle armor, their weapons ready. The one in the lead took a menacing step toward Geary. "Alliance scum."

"Where's Aragon?" Michael asked. "Executive Aragon?"

The Syndics hesitated, their weapons not yet aimed at him. "How do you—? Wait. This is Rispoli. Yes, Executive. He's Black Jack's? I understand and will comply."

The Syndics stepped back, their weapons still ready, but not directed toward him. Their attention seemed to be divided between watching him and watching the passageway outside of the cell, where other Syndics in full armor could be seen. Were they really guarding him? Michael waited, hearing the alarms shut off and wondering what that meant.

More Syndics arrived, the one in the lead wearing battle armor scarred by recent damage. "Lucky for you, my workers believe what I tell them," Aragon told Geary. "Otherwise, one of them would have accidentally put a shot through your heroic head."

Michael glared at her, triggered by a word he'd avoided ever

Michael took a moment to calm himself, knowing that losing his temper wouldn't help anything. If there was any chance Aragon would keep her promise to release other Alliance prisoners here, he had to keep this deal on track. Swallowing his pride would be a small price to pay. "At least tell me what the target is," he said as the shuttle lurched into motion, rising and heading out of the hangar. "What sort of ship are you trying to hijack? A freighter? A Syndic troop transport? A passenger ship?"

Aragon raised her face shield so he could see her grin, the large scar on her right cheek more prominent because of the expression. "A freighter wouldn't get us through Syndicate space in one piece. We need something big and tough."

That smile of Aragon's was really disturbing, Michael thought. "Big and tough? What the hell are you thinking? What's our target?"

"A mobile forces unit."

A warship? "There's a Hunter-Killer or light cruiser near us?"

"Too small," Aragon said. "Our target is a battle cruiser. We're going to take a Syndicate battle cruiser."

He stared at her, momentarily shocked into silence. "Ancestors save us," Michael finally got out. "You're crazy."

Aragon's smile didn't waver. "Probably. Everybody dies sometime, Captain Michael Geary. Let's find out if today is our day."

using about himself. "It wasn't heroism. You gave me your word. I trusted that you wouldn't have your own soldiers kill me."

"Trust is for fools," Aragon scoffed. She tossed him a bundle that expanded into a lightweight survival suit. "I made a deal. I keep my deals. Get into that suit, fast. We have no time to waste."

He pulled on the suit and its helmet, life support automatically coming on. Aragon moved the moment he was done, leaving him to follow, the Syndic soldiers following behind both of them. He wouldn't have lagged anyway, but that escort still felt more like a threat than a protection.

As they moved through the halls, Michael saw piles of bodies. His suspicions that the 'revolt' might be some sort of trick faded a bit. It seemed unlikely even the Syndics could get away with murdering so many of their own in order to create an image of realism. "Lot of dead," he said. "No mercy, even for your own, huh?"

"They're not our own," Aragon said, loathing easy to hear in her voice. "They were snakes. They never showed mercy to anyone. We showed none to them."

The group ran out into a hangar where ranks of shuttles waited as well as a lot more soldiers. He guessed at least a couple of hundred Syndic soldiers were here, which might be a lot or too few depending on whatever Aragon was planning. "We're leaving?" Michael demanded. "Where are the other Alliance prisoners?"

"They'll follow us," Aragon said as she led him into the nearest shuttle. "The first shuttle runs are all assault troops."

"If they don't come with us, I don't take you anywhere!"

Aragon shoved him into a seat, the strength of her battle armor easily overcoming his resistance. "If we don't take that mobile unit, nobody is going anywhere. Sit back, strap in, and shut up. I keep my bargains. I won't tell you that again."

He almost snapped back at her. *Damn, arrogant Syndic.* But

2

GIVEN the insanity of what Aragon was proposing, Michael wondered if she was joking about their objective. Why should he believe anything a Syndic told him? But as the shuttle closed on their goal, the view on the display screen clearly revealed the massive, shark-like shape of a Syndic battle cruiser. Like Alliance battle cruisers, it was designed for speed and maneuverability, lacking the armor and some of the weaponry of battleships. With those savings in mass, the massive main propulsion units aft could swiftly accelerate a battle cruiser. It could catch anything it wanted to destroy, and outrun anything it wanted to avoid.

But right now this battle cruiser was only going in very, very large circles near the facility that had been Michael's prison. He looked at another display, seeing a barren planet that both the prison and the battle cruiser were orbiting around. The planet reminded him of images from humanity's early space exploration, showing what Mars had been like before terraforming made it habitable, a lifeless waste of rock and dust and thin sheets of ice near the poles. But with jump drives and the hypernet allowing easy interstellar travel, no one needed to waste resources anymore fixing barren worlds when nicer ones were always to be found around another star.

All of this time he'd been wondering where he was. Now he knew. Orbiting a nothing world in what was probably a nothing star system, the perfect place to hide prisoners the Syndicate Worlds didn't want anyone knowing about. "What star system is this?" Michael asked Aragon.

She eyed him as if deciding whether to answer. "Augusta."

"Augusta? I've never heard of it."

"That's because there's nothing here worth hearing about."

He looked toward their objective again, the battle cruiser growing in size as the shuttle drew nearer. "How many soldiers do you have?"

Aragon favored him with another of those unnerving smiles. "We had to leave some workers watching things at the prison. All the rest are going in with me. Two hundred and forty."

"Two hundred and forty?" Michael repeated, not sure he'd heard right. "Are you insane, Aragon? Trying to capture a Syndic battle cruiser with a force this small?"

"Not 'trying.' We're going to do it," Aragon said.

"It's impossible."

"Maybe I know something you don't." She leaned closer to him for a moment, intimidating in her battle armor. "We made a deal, Geary. We get the mobile forces unit, you get us home. Are you backing out? Despite your *word of honor*?"

Michael felt his face warming with anger. "I'll carry out my end of the deal, if we survive this. Honor still means something in the Alliance."

"It means you're an idiot," Aragon said before flipping her face shield shut. The shuttle was very close to the battle cruiser now, the bulk of the warship's hull looming ahead. "Let's go!"

Her soldiers moved, leaping from the shuttle toward a narrow platform on the hull of the warship, Geary trying to stay with them, acutely aware of how flimsy his survival suit was compared to their battle armor.

Sailing alone through space had always terrified him, the infinite depths on all sides promising a slow death and an eternity of drifting for his remains if he missed his target.

He hit the side of the battle cruiser, trying to get a grip, rebounding back into space…

One of the soldiers grabbed him and pulled him back.

"Try not to drift off," Aragon told Geary. "Hackers, I want in now."

"We're in, Executive!" another voice called over the circuit. "Access codes overridden."

Massive loading hatches swung open, revealing wide cargo hangars. The soldiers swarmed inside, landing amid crates secured to the deck. "Seems no one's expecting us," a Syndic woman commented.

"Don't be overconfident, Sub-Executive Nedele. Our luck won't hold forever. Stay alert." Geary saw Aragon, distinctive in her battle-scarred armor, looking around. "How does it look, Harbin?"

A man's voice replied. "We're ready, Executive."

Geary stared about the hangar, wondering why no one had come to check on the opened loading hatches. Where was the crew? Syndic warships didn't have crews as large as Alliance warships did, but a battle cruiser should still have five or six hundred.

A moment later, Aragon answered his unspoken question as she called out orders. "Listen up! There's only a skeleton crew aboard this mobile unit. All snakes. All of them complacent, thinking they've got nothing to fear. Hit them fast before they realize we're aboard. Make sure they don't manage to hole up inside the citadels. My group will take the bridge. Harbin, take engineering. Nedele, fire control."

"Do we need prisoners?" Harbin asked. "To operate the ship?"

"They're all *snakes*," Aragon repeated. "No prisoners. Operating the ship is why we have Black Jack's scion with us. All units, go!"

Aragon pulled Michael Geary into motion so he was running alongside her as their group of soldiers poured out of the hangar and into a wide passageway. He fought down another burst of anger at the way she was yanking him around, realizing that she was ensuring he was safe during this fight by keeping him close to her. Approaching a wide cross-corridor, they saw two figures walk into sight and stare at the oncoming soldiers. A flurry of shots knocked both sprawling before either could react.

"Why aren't you trying to take them prisoner to operate the ship instead of depending on me?" Geary asked Aragon as the group turned the corner, the two dead snakes staring sightlessly at the passing figures.

"Weren't you listening?" Aragon said, her words sharp and fast. "There are only snakes aboard. They won't surrender, we won't take them prisoner, and we couldn't trust them even if we let some live. Now shut up and try not to get killed."

Michael shut up, trying to stay close to Aragon as the soldiers headed for the bridge. He knew what the Syndics were trying to do. Syndic warships were designed with interior, armored citadels protecting critical command areas. One citadel was in engineering, a second in the fire control area, and the third was the bridge, where the ship's senior officer would be. According to what he'd heard, the citadels weren't intended only to defend against Alliance boarding parties. They were also protection against mutiny by the crew of the ship, because the Syndics didn't trust the "workers" they exploited and mistreated.

But he doubted the Syndic designers had expected this strong of an attack on a warship that had so few defenders aboard.

Maybe Aragon wasn't crazy after all. Maybe she had the cunning of a veteran who had survived this long in a war that ate lives like an insatiable monster.

Patched into the communications net being used by Aragon and her soldiers, Michael heard the assault teams hitting engineering and the fire control spaces.

"Traitors!" an unfamiliar voice screamed on the circuit, high pitched with outrage and fear. "Your families will suffer!"

"Snakes already killed my family," a woman shouted in reply.

"Trai—" The voice cut off with an agonized grunt as the snake died.

"I've waited a long time for this," another soldier said, the sound of weapons firing audible in the background.

Michael saw the entry to the bridge was right ahead. He was still running with Aragon, and suddenly all too aware that he was probably the only person on this ship without a gun. "Give me a weapon!"

"Move it, Alliance slug," Aragon called in reply. But her hand moved to draw her pistol and toss it to him.

They spilled onto the bridge, where three snakes were huddled around the command seats. All three died as they tried to bring up their weapons.

Michael heard another shot behind him and spun about to see a fourth snake had been aiming at him, but was falling. One of Aragon's soldiers stepped closer and fired again at the prone snake.

"Thanks, Syndic," Geary said.

The soldier turned to look at him. "You're welcome, Alliance scum."

For at least the second time today, he owed his life to a Syndic. Michael paused to catch his breath, wondering what that meant.

Aragon was speaking again as she paced about the bridge. "Harbin, Nedele, status."

"Engineering secured."

"Fire control secured."

A soldier at one of the bridge consoles waved to Aragon, who came over to look. "Harbin, Nedele, I'm tagging the locations of a few snakes still left alive. Looks like they're asleep in their quarters. Each of you detach a squad to deal with them."

Geary walked to what he thought was the secondary command seat, looking at the unfamiliar display. "It looks like the, uh, snakes were trying to trigger a power core overload."

"Probably," Aragon said. "Armageddon response to a successful mutiny. Harbin would have blocked the commands in engineering, though. We were ready for standard snake tactics." She pointed at the controls. "Can you operate these?"

"I think so," Michael said. He tried a tentative command, seeing the expected response. "But we're not going anywhere until you enter the codes to activate these controls."

Aragon turned to some of the soldiers with her. "Hackers. We need into these controls. Now."

The soldiers straightened and rendered Syndic salutes, rapping their left breasts with their clenched right fists. "We understand and will comply, Executive Aragon."

"You don't have the codes," Michael said, gazing unhappily about the bridge.

"Not yet," Aragon said. "My workers are good. They'll get the codes. See anything familiar? Have you ever been aboard a Syndicate battle cruiser?"

"Yeah," Michael said, images of blood and death filling his memory. "A boarding action."

"Did you win, Captain Michael Geary?"

"Yeah, we won," Michael said. "Then we evacuated the ship and blew it up."

"Sure you did," Aragon said. "After how many of you died capturing it?"

"Too many."

"Was it worth it?"

He glared at her. "What the hell kind of question is that?"

"You never asked it yourself?" Aragon said, her voice calm.

Michael nodded. "Yeah. I have. I didn't realize Syndics would ask themselves that."

"All the time," Aragon said. "All the time."

MICHAEL could do nothing but wander about the bridge while waiting for access to the controls. He was acutely aware that two of Aragon's soldiers were watching every step he took, and made sure to always move slowly. Destina Aragon had yanked a dead snake out of the senior command seat and sat down there. Even though his survival suit readouts said the air inside the ship was fine, none of the Syndics had opened their suits to breathe it, so Geary didn't either.

A few soldiers came through collecting the bodies of the snakes and hauling them off to wherever the Syndics were depositing them. Michael watched the dead being dragged away, thinking of how many dead he had seen, Alliance and Syndic, in how many places. Somehow he doubted that these Syndics intended to give the dead "snakes" what the Alliance considered honorable burials in space, launched onto trajectories aimed at eventually entering the flames of the nearest star.

"We've got the codes, Executive," one of the Syndic soldiers reported. "All primary controls are accessible."

"Good work," Aragon told her. "Captain Michael Geary, it's your turn."

He went back to the secondary command seat next to her, trying a few simple access commands. "It looks like everything is fine." It seemed a good time to push an issue that hadn't been resolved. "What about the rest of the Alliance prisoners?"

"What about them?" Aragon gave a brief, harsh laugh. "Sub-Executive Harbin, take two platoons back to the prison. Assume command of the soldiers left there. Get them and the remaining Alliance POWs aboard this unit."

"All of them?" Harbin questioned.

"You heard me," Aragon said. "All of them. Alive."

"I understand and will comply."

Aragon finally raised her helmet's face shield. "The last snakes aboard are dead," she told her soldiers. "You can unseal your armor."

Geary did the same, breathing the air cautiously. Unsure when he'd last slept, realizing that he'd be living his life again by the rhythms of day/night cycles and clocks, he gazed with a vague sense of wonder at his display, where the seconds and minutes were going by.

"Executive," Harbin called in. "These Alliance scum are giving me trouble. Request permission to make an example of one of them."

Geary bolted to full alertness. "No," he told Aragon. "If he does shoot one, they'll think they're all being taken for execution! Then they will fight, and your soldiers will have to kill them all."

Aragon laughed. "You say that like it's a bad thing."

Was she really amused, or just yanking his chain? "I can't drive this ship on my own! If you want to get home, I'll need help—a lot of help!"

"Sure," Aragon said. "Here. You're linked to the announcing system on the prison. Talk to them."

He hadn't prepared anything to say, and had no choice but to speak off the top of his head. "All Alliance personnel, this is Captain Michael Geary, Alliance Fleet. These Syndic soldiers have mutinied against the Syndicate Worlds. You're being moved to a battle cruiser orbiting near the prison, to assist in taking them to their home star system. Then we'll be allowed to go home as well. That's the deal I've made with them. It's our best shot at life and freedom on honorable terms."

A pause.

"They're talking it over," Harbin complained.

Aragon looked toward Geary before replying. "Give them a few more minutes."

Another minute.

"They are complying," Harbin said. "They are being moved to the shuttles now."

A display popped into existence before the command seats, showing a 3D image of the star system. A symbol pulsed near the edge of it. "What does that mean?" Geary asked Aragon.

"It means it's a friendly. Meaning Syndicate, so not friendly to us. Heavy cruiser. Is this the…uh…jump place?"

"Jump point," Michael said. "Yes. I think so. That ship must have just jumped in." He looked around the display. "I'm seeing only one jump point. There's only one way out of this star system?"

"You tell me, Alliance Fleet officer," Aragon said. "The display is only showing one symbol like that."

Geary shook his head, studying the information and trying make sense of Syndic symbols and notations. "If I'm reading this right, the jump point is three light hours away. Meaning that cruiser has already been here for three hours. He's coming in hot toward us. I think this says he's at point two light speed. That means we only have twelve hours left before he reaches us. But the only way out of this star system is by going past him. If we don't get this battle cruiser moving soon and figure out how to operate its shields and weapons, we'll be shot to pieces."

"It sounds like a great opportunity to excel, Captain Geary," Aragon said in a dry voice.

It was weird to hear a Syndic using the same, sarcastic phrase employed in the Alliance to describe a very tough situation.

"Or a great opportunity to meet our ancestors really soon," Michael said.

"Your fellow scum are being off-loaded in the same cargo hangars we came in through," Aragon said.

He nodded, his thoughts fixed on the problems facing him. "I need to talk to them in person."

"Let's go," Aragon said. "Why don't you shed your suit, first?"

He pulled off the Syndic survival suit, noticing none of the Syndics were making similar moves. "You're keeping your armor on?"

"Just in case," Aragon said.

HE came through the door into the hangar, trying to act as if he were a commanding officer aboard their own ship. There were times when Authority with a capital A was needed, and that's what he had to be now.

Syndic soldiers were stationed along the walls, their weapons ready. A few hundred men and women in a variety of Alliance uniforms were in the middle of the hangar, casting worried and defiant looks toward the Syndics.

"Maybe four hundred of them?" Geary murmured to himself.

"Good guess," Aragon said. "Four hundred twelve. Counting you."

The great majority wore the blue of the Alliance Fleet. The second largest group wore the red uniforms of the Alliance Marines. A few others were in the green of the ground forces. All of their uniforms, Geary saw, were like his, bearing the marks of whichever losing battle had resulted in their capture.

A woman shouted in surprise. "Captain Geary! You *are* alive!"

To his surprise, Michael recognized the person who'd called out, a woman with the naturally bright green hair that marked her origin in Eire Star System. "Lieutenant Bailey? The last I heard you were on *Audacious.*"

Bailey nodded, smiling with relief. "Yes, sir. We were destroyed at Lakota. The fleet got away, but after that I don't know."

"Lakota?" Michael said, trying to remember where that star system was.

Aragon flipped up her face shield again and spoke in an annoyed voice. "Black Jack won. I told you that. I thought we were in a hurry, Captain Michael Geary?"

He took a deep breath before speaking in his best command voice. "Listen up, all of you! This battle cruiser needs a crew. It has Syndic controls and protocols in every system. We have to learn how to operate them fast, because there's a Syndic heavy cruiser coming this way."

"But…these are Syndics!" Lieutenant Bailey protested.

"Not anymore," Geary said. "As I told you earlier, they mutinied. They need someone to operate this ship. I made a deal with their commander. We have to get them home. Then we get this ship, and we go home."

"We can't trust Syndics!" another prisoner called out.

"We don't have to trust them," Geary said. "We have to work with them, against the Syndicate Worlds, or we'll die here. Who *wants* to die? Show me some hands. No one? Now listen up. I am the senior Alliance Fleet officer here. I'm in command. Anyone with experience in engineering, head for the engineering central compartment."

"Citadel," Aragon corrected him.

"The engineering citadel," Geary said. "You know how the Syndics design their ships. Some of these soldiers will escort you, so no other soldiers will wonder why there are Alliance personnel running around the ship. They are not guards, they are escorts. Don't do anything stupid. Anyone with fire control experience, I need you there. Anyone with bridge systems experience, follow me there. These…former Syndics have already broken into the control systems. Start trying to figure out how they work."

"What about the rest of us?" a Marine called.

"You'll have to stand by while we get this ship operational and moving," Geary told him. "You've all been in a Syndic prison for a long time. You can wait another half-day while we sort this out. Can they go to a more comfortable space?" Geary asked Aragon.

She snorted in derision. "The Syndicate doesn't do *comfortable* for workers. But, yeah, there's places with chairs and stuff. Some of my workers will escort them there."

"Let's go!" Geary called to the former prisoners.

There was a momentary pause.

"You all heard the captain!" Lieutenant Bailey shouted. "Move it!"

As Geary led the group heading for the bridge, Aragon walked beside him. She'd finally removed her helmet. "What do I call you?" he said.

She glanced at him. "Executive Aragon. Unless you're planning to ask me out on a date, and then you call me Esteemed Executive Aragon."

Michael shook his head. "I don't mean you personally. I mean you as a group. If you're not Syndics anymore, what are you?"

Aragon gave him another glance, this one holding a hint of pride in it. "We're all from Anahuac Star System. They call us Tigres."

"Tigres? Why?"

"Because we're from Anahuac. Where are you from, Captain Michael Geary?"

"Glenlyon Star System."

"So what are you called?"

He paused before answering. "A Geary. One of Black Jack's family. That's all I've ever been known as. That's all that ever mattered to anyone else."

Aragon grinned. "And that's still all that matters! If you hadn't been Black Jack's scion, we never would have made our deal. Happy?"

He gave her an angry scowl in reply. "Go to hell."

She shook her head, still smiling in a way that held no hint of humor. "Already been there. Just like you, Captain Michael Geary."

He knew what she meant, wondering exactly which hells, which battlefields, she had experienced, and whether he had ever been nearby, fighting on the opposite side.

They reached the bridge, the Alliance personnel slowly spreading out to start trying to activate and learn the controls, Tigre soldiers among them watching every movement with suspicion.

Aragon finally removed the rest of her battle armor, stretching with obvious relief. "Sidearm?" she said, extending a hand toward him.

He had still been holding her pistol. What would happen if he asked to retain it? But there were other fights to worry about right now. Geary reached out to give back the weapon.

Aragon returned her sidearm to her hip holster, ready for use. She gave Michael a long look before moving with clear intent and sitting in the secondary command seat, leaving the primary command seat for him. It was an important gesture. He still hadn't decided whether he could ever like Destina Aragon, but she seemed more and more like someone he could work with.

Michael sat down in the command seat, watching the other Alliance officers and enlisted work, itching to jump in and try to fix things himself, but knowing the best thing he could do was stay back and let them do their jobs.

"You let your workers operate without much supervision?" Aragon asked him.

He frowned at her, not sure whether or not she was baiting him again. "You mean the officers and sailors? Of course I do. They know their jobs better than I do. I give them direction, and they know how to carry it out."

"Of course?" Aragon sat back with a sigh. "Not in the Syndicate. We're supposed to micro-micro-manage. Smart people realize workers need guidance, but should know their jobs, like you say. But, you know, being smart isn't a requirement to be promoted in management. Giving your workers room to work has to be done on the down-low. Don't let your own bosses know. I guess it's not like that in the Alliance?"

"It can be," Michael said, remembering some of the officers he'd served under. "It's not supposed to be, but it can be."

Another display flared to life before him, a virtual comm window showing Lieutenant Bailey. "Captain Geary? Praise our ancestors, I got this working. I'm in fire control. The weapons controls are a mess. Every time we think we've identified the firing authorization codes, we run into another wall."

Aragon nodded. "Firing weapons requires cascading authorization codes from multiple levels of command. That should be obvious."

"Cascading authorizations?" Michael demanded. "That's insane."

"No," Aragon said. "That's Syndicate. The CEOs don't trust anybody. Who is that? What is she? A sub-executive?"

"I'm a *lieutenant*," Bailey said in an icy voice.

"Sure, loof-ten-ant," Aragon said. "Can you get it working knowing that?"

"Of course I can!"

"Get it working, Lieutenant Bailey," Michael said. "I know you can do it."

As the display showing Bailey vanished, Aragon cast a sidelong glance Geary's way. "You were in the same unit with her?"

"A few years ago," Michael said. "Lieutenant Bailey was one of my officers on the heavy cruiser *Adamant*. She's very capable."

"No personal relationship?"

He gave her a disapproving look. "She was my subordinate."

"Ah." Aragon nodded. "You follow rules like that?"

"Of course I do."

"Why?"

He hadn't had that question put to him before and had to think for a moment. "Out of respect. For them. My subordinates."

"Huh," Aragon said, her expression revealing little.

"Earlier, you jokingly said something about me asking you on a date. You weren't serious."

"No, I wasn't," she said. "And don't. But the Syndicate…there's not a lot of respect for subordinates or workers, Captain Michael Geary."

"You've been harassed?" he asked.

"Harassed? Interesting word." Aragon bent a crooked smile his way. "This one executive, he made it clear that if I did what he wanted, he'd make sure I got promoted, or if I didn't he'd make sure I ended up busted to a worker."

Michael stared at her, trying to guess why she was telling him this. "What did you do?"

"I didn't have to do anything," Aragon said. "We were going into a fight the next day, and he was way back, trying to stay safe while he 'supervised' the attack. But there was a glitch in the command net. All of our battle armor lost their links and data for about thirty seconds. When it came back, it turned out that executive had taken a bullet right in the center of his face shield. It must have been a really lucky shot by an Alliance sniper, you know?"

"A lucky shot." Michael nodded to her, knowing exactly who had really fired it. "Too bad for him."

"Yeah. He had bad judgment." She looked steadily at him. "I'm glad to hear you have good judgment, Captain Michael Geary."

"Thanks," Michael said. *Message received,* he thought. Given her experiences in the Syndicate Worlds, and her low opinion of Alliance officers, it wasn't hard to see why Aragon had made sure he understood what lines not to cross.

A minute later, his display sounded an alert, the symbol representing the Syndic heavy cruiser pulsing. "I think this is telling me he's strengthening his shields. He's doing it way early, either to let us know we've got a fight on our hands, or because whoever is in charge isn't too experienced. By now he'll have seen your soldiers going aboard this ship."

Aragon nodded. "He'll also be expecting a message from the snake CEO who commanded the prison."

"Couldn't you fake one?"

"Only the snake CEO knew the right code phrases," she said. "That heavy cruiser knows something is wrong. As soon as he figures out exactly what it is, he'll show no mercy."

"Hey!" The worried shout made Michael jump to his feet and spin to see what was happening.

A female Tigre had her weapon pointed straight at an Alliance chief petty officer, who was facing her with raised fists and an expression combining fear and defiance. Other soldiers and former prisoners were also turning to look, but hadn't reacted yet.

"Worker, stand down!" Aragon shouted.

"He was—" the soldier began.

"Worker! Comply!" Aragon's voice this time held a steely ring of menace as well as authority. Geary realized to his shock that she had her pistol out and was aiming it at her own soldier.

The Tigre lowered her weapon and raised one hand with careful movements. "I understand and will comply."

Aragon reached the two before Geary did. "Explain!"

The soldier cast a harsh look at the Alliance chief. "He was trying to sabotage these controls, Executive."

"If you think you see that, you notify your superior to inspect!" Aragon said. "Next time, you will not be given a second chance to comply. Understand?"

The Tigre, a woman who to Michael's eyes looked fearfully intimidating in her battle armor, nodded meekly. "I understand and will comply."

Geary looked at the chief. "What happened?"

"I'm Chief Okoro, sir." He pointed to the panel near him. "I guess I hit something out of sequence and got a warning."

"That's a lockout warning," Aragon said. "Clear it with the sigma code."

"Whatever you did," Michael said, "don't do it again."

"Yes, sir," Chief Okoro said, clearly still rattled by the confrontation. "Can't we get these Syndics off the bridge?"

"No," Geary said.

"The worker understands that if she overreacts again, she'll be shot," Aragon told the chief. "Now do your job."

"Do it," Michael said before turning to Aragon. "Is that how you work? Threaten to shoot people who mess up? How can you run an organization that way?"

"How can you run one without doing that?" Aragon asked scornfully. "If you want to coddle your workers, fine. But they'd better get the job done."

"They'll get the job done."

As if prompted by his words, an Alliance lieutenant let out a triumphant yell. "I figured it out! Captain, they enter commands *backward*. I've got the maneuvering control systems online."

Michael gazed at her work in disbelief. "Cascading authorizations. Backward command sequences. Death threats for motivation. How the hell did we fail to beat the Syndics for a century?"

Aragon answered him as she walked to check on some of her other soldiers. "Maybe you're not as good as you think you are, and maybe we're better than you think we are. Are you finally ready to get this mobile forces unit moving?"

"Almost," Geary said. Sitting back down, he cautiously entered some commands, seeing an internal communications window appear before him in response. "Engineering? How does it look?"

To his surprise, a familiar face appeared. "Just about got it, Captain. Hey, Sindi, are we ready to cook?"

"Chief Taman," Michael said, surprised and happy to see a fellow survivor. "You made it off *Repulse*."

Taman nodded. "A bunch of us did, sir. I don't know where all the others ended up after the Syndics grabbed us, though." He gestured toward a woman who entered the picture. "This is my sister, Chief Sindi Taman. I thought she'd died at Fenris four years ago, but she's here. She's almost as good at engineering as I am."

"Better, you mean," Chief Sindi Taman said. "Captain, we've got basic functions working. If you send down thrust commands,

they should go through fine. But we're having an awful time getting to status and operating sub-routines."

Michael Geary nodded. "I guess the Syndics don't like their
people knowing what's going on or messing with preset operating
parameters. Keep on it." He looked at Aragon. "We can move.
The ship's shields are still at regular operating strength because we
haven't figured out how to maximize them, but we can use the
main propulsion and maneuvering thrusters."

Aragon looked back at him. "So, go."

"All of your people are off the prison? And all of the Alliance
prisoners who were held there?"

"All of them," Aragon said. "Nobody is left there except the
bodies of dead snakes."

He had no choice but to believe her. Geary carefully entered
a sequence of commands, seeing the projected track toward the
jump point spring into existence. Hitting the execute command,
he felt the welcome push of the ship's main propulsion for an
instant before the inertial dampers kicked in to protect the crew
and the ship's structure. "We're going to start out easy, accelerating
to only point zero five light speed. That will give us more time to
get the rest of the systems on line before we encounter that cruiser."

"Fine." Aragon was entering some commands into her palm
unit.

"Captain Geary?" An ensign was squinting at the display
before him. "I think this is telling me that the power core on the
prison is displaying fluctuating output."

Geary eyed Aragon. "Did you do something?"

"Me?" Aragon said. She gave him that disconcerting smile.
"Maybe."

Five minutes later, the orbiting prison, already far from them,
disappeared in a titanic explosion.

"You caused the power core to overload?" Michael asked Aragon. "Why did you do that? Not that I disapprove of destroying Syndic property, but why?"

"We don't want to leave any more evidence of what happened here for the Syndicate than we have to, Captain Geary." She gestured toward his display. "Which also means destroying that cruiser. Can you do it?"

He couldn't promise that yet, not when the battle cruiser's shields and weapons were still refusing to cooperate with the efforts of the Alliance officers. "We'll do our best."

She gave him another sidelong look. "That had better be good enough."

"Or, what, you'll shoot us?"

"I won't have to, Captain Michael Geary. If the Syndicate gets its hands on this mobile unit, we'll all be shot."

"We're still trying to unlock the weapons, and without our shields at full strength, that heavy cruiser might be able to do some serious damage to us."

Aragon rested her chin on one fist as she looked at him. "I assume that means no, you can't destroy the cruiser."

He bit back his first, angry reply, thinking. He'd had to do that a lot in life, responding to people wanting to know why a Geary couldn't produce miracles on demand. "What's your priority, Executive Aragon? Getting home? Or trying to destroy that heavy cruiser? Because I'd love to take it out, but it might beat us up so badly we couldn't get you to Anahuac."

She didn't answer for a moment, gazing at her own display. "I told my workers that I'd try to get them home," Aragon finally said. "I can't command a mobile forces unit like this one. Use your best judgment, Captain Michael Geary."

To his surprise, the next protest came from the lieutenant who'd figured out the maneuvering commands. "We can't just let that cruiser go, sir. We have to fight."

The ethos of the Alliance Fleet. The so-called "fighting spirit" that had cost countless lives. Supposedly the example embodied by the greatest of all Alliance heroes, Black Jack himself. But Michael had seen enough of his granduncle to suspect that example didn't really reflect the way Black Jack thought and acted. And he knew what this situation called for.

"We have to survive," he said, projecting his voice so everyone on the bridge could hear him clearly.

"But—our *honor*," the lieutenant began.

"I gave my word I would get these people home! That is *my* honor! If you want to die in a glorious battle after that, I'll be happy to lead you! *After* I've fulfilled my promise!"

It was the sort of argument no one in the Alliance Fleet could refute. The lieutenant looked startled, but nodded in agreement, voicing no more objection.

Michael, aware that Aragon was giving him a look of sardonic amusement in reaction to the discussion of honor, entered another internal communications command to fire control. "Lieutenant Bailey, there's a Syndic heavy cruiser coming straight for us. What have I got to work with?"

"We've got fire control online," Bailey said. "But we've only been able to unlock one hell-lance battery."

"Only one hell-lance battery?" Michael Geary demanded. "How the hell am I supposed to face down a heavy cruiser with that?"

Lieutenant Bailey looked back at him in momentary confusion. "You're a Geary...sir."

You're a Geary. The same old statement. The same old expectations. *We need this. You're a Geary. Make it happen.*

But he couldn't blow off those expectations. There were more than four hundred Alliance former prisoners of war depending on him for not just their freedom but also their lives. Not to mention roughly three hundred Tigres, who were former Syndics but who also had his promise to get them home.

You're a Geary. With only a single working hell lance, you have to defeat or at least hold off a heavy cruiser. Figure out how to do it, or seven hundred people will die.

No pressure.

3

"**THAT** is *my* flagship," the Syndic CEO said. "You have one chance to earn my possible forbearance, and that is by surrendering the ship to me. If you don't, you will all die, and your families will be listed as those of traitors to the Syndicate Worlds. Workers! If you have been misled by your supervisors, mistakenly following orders you thought must be obeyed, I will take that into account if you remove those superiors and throw yourselves on my mercy. For the people, Clovis, out."

Executive Destina Aragon, still seated on the bridge of the mobile unit, glanced at Michael Geary to see how he had taken the threatening message sent from the heavy cruiser. He hadn't said much for the last couple of hours, aside from acknowledging reports from his workers on their progress, or mostly their lack of progress, on getting more weapons online and the shields of this unit strengthened.

"How will your people respond to that?" Geary asked. "Will they believe those promises?"

Aragon laughed. "Promises? What promises? She talked about possible forbearance and the workers begging for mercy. To those who've grown up in the Syndicate and listened to CEOs all their lives, the only thing that message did was threaten. My workers realize that CEO didn't say she wouldn't have us all shot, maybe after some torture to get confessions from the leaders or anyone else chosen at random."

Michael Geary eyed her, seemingly disconcerted by her frank assessment. "That was a CEO?"

"Couldn't you tell by the suit?" Aragon asked, surprised by the question. "And the attitude. That's a CEO suit."

He glanced at her. "Do you have a suit like that?"

"Sure, I've got an official suit." She shrugged. "Required, you know. Not nearly so well tailored or made of the expensive fabric a CEO suit is, but that's fine with me."

Michael Geary shook his head. "I'm trying to imagine you in a civilian suit."

"Not a civilian suit. An executive suit, cut to show I'm in a ground forces unit." She eyed him. "I've got to admit, I do envy you Alliance scum for your uniforms."

He laughed shortly. "Yeah, we look great in them, don't we? Especially at funerals."

At funerals. That told her where his thoughts had been. "Where are you at, Captain Michael Geary?" Aragon asked.

"What do you mean?" He didn't look at her as he asked that, instead staring at his display again.

"I mean, you've been locked up for a while. That can mess people up. How they think, how they feel."

Geary kept his gaze on his display. "Have you been a prisoner? Are you speaking from experience?"

"You mean aside from living in the Syndicate?" Aragon sighed. "Captain Michael Geary, if you live in the Syndicate, you don't just deal with all the rules all of the time, you also know people who've been to labor camps or worse. Friends, family, coworkers. The lucky ones survive their reeducation and come back. But sometimes the person who comes back isn't the same person the Syndicate took. Do you understand? It can change people."

He nodded slowly, thoughts moving behind his eyes. "You're

wondering if being locked up for so long changed me. Whether I can still command a ship in combat."

"That's right," Aragon said. "What's the answer, Captain Michael Geary? I've got a personal interest in knowing."

He finally glanced at her, a tight smile showing. "We all do. The truth is, I don't know. I think I can handle this. But it's a tough situation. Very tough."

"You're a Geary. Black Jack's scion."

She saw a flash of anger appear. "Do you have any idea—" He broke off, his jaw tight. "Even you think a Geary can do miracles."

"Black Jack beat the Syndicate. He smashed the Syndicate mobile forces in fight after fight. Maybe the Alliance just expected that, but from this side we saw a commander who couldn't be matched."

Michael Geary nodded again. "Why did you tell me he was for the people?"

"Black Jack?" Aragon ordered her thoughts, realizing that Michael Geary wouldn't know the same things everyone else did. "He stopped your fleet from bombarding worlds. Yes. We heard, and we saw. Only military targets have been hit while he was in command. He ordered his fleet to never kill another prisoner. We captured a lot of Alliance workers who told us that. He saved workers, Syndicate citizens, going out of his way, risking his ships, to save ordinary workers who were trapped. Syndicate CEOs say 'for the people' and don't mean a word of it. But we see what Black Jack has done and we know that, whether or not he ever says 'for the people,' he really is like that."

Aragon shook her head at him. "As long as the Alliance kept acting like the Syndicate, killing indiscriminately, we had to keep fighting. No one expected mercy from the people who were wiping out the populations of planets."

"We were doing that because the Syndics started it!" Michael Geary objected, angry again. "It was retaliation."

"It was stupid," Aragon said. "Did that make the Alliance give up? No? Then why did you think it would make the Syndicate give up? The workers figured if they didn't fight, either the Syndicate would kill them and their families, or the Alliance would. Better the lawyer you know, right?"

He stared at her. "You mean better the devil you know?"

"Lawyer, devil. Same thing."

Michael Geary kept his eyes on her for a long moment. "I could tell," he finally said. "I only had a few brief conversations with my great-uncle, the man you call Black Jack, before *Repulse* was destroyed. But even those told me he wasn't the 'hero' I'd been told about all my life. Do you how many things have been justified by saying that's what Black Jack would do, that's what Black Jack would expect? All of my life, I've run into these expectations of what a Geary is, what a Geary can do, what a Geary must do. Based on a false image of a real man who, from what I saw, from what you say, was a lot better than the myth we were fed." He looked about the bridge. "But they're still expecting it of me. Expecting me to be a Geary. To get us through this. Because they've been told that."

Aragon uttered a short, scornful laugh. "Hey, Captain Michael Geary, guess what? Nobody told me Black Jack was some special guy. He was just some legend the Alliance clung to like their stars thing and their ancestors thing and their honor thing. But *I'm* expecting you to get us through this. So are my workers, who believed me when I said I would try to get them home. I made a deal with you because you're Black Jack's scion. You think I would've dealt with any other Alliance officer?"

"What do you expect me to do?" Michael Geary demanded.

"I expect you to get your head out of the cell the Syndicate kept you in, and get it onto this mobile unit, and figure out how to win this fight. Because if you don't, that precious word of honor you gave me wasn't worth anything."

He stared at her, clearly angry. Good. Sometimes someone needed a good swift kick to get them motivated.

"All right, Executive Aragon," Michael Geary said, biting off each word. "Yes, I'm a Geary, too. And I don't give a damn about Black Jack, or about you, but I don't want to let down the other Alliance personnel on this ship." He paused, eyes narrowing in thought. "I'm a Geary, too. The guys we're fighting don't know that, though. They think everyone on this ship is a Syndic."

"What are you thinking?" Aragon asked.

"That heavy cruiser." He looked at his display again, but this time with an expression that reflected ideas forming. "They think this ship is commanded by Syndics, and will use Syndic tactics. Check me on my thinking. In a situation like this, Syndics would make their firing run as close as they could to hit the heavy cruiser as hard as possible."

Aragon nodded. "That's what they'll expect us to do. Isn't that what Black Jack would do?"

"No," Michael Geary said. "I didn't see much of him before *Repulse* was destroyed, but at Prime when the Alliance Fleet was trapped, he didn't charge straight in seeking a glorious death or an impossible victory. Black Jack gave orders to do something no one expected." He looked back at her with what seemed to be grudging admiration. "Like you did on that prison. Those 'snakes' weren't expecting you to hit them, were they?"

She shrugged, surprised by the praise and the implicit comparison of her actions to those of Black Jack. "The snakes always expect workers to do wrong, but they didn't expect anything as strong, organized, and swift as what we Tigres hit them with. That's just smart tactics, right?"

"It is."

An Alliance officer called out a warning from one of the bridge consoles. "The Syndic cruiser is twelve light minutes away. At the current rate of closing, we'll reach engagement range in one hour."

"One hour," Aragon said. "And this mobile unit is still far from combat ready. Do your workers need motivating, Captain Michael Geary?"

Before he could reply, a communications window appeared before him. "Captain Geary! This is Chief Taman in engineering. Sindi got us through into the status sub-routines. You now have full control of engines and maneuvering."

"Excellent work," Geary said. "Get a little rest. We've got one hour before we meet the enemy." He smiled at Aragon as the comms window vanished. "You were saying?"

"We've got legs," Aragon conceded. "What about weapons?"

Once again his reply was interrupted, this time by the urgent chime of her comm link. "Executive! The Alliance—"

Was this betrayal? There was only one way to learn the answer. She turned the link so Geary could see the images on it, a chaotic whirl of motion in which it was possible to make out men and women in Alliance Marine uniforms attacking the sentries outside the compartment they'd been resting in.

MICHAEL bolted to his feet. "Damn! I let a bunch of Marines get bored and now they're trying to be heroes!" He paused, staring at the images. "Your soldiers aren't shooting. They're not trying to shoot."

"They have orders not to shoot!" Aragon shouted at him.

"Because we made a deal! If your Marines kill some of my workers—"

"I'll stop them!"

"Then come on!" Aragon turned and ran off the bridge.

Geary managed to keep up with her, catching glimpses on her comm link of what was happening to the sentries and the Marines, able to overhear what was said.

The senior sentry had been knocked down onto the deck and was looking up at a group of Marines, two carrying weapons that they'd taken off him and the other sentry.

"Kill the Syndic and let's go!" a Marine shouted.

A female Marine with one of the weapons shook her head. "Major Guerrero, he's a prisoner."

"So what, Lieutenant Pradeesh? Kill him!"

"I served under Black Jack before I was captured at Lakota, sir! He commanded us to never kill prisoners."

Major Guerrero hesitated, staring at Pradeesh in disbelief. "Captain John Geary was—*is*—the greatest hero in the history of the Alliance. Why would he give such an order?"

"It's true, Major," a sergeant spoke up. "I was captured at Lakota as well."

"Black Jack told us killing prisoners dishonored us, and dishonored our ancestors, who would never have done such things," Lieutenant Pradeesh said, though her weapon still pointed at the downed sentry.

"We'd turned our backs on our ancestors, sir," the sergeant said. "That's what Black Jack said. He'd *know*. Maybe that's why we could never win the damned war."

The sentry finally spoke, laughing scornfully despite his peril. "Idiots! Your Black Jack beat the Syndicate! The war is over!"

"Shut up, Syndic," Pradeesh warned, steadying her aim at him.

From the sentry's perspective—the way Michael could catch moments of imagery—the muzzle of the weapon in her hand was a deadly black hole.

"Go ahead and kill me, Alliance scum," the sentry yelled. "But I will die a free Tigre, not a slave of the Syndicate!"

At that moment, Geary followed Aragon around a corner to face the group of Marines and the two downed sentries. But before anything could be said, the tromp of heavy footfalls warned of a group of soldiers in battle armor also racing to the scene, their weapons raised.

Even though she wasn't armored, Aragon didn't hesitate at all, running to place herself between the charging soldiers and the Alliance Marines. "Stand down!" she shouted, holding out one hand in a demanding 'halt' gesture. "Safe all weapons! No one is to fire. Anyone who fires will be terminated immediately by me! Comply!"

Whatever else could be said of her, Geary thought, Destina Aragon had a command voice that could probably bring the dead springing to attention. Even the Alliance Marines froze as if awaiting her next command.

The soldiers stumbled to a halt, their weapons coming down.

Aragon spun to angrily face Michael. "Deal with your workers, Captain Michael Geary!"

"My Marines," Geary corrected her. "Just what the hell are you doing, Major Guerrero?"

One of the soldiers behind Aragon spoke. "The Alliance is betraying us, Executive Aragon. We should—"

Aragon silenced her with a gesture. "Let Black Jack's scion speak, Sub-Executive Nedele. I will not allow betrayal. Neither will the scion of Black Jack."

Major Guerrero looked as abashed as any Marine could, taken aback by the unexpected reactions. "Captain Geary, we…I…"

Michael gestured to him. "With me, Major. And the rest of you. Now." He led the way back into what must be the Syndic version of a rec room, waiting until the Marines had joined him. Chewing them out in front of the Syndics would generate bad feelings, and in any case he had always followed a policy of chewing out in private while commending in public.

"There's a Syndic heavy cruiser approaching us, Major. We'll engage it within about half an hour. But instead of preparing to battle the enemy from the bridge, instead of overseeing our attempts to get the weapons on this ship operational, I am down here trying to keep my own Marines from violating my clear orders. Does my rank mean so little to you, Major Guerrero?"

Guerrero had recovered his mental balance, now facing Geary with both respect and defiance. "It's our duty to fight the enemy, sir."

"It's your duty to obey lawful orders! I gave my personal word to these *former* Syndic soldiers. Does my honor mean so little to you?"

"I would not question the honor of a Geary…" But the major's words trailed off. "Syndics have no honor!"

Michael shook his head. "I am a Geary." He had rarely used that, but sensed that now was such a time. "Would I ever betray the Alliance? Would I ever betray any member of the Alliance Fleet? Would I ever betray the Marines, whose loyalty to the Alliance has never been questioned?"

After a long moment, Guerrero let out a deep breath. "No, sir. That could never happen."

"Come here. All of you," Geary said, leading the Marines out into the passageway again, where Aragon and her soldiers as well as the two sentries waited. "This is Executive Aragon, commanding officer of this unit. They call themselves, she calls herself, Tigres. They no longer bear any allegiance to the Syndicate

Worlds. I witnessed them killing the security personnel who had terrorized them into following orders."

Aragon spoke up, speaking casually but with force. "We made a deal with Black Jack's scion that benefits us. Why would we break that deal? The Syndicate has been slain by your Black Jack, but like a slowly dying monster it continues to lash out and kill all that it can. We want no part of that. You want to go home. So do we."

"Why should we trust you?" Lieutenant Pradeesh asked.

"Trust?" Aragon said mockingly. "What is that? You believe us, because our interests coincide. Captain Michael Geary, if your Marines need weapons to feel safe, they can keep the weapons they took from the sentries. There are armories aboard. They can draw more weapons if they wish. But they must leave my workers, my *soldiers*, alone!"

"You have no objection to them having weapons?" Geary asked, as surprised as the Marines.

Aragon smiled thinly. "Alliance Marines are supposed to be very well disciplined, at least in combat situations. If you confirm that they will follow your orders from this point on, I see no grounds for us to be concerned about them." She paused before speaking with extra force to the Marines. "The war is *over*. You won. Congratulations."

Major Guerrero studied her for a long moment before turning to Geary and saluting. "I apologize to the captain for my failure to understand and obey his orders. I did not intend any disrespect toward you."

Geary returned the salute. "Accepted. You have my confidence, Major Guerrero. Do you understand your orders now?"

"Yes, sir."

Michael faced the other Marines. "You are authorized to defend yourselves if necessary. But anyone who starts a fight, anyone who fires the first shot, had better be on good terms with their ancestors, because I will personally send that person to meet them! Is that clear, Marines?"

"Yes, sir!" the Marines chorused, their hands all coming up in salutes.

Geary returned the salutes. "Carry on. I've got a battle to fight."

He headed back toward the bridge, grateful when Aragon joined him since he wasn't sure of the entire route. "You've got a lot of guts, Executive Aragon," he said. "Facing down those soldiers, and Alliance Marines."

She gave him an impassive glance. "Sure. I ought to be dead by now, taking chances like that. So, Captain Michael Geary, you threatened to shoot any Marine who disobeyed your orders."

"That's right," he said. "In a battlefield situation, which this is, fleet regulations authorize summary judgment and, if appropriate, execution of offenders by a commanding officer of sufficient seniority."

"And yet you acted so shocked when I threatened to shoot one of my workers."

"That wasn't——" Michael paused as he realized he didn't have a good counter-argument. "All right, you've got a point. I guess our moral superiority over the Syndics isn't as clear cut as I'd thought."

To his surprise, Aragon shook her head. "There is a difference. I could shoot any of my workers without cause. Just to provide an example. To demonstrate control, and consequences. The Syndicate would approve. You made it clear you would only shoot one of those Marines if they violated your orders. As punishment for actions committed. Which system is better?"

"You know my answer," he said. "I'm surprised to hear it from you."

"Why? I had to live with that. Do you think I liked it?"

Geary took another look at her, thinking. "You know, Executive Aragon...Tigre, sometimes I think I might someday respect you."

She snorted. "Am I supposed to swoon because you said that?"

"I don't think you're the swooning type," Geary said. As they walked back onto the bridge, he looked about. "Status!"

"Engineering reports internal tests confirm full propulsion and maneuvering capability," one of the Alliance officers at a console responded.

Geary sat down in the command seat, calling up the link to fire control again. "Lieutenant Bailey, where are my weapons?"

Bailey, who looked worn out but determined, grimaced. "We've managed to get a second hell-lance battery on line, sir. But when we got into missile controls we discovered there aren't any missiles aboard. Inventory is zero. All grapeshot launchers are loaded, but we've only managed to power up three of them."

Geary checked the display before him. "And shields remain at standard strength. Ancestors save us. Are we making any progress on the shields at all?"

Bailey shook her head. "Not yet, Captain. The shield controls were damaged, I guess during the fighting on this ship. They aren't responding, no matter what we do."

"Lieutenant Bailey," Michael said, "we're twenty minutes away from combat with that Syndic heavy cruiser. I need those controls working and the shields up to maximum as of five minutes ago."

"Chief North is working on the shields, sir. She's very capable. Chief! Status!"

Michael heard Chief North calling out. "The controls are broken, Lieutenant. This gear is junk. The Syndics wanted their so-called techs to just replace busted equipment instead of repairing it, so it seems to be designed to be impossible to fix."

"Impossible?" Bailey asked. "Are you saying you can't fix it?"

"Of course I can fix it, Lieutenant! But since it's impossible, it's going to take a few more minutes."

"Captain—"

"I heard," Michael said. "Keep on it."

He sat back, gazing at the display showing the movements of the heavy cruiser and this battle cruiser.

"Why did they slow down?" Aragon asked. "Do I read this right? The Syndicate heavy cruiser is now moving at point one light speed?"

"Yes," Michael said. "You're reading it right. They just finished braking velocity a lot."

"Why? Why would they slow down before a fight?"

He was momentarily surprised. Aragon had been so competent, he'd forgotten that as a ground forces officer she wouldn't know much about space combat. "Because the faster we're moving, the harder it is to hit a target. Point one light speed is, um, about thirty thousand kilometers a second. We're both going that fast, so relative to each other the two ships will be moving twice that speed. Point two light speed is the upper limit for successful engagements. If we're going faster than that, the fire control systems lose effectiveness."

Aragon frowned at him. "It's just leading the target, right? Why can't the systems just lead more if they're moving faster?"

"Relativity," Geary explained. "The faster you go, the more your outside view of the universe distorts. Both the Alliance and the Syndics have managed to develop fire control systems that can compensate for that distortion up to a certain point. Past point two light speed, the distortion is too great. We can't see exactly where the target is, or exactly what its vector is. And that means we can't hit it."

"Ah." Aragon nodded, gazing at her own display. "And that CEO wants to make sure she gets hits on this mobile unit. How well can they aim? Because I'm sure that CEO wants to cripple this ship so we'll have to surrender."

"They can tell their fire control systems to try to hit our main propulsion," Michael said. "But with the window for firing at each other literally a tiny fraction of a second, in practice the hits could strike anywhere. They could only precisely target hits if our relative speeds are a lot lower." He paused. "You think they'd let us surrender?"

"Sure. To save this mobile unit for themselves." Aragon gave him a humorless smile. "*Then* they'd kill all of us."

"That's what I thought," Geary said. "I guess the Syndicate Worlds doesn't have a Black Jack to tell them to knock that off."

She shook her head. "If any CEO showed signs of being that capable, the other CEOs would find ways to tear them down or isolate them. Like Drakon. He got sent to Midway because it was an out-of-the-way place where he couldn't win any high-profile victories or accumulate supporters. Apparently that gave Drakon room to revolt, but he couldn't have managed that until Black Jack smashed most of the Syndicate's mobile forces."

"I hope he's grateful to Black Jack," Michael said. "Lieutenant Bailey?"

Instead of replying directly, Bailey turned to yell. "Chief North, hurry!"

"I am hurrying!" North shouted back.

Geary studied his display again. "We can't avoid that heavy cruiser. He's maneuverable enough to force us to engage him while we're trying to learn how to operate this ship. If we try to turn away, he'll be able to hit our rear shields and have a lot better chance of damaging our main propulsion. But if we go head to head with our bow shields this weak, that cruiser might do a lot of damage to this ship."

"Why can't you dodge?" Aragon demanded.

"Dodge?"

"Zig. Zag. Make it harder for him to hit us."

"We don't—" Michael paused, thinking. "We never do that in space battles. We don't flinch, Alliance or Syndic. We charge straight in and fight. Just like we're doing now. That's supposedly what Black Jack would do. But he didn't do that at Prime."

"Five minutes to contact," an Alliance officer reported.

They were all watching him, Michael knew. Counting on a Geary to win a fight despite the currently lopsided firepower and shields that gave the Syndic heavy cruiser a substantial advantage. "When Black Jack took command of the Alliance Fleet at Prime, he did the one thing no one expected. Instead of charging the enemy, he repositioned. He avoided combat."

"Captain Geary!" Lieutenant Bailey called. "Chief North got the controls working! Shield strength is finally building."

Geary checked his display. "Check me on this, Lieutenant. The shields won't be able to get close to full strength before we meet that heavy cruiser."

"I concur, sir," Bailey said heavily. "They won't."

"You and Chief North did one hell of a job," Michael said. "We've got a chance now. Let's see what I can do with what we've got."

He knew what to do. It went against everything he'd been taught in the fleet. It went against the supposed example of Black Jack. But, somehow, Michael thought the granduncle he'd finally had the chance to talk to would approve of what he was planning.

Only two hell-lance batteries operational. No missiles. Only three working grapeshot launchers. Shields still far from full strength. It made no sense to trade blows with a heavy cruiser that had shields at maximum and all of its armament available.

His hand rested on the maneuvering controls. They weren't hugely different from those on Alliance ships, because the requirements were the same. And he had a decent idea of how this battle cruiser could maneuver because he'd seen and fought against Syndic battle cruisers any number of times.

Talking to Aragon had given him an idea. Why did honor demand taking a heavy blow? It was one thing to stand up and take the hits when that accomplished something, as with the loss of the *Repulse* that still haunted him. But doing that because avoiding the blow was dishonorable? His sister Jane had scoffed at the idea that battleships were less honorable commands because of their heavy armor and very powerful shields. "I can be a Geary without throwing my life away," she'd told him.

He'd already suggested that he would avoid combat completely if that was the best way to keep his word. That hadn't been possible when there was only one jump point to head for and this ship's maneuverability had been limited. But, now…

Relativistic distortion wasn't the only way to throw off fire control systems. Doing something unexpected could also achieve that, if it happened at the last possible moment so fire control systems didn't have time to compensate while two warships were tearing past each at a combined velocity of sixty thousand kilometers per second.

He was vaguely aware of shield strength climbing on this ship, climbing too slowly with only seconds left. He could sense the other Alliance personnel on the bridge watching him, either confident that a Geary would win or anxious to see if the Geary legend also applied to Black Jack's descendants. In the secondary command seat next to him, Aragon leaned back as if unconcerned, her attitude calming the soldiers still stationed on the bridge. But Michael kept his primary focus on the oncoming heavy cruiser, trying to judge the right instant to act.

"The heavy cruiser is firing missiles," an Alliance officer reported, his voice tense.

Geary's fingers twitched as if of their own accord, hitting the thruster controls, holding briefly, then releasing them. Thrusters fired on the battle cruiser, shoving the ship to one side and up, altering its vector very slightly.

A very slight change in vector made a big difference over the span of sixty thousand kilometers.

The heavy cruiser had been far off, then suddenly there, the moment of closest approach too vanishingly brief for human senses to really spot, human brains generating the image they thought should have been seen, then the enemy was far behind. In the wake of that moment, Geary finally registered the shuddering of this ship as some of the enemy shots managed to score lucky hits, a particularly violent shake marking the detonation of a missile just too far off to cause significant damage.

"Most of the enemy shots missed," another Alliance officer said. She continued, a bit breathless but keeping her words clear. "We suffered spot failures to shields midships and aft. We took minor damage to two compartments aft."

Geary nodded, trying to keep his own voice steady. "Very well." His desperate ploy had worked. The heavy cruiser's fire control systems had seen the thrusters firing, and had anticipated they would keep firing, changing the vector of the battle cruiser more and more. By cutting off the thrusters again so quickly, Geary had thrown off the enemy estimates of where the battle cruiser would be, and most of the enemy shots had torn through empty space, the missiles unable to change their own tracks in time to manage intercepts.

Of course his own weapons, a mere two hell-lance batteries, had done no damage to the heavy cruiser, only temporarily weakening its shields in places.

"So," Aragon said in the casual tones of someone discussing the weather, "you dodged him. That didn't seem too hard."

"I got lucky," Michael said.

"Now we head for the jump point?" Aragon asked.

"No. He's too close. He can volley missiles at our weaker stern shields and might damage our main propulsion. If we're going to be hit again, it will be while we're attacking, not running away."

"Fine," Aragon scoffed. "Why should next time be any different?"

"Because of this," Geary said, grinning as he pointed to part of his display. "Lieutenant Bailey, confirm this for me. Are all of our weapons unlocked?"

"Yes, sir!" Bailey reported, her own smile relieved and triumphant in equal measure. "We'll start powering them up immediately—"

"No!" Geary ordered. "Not yet." He was maneuvering the ship, bringing the battle cruiser up and around to reengage the heavy cruiser, which was looping down and to the side to stage another attack run. How could he ensure this exchange of fire did the most damage possible to an enemy who might become wary when faced with a battle cruiser's full armament? "Lieutenant, what's the latest we can start powering up those weapons and have them ready to fire when we met that heavy cruiser again?"

Chief North answered him. "Captain, if we do all the prep work, the hell lances can power up in three minutes."

"These are Syndic systems. Are you confident of that, Chief?"

"Hell, yes. Sir."

"What about the grapeshot?" Michael asked.

"One minute to fully charge the rest of the launchers," Lieutenant Bailey said.

"We'd have time it just right," Michael said.

"Captain?" Chief North gestured toward the equipment behind her. "I should be able to link powering up the weapons to the fire control system estimate of time to engage. That would cause the fire control to start the powering-up sequences at exactly the right instant. Assuming we and the enemy don't maneuver at the last moment."

There would be a risk if he did this. But they might be able to hit that heavy cruiser hard enough to disable it. And the battle cruiser's own shields would be at maximum strength this time. "Make it happen," Michael said. "If you run into potential glitches, I need to know immediately." He took a careful look at his display, where both warships were making immense loops through space to reengage each other. "We have an estimated twenty minutes until the next exchange of fire."

"We'll be ready, Captain Geary!" Lieutenant Bailey promised.

"Executive Aragon," Geary said. "What's the CEO running that heavy cruiser thinking and doing right now?"

Aragon smiled. "She's raising hell because so many shots missed. Telling her workers they'd better score one hundred percent hits next time. Threatening to shoot certain people if they don't hurt this ship pretty bad this time."

Michael nodded. "The heavy cruiser will make its firing run as close to us as possible, trying to score maximum hits and inflict maximum possible damage. Especially since it still looks like we only have two working hell-lance batteries. Do you think they'll veer off when they see us starting to power up the rest of our weapons?"

"You're going to sucker punch them?" Aragon smiled again. "Good plan, Captain Michael Geary. Maybe not so *honorable*, but good plan. Because even though the executives on that ship might see what's happening and want to dodge themselves this time, that CEO is mad and will insist they keep going, hoping to still hit us before those weapons of ours are ready to fire. Of course, if they're not great executives on that ship, they'll be so afraid of making the CEO angrier they won't even suggest dodging. They'll just stay straight on, following orders, not questioning whether changing circumstances mean they should rethink their plan."

Geary spared a moment to study her impassive expression. "It sounds like you're speaking from experience."

"Sure, I am. I notice you're not saying I must be wrong," Aragon said. "Maybe your experience is the same?"

"It has been at times," Michael said. "Too many times."

She grinned. "But not this time. Not on this unit. Eh?"

"Not this time on this ship," Geary agreed. He played with the thrusters, altering the battle cruiser's vector to line up for an intercept with the Syndic heavy cruiser, which was also coming out of its loop and steadying on a course aimed at another attack.

They would come straight in, the arcs forming the intercept paths for both ships meeting far ahead.

"We're going to hit him with everything we've got," Michael told the other Alliance officers on the bridge.

"Our shields are at maximum but our other weapons haven't powered up yet, Captain," one of them noted in a worried voice.

"They will," Michael said, drawing looks of relief and confidence. "Introduce yourselves, please."

"Lieutenant William Law, Captain," the man said.

"Lieutenant Esther Kuei, Captain," the woman officer said.

"And Chief Okoro, right?"

"Yes, Captain," the chief replied. "Harshan Okoro."

"You're all already a good bridge team," Michael said, "giving me all the support I need." He'd observed how important it was to notice and comment on such things long before he became a commanding officer himself, sometimes by watching good examples from his superiors, and sometimes by experiencing bad examples. "What ships are you off of?"

"Chief Okoro and I were on *Renown*, sir," Lieutenant Law said.

"I was on the heavy cruiser *Sallet*, Captain," Lieutenant Kuei said. "I think almost all of the prisoners with us were either taken at Lakota, or from *Repulse*."

Michael nodded, not trusting himself to speak as he thought about the rest of the crew of *Repulse*. Chief Taman was here. What had happened to Commander Estrada, Lieutenant Aiko, and so many others? Held at other prison camps, or killed during the battle or afterward?

He couldn't focus on that. Not now.

Maybe never.

He kept his eyes on his display, trying to think of nothing but the upcoming engagement.

At exactly three minutes before the projected intercept, an alert appeared on Geary's display.

"Hell lances are powering up, Captain!"

Aragon gave him a measuring look. "You can be pretty sneaky when you want to be, can't you, Captain Michael Geary?"

"Only against my opponents," he replied, returning her look. "Anyone on my side has nothing to worry about."

One minute to intercept.

"All grapeshot launchers are powering up, Captain. Fire control is locked on the Syndic."

He didn't maneuver as the ships closed on each other, wanting his own shots to have the maximum chance to hit. A heavy cruiser was seriously outclassed by the full armament of a battle cruiser. Maybe the heavy cruiser's crew would have rethought their actions if they'd known this ship would have all of its weapons ready as well as shields at maximum. But they hadn't learned that until after committing to this firing run, and Geary knew from bitter experience that even a lot of Alliance officers wouldn't have altered their approach at this point. Not if that made them look like they were avoiding a fight.

The battle cruiser shuddered as the moment of engagement came and went in a millisecond's time, automated firing systems handling a job that human reflexes were far too slow to manage. Every hell-lance battery on the battle cruiser unleashed particle beams, while the grapeshot launchers hurled out fields of metal ball bearings, even more deadly in space against fast-moving objects than their ancient counterparts had been.

"We sustained numerous hits on forward shields!" Lieutenant Kuei reported. "Spot failures. We've lost hell-lance battery 3A. Several compartments holed forward. No serious damage."

"Very well," Michael said. "What about the Syndic?"

"Damage assessments coming in. Damn, Captain, these Syndic systems…Wait. We hurt him, Captain Geary. Estimates show major damage forward. His shields have totally collapsed. They are not rebuilding. He must have lost his shield generators. At least half of the Syndic's weapons are knocked out. With that much damage he must have lost a lot of his crew as well."

"He's not maneuvering," Lieutenant Law reported. "We must have crippled his maneuvering systems."

"Good," Geary said. He had already begun bringing the battle cruiser around again in a vast arc through space. "He won't be able to avoid our next attack. We'll finish him off."

Maybe once upon a time, when the war began, the Syndics would have been offered the chance to surrender. That rarely happened now. Too many decades of war had swept away such merciful concepts.

But Black Jack had ordered that prisoners not be shot. Had his great-uncle also revived the tradition of offering a stricken enemy a chance to surrender before being destroyed?

"What's he doing?" Lieutenant Law wondered.

The Syndic heavy cruiser had abruptly shut off its main propulsion, then just as suddenly reactivated it. Then it cut off again.

"Discipline is falling apart on that unit," Aragon said, her voice toneless. "The workers, knowing the ship is doomed, want to abandon it. The CEO and the snakes enforcing her authority are killing everyone who refuses to fight to the last. Maybe the executives are striking back, trying to keep from dying. Expect to see the unit's workers beginning to abandon ship."

Michael stared at her, trying to imagine such an outcome.

"One Syndic escape pod has launched from the heavy cruiser! Targeting—"

"Negative!" Michael ordered. "I've learned that Black Jack has forbidden anyone in the Alliance Fleet killing prisoners. I consider all of us bound by that order, and those fleeing Syndics to be effectively prisoners. Do not target any escape pods. Make sure every shot is aimed at that heavy cruiser."

A few more escape pods leaped away from the heavy cruiser as Michael lined up for a firing run that would surely destroy the Syndic warship.

Chief Taman called in from engineering. "Captain, if I'm interpreting these Syndic sensors right, readings from the heavy cruiser's power core are going critical."

Michael Geary hit the maneuvering controls, swinging the battle cruiser off its intercept with the Syndic warship.

A moment later the heavy cruiser vanished in a burst of unleashed energy that flared outward to engulf the fleeing escape pods.

"How did that happen?" Lieutenant Law gasped. "Captain, we didn't have any warning signs coming off that ship's power core. The readings off it didn't show any signs it had been damaged by our fire. Then suddenly it went out of control."

"The snakes," Aragon said, her voice flat. "Armageddon response. The crew had mutinied, was trying to run, so the surviving snakes, maybe the CEO, triggered a deliberate power core overload. We'd been warned that would happen to anyone who revolted, that success was impossible because the Syndicate would ensure we all died."

"Captain," Lieutenant Kuei said, her voice shaken, "all of the escape pods that managed to launch were still inside the blast radius when that power core blew. None of them survived."

It was one thing to know opponents were dying during a battle. It was another to watch them be murdered by their own side.

"Do you understand now, Captain Michael Geary?" Aragon said. "You and all of the other Alliance prisoners of war? Do you understand why revolt was so difficult, when similar methods would be employed against entire rebellious cities? When snakes and Syndicate citizens still loyal would be willing to kill so many just to ensure anyone who wasn't loyal didn't win? And do you understand why my workers killed every snake instead of giving them any chance to surrender?"

He knew the questions were aimed not just at him, but at every Alliance Fleet officer and sailor who could hear her. Did Aragon know about the arguments on Alliance warships wondering why the Syndics kept fighting, kept supporting a government that did such awful things? And the conclusions that the average Syndic must be in favor of those things, must want the war to continue, because why else would they let their government stay in power?

Easy questions to ask when you didn't have to worry about

fanatical security agents willing to destroy a ship, or a city, if anyone mutinied against the government.

"Why did you act at this time?" Geary asked her. "I understand why revolt was so…hard. But what made you risk it?"

Aragon shrugged. "I told you. Black Jack tore most of the Syndicate mobile forces to pieces. They were the ultimate enforcers,
you know. Suppose you gained control of a city, took it from the
government. The Syndicate didn't have to send troops, didn't have
to fight to get the city back. The Syndicate had plenty of cities. It
would send a battleship to orbit that world and drop rocks on the
city. Everyone in the city would die, unable to defend themselves.
And the citizens in every other city on every other world would
be told of it, and know what would happen to them.

"But when Black Jack smashed so many Syndicate warships,
the Syndicate couldn't threaten that anymore. And everyone
knew Black Jack had taken the Alliance Fleet back to Prime and
forced the CEOs to surrender on his terms. They weren't all powerful. Not anymore. That's why now, Captain Michael Geary.
Because the war ended, and the Alliance is no longer a threat to
our worlds, and under Black Jack your fleet has *protected* some
of our worlds, and the Syndicate is so weakened it can no longer force compliance. We've heard. The Syndicate tries to keep it
secret, but we have heard. Star systems like Midway have fought
and gained their freedom. We will, too."

Michael looked around, seeing the other Alliance personnel
watching Aragon with newfound understanding. "Do you know
anything about the surrender terms? Were the Syndicate Worlds
supposed to return all prisoners of war?"

"Sure, they were supposed to," Aragon said. "They returned
some, the ones the Alliance knew about. But the Syndicate has
held on to other prisoners, like you guys. Probably as future

bargaining chips. But something convinced the Syndicate you were liabilities now, not valuable property. Maybe they're scared of what Black Jack would do if he found out they've been holding his scion instead of returning you. So you all would've been blown to dust after they pulled my unit and all of the snakes off that orbiting prison."

"I admit," Michael said, "that I'd wondered if even Syndic CEOs could be that ruthless. But after watching that heavy cruiser be destroyed, I'm not doubting you." He sighed, checking his display. "Get us on a track to enter that jump point, Lieutenant Law. Do we know where it leads?"

"Ravana Star System," Lieutenant Kuei said. "I had some time to look that up. But there's no information that I can access about Ravana."

Aragon stood up, grimacing. "Information like that, even if widely known, is classified in the Syndicate. The files would only be accessible to the CEO and top executives on a unit like this." She raised her comm link. "Sub-Executives Harbin and Nedele, inform all of your workers that the Alliance prisoners have defeated the Syndicate heavy cruiser. Our path out of this star system is clear. Get your hackers working on access to the senior executive files. We're going to Ravana. I need to know what's waiting for us there."

4

MICHAEL looked around the conference room, impressed despite himself at the quality of the equipment and the comfort of the seats. "This is a surprise. Based on what I've seen of most of the ship, I thought this would be a bare-bones setup in here."

"This is the executive conference room," Aragon said, sitting down and leaning back in one of the chairs. "That super comfy chair you're relaxing in? That would be for a CEO. Have you been to the command executive or CEO's quarters aboard this unit?"

"Not yet," he replied with a yawn. "I've been making sure the other former prisoners have decent quarters. Most of the berthing available on this ship looks pretty much the same as the prison facilities."

"Yeah. Standard worker accommodations," Aragon said. "Life in the Syndicate is pretty good for those at the top. Not so good for those at the bottom." She paused. "My family was at the bottom until my grandmother pulled us out. The woman was like a demon. Unstoppable. She dragged her husband and children with her out of worker level and up to the executive ranks."

Geary studied her, trying to judge Aragon's feelings. "That sounds like someone the Syndicate Worlds would want."

"No," Aragon said, her gaze on the table. "It made the family suspect because we'd risen from the worker ranks. Maybe we were still too sympathetic to the workers. The snakes always kept a close eye on us. Closer than usual, that is. My mother disappeared several years ago. She might be in a labor camp somewhere. Or she might be dead. I don't know."

"I'm...sorry," Geary said, knowing the words were totally inadequate. "Do you have any siblings?"

"A brother. Supposedly he died two years ago fighting the Alliance."

"Supposedly?"

"That's what the Syndicate told me. Maybe it's true. Maybe he was really taken prisoner. Or maybe he's in a labor camp." She inhaled deeply, letting it out slowly. "Are you married, Captain Michael Geary?"

He tensed inside. Aragon couldn't know how heavily charged that question was for him. But then, she knew nothing about what it had been like to grow up as a Geary, or the broken promises once made with his sister. "I was." Why had he told her the truth?

"Was?" Aragon looked at him.

"She died. In an accident. While I was a long way off, fighting in the war," Michael said.

Aragon kept her eyes on him. "You loved her, huh? I can hear it."

"Yes. I loved her." He had to move this conversation away from him. "What about you? Do you have a spouse anywhere?"

"Had one," Aragon said as if indifferent. "He met a higher-ranked executive who looked like she was on her way up, and traded me for her. Just business, you know? Very Syndicate. Any kids, Captain Michael Geary?"

He hesitated. "Yes. I...don't know where...how they're doing."

Aragon nodded. "Funny we have that in common. I've got a son. He should be six years old. Back on Anahuac. I don't know, though. Where he is, what happened."

Geary stared at her, startled to feel such a strong burst of empathy for a Syndic. "This war sucks."

"I bet every war sucks," Aragon said. "You're wondering why I'm talking about this stuff, right?"

"Yes, I am."

"We found the files on Ravana. I'll pass you the links. Here's the important thing," Aragon said. "There's a labor camp at Ravana. The snake files on this ship had data on the prisoners there." She leaned forward, forearms on the table, her gaze fixed on him. "My unit is the 1233rd Regiment. The prisoners at the labor camp in Ravana are almost all from the 1234th Regiment. Survivors of the 1234th. They're Tigres from Anahuac, just like me, just like my workers."

Michael gazed back at her, feeling cautious again about what Aragon was driving at. "Did they mutiny, too?"

"Huh? No. If they had, they'd all be dead. They were cut to pieces fighting the Alliance, but failed to take their objectives. It was the fault of the CEO in command, but CEOs can't be blamed for failures. The survivors of the 1234th were punished for the failure, to serve as an example to others. The labor camp is a mining facility orbiting a gas giant." She leaned a little closer, her eyes intent. "We're going to Ravana anyway. You *must* take us to that labor camp so we can liberate our comrades."

Geary sat back, spreading his hands helplessly. "Executive Aragon, we're deep in enemy territory in an undercrewed and inadequately supplied enemy warship. We don't know what kinds of defenses Ravana has, but I assume these labor camps have guard forces. How could we—"

"How could we leave them?" Aragon demanded. "How could we fail to help our comrades, our fellow Tigres? You speak often of honor, Captain Michael Geary. Where would be the honor in abandoning our comrades? You would not allow any of your fellow prisoners to be left behind. If there is any of this honor in us, it is that we will not leave our friends in a Syndicate labor camp without trying to save them."

He closed his eyes for a moment, breathing slowly, before looking at her again. "That is the honorable thing to do. We understand each other when it comes to that. But…"

"It's not part of the deal we made. You want to renegotiate."

Michael scowled over her misinterpretation of his hesitancy, shaking his head. "No."

"I haven't got anything else to offer you in exchange for this, Captain Michael Geary. Are you willing to accept an IOU in the event you need something outside the deal?"

He looked at her, slowly realizing that this was how Aragon thought because of her experiences in the Syndicate Worlds. She needed the framework of an agreed-upon deal between them. "Yes," Geary finally said. "I'll accept that IOU."

"It's not a blank check," Aragon cautioned him, her gaze on him growing harder. "When you want to cash in that IOU, we negotiate the terms."

"Fine," Geary said. Why was she so insistent on that? And what was she clearly warning him *not* to ask for?

Then he remembered Aragon's story of the supervisor who had demanded physical favors from her. Did she still think he'd do something like that? Michael realized he was scowling again in response to his thoughts and smoothed out his expression. "Fine," he repeated. "I'll need to discuss it with the other Alliance personnel, let them know what's going on, but they should understand your reasons."

Aragon sat up a little, watching him with hope and skepticism mingled. "You agree? We raid that labor camp, we rescue our comrades. You get an IOU with limits."

"Yes, I agree. If we can figure out a way to do it." Geary waved around him. "We've got one ship, which doesn't have enough crew and is lacking missiles. And we've got your limited number of soldiers. I've seen how good your soldiers are. I think my Alliance personnel, some of whom are really rusty after years in prison, and all of whom need to train more together, can also do a lot. But all of that's not much."

"My Tigres can handle their end," Aragon said. "What about your Marines? Are they any good at anything besides tackling sentries?"

"Anything any former Syndics can do, my people can do better," Geary said. "Even the impossible," he added, remembering Chief North's comments about the equipment on this ship.

Aragon gave him a fierce grin. "Then let's go do the impossible. If you dare, Captain Michael Geary, Black Jack's scion."

He shook his head. "You're a very dangerous woman, Executive Aragon. You've talked me into it. But you do realize, if this is a raid, you might lose a lot of your own people trying to liberate those other Tigres."

She nodded. "Better to die at Ravana, trying to save our comrades, than on some hellhole of a world where the Syndicate sent us to try to suppress another rebellion."

"That's your call to make," Geary said. "Do you have any idea where the Syndics were going to send you?"

"I know exactly where they were going to send us," Aragon said. "Some star named Kane, aligned with Midway. Meaning we'd be going up against Drakon. Meaning we'd all die." She stood up. "Thank you, Captain Michael Geary. Sometimes I think I might someday respect you."

He couldn't help laughing for a moment.

His good humor died when he finally got to the commanding officer's stateroom, and saw that Aragon hadn't exaggerated when she said how luxurious it would be. He also saw the few personal possessions of the Syndic internal security service "snake" who had commanded this ship before being killed by Aragon's soldiers. A small projection just above the desk held Michael's attention as it cycled through pictures of a family. Cheerful mother, three kids, proud father. Michael recognized the man, whom he'd last seen sprawled lifeless in the primary command seat on the bridge. He gazed at the images of the happy family, wondering how many other families had been hurt by that same man. His spouse in some images wore a similar suit, so she must also be an internal security service agent. Did they ever think about how their actions had torn apart other happy families? Did their children know what their parents did?

Did monsters ever look in the mirror and see a monster?

He had never been happy with the legacy of being a Geary. But at least Gearys had a heritage based on defending the Alliance. Suppose instead his parents had been "snakes," ruthlessly enforcing the will of a despotic government that had started the century-long war? How would he have dealt with that? Would he have rebelled against that legacy, or gone along with it, tried to justify it, rather than confront the truth?

What if the Black Jack he had briefly met had turned out to be an ambitious, cold-hearted spender of human lives, interested only in whatever benefit their deaths might bring him? At least the living stars had spared him that awful dilemma.

He'd had other things to distract him until now, but finally had to confront his own fears about this strange arrangement he had agreed to. Was Executive Destina Aragon what she seemed, a professional with her own code of "honor," though she'd probably laugh at the word being applied to her? Or was she putting on an act with him so he wouldn't realize she was the sort of person who would commit atrocities without hesitation? Could he ever trust a Syndic, even one that had rebelled against the Syndicate Worlds?

Had everything she told him been true? What did "truth" even mean to a Syndic? At least he could check some of Aragon's story in the files aboard this ship.

Michael shook his head, realizing that even though he was out of that cell and apparently in command of a battle cruiser, he still had no choice. The only hope for getting the rest of the former prisoners of war home required working with Aragon. And hoping that partnership wouldn't stain his own honor beyond any hope of redemption.

He needed to sleep without the nightmares the personal items of a dead man might bring to him. Michael shut off the projection after deleting all of the images, and shoved everything else into the waste recycling or disposal units, including the sheets on the oddly large stateroom bed.

MICHAEL rubbed his eyes as he sat back down in the command seat on the bridge of the battle cruiser. He hadn't slept at all, but wanted to ensure he was on the bridge when they entered jump for Ravana.

Executive Aragon dropped into the secondary command seat. "You're moving into the commanding officer's quarters, right?"

"Right," Geary said. "I'm already in there. The CEO quarters are…too plush. Where are you going to stay?"

"Second-in-command's stateroom. Not as fancy as yours, but it's got all I need."

"Captain Geary," Lieutenant Law said, "we're five minutes from the jump point."

"Good," Michael said.

"Captain? What's the name of this ship?"

Geary gave Law a startled look, seeing that the other Alliance personnel on the bridge were watching and listening, intent on the answer. "I don't know. Executive Aragon, what's the Syndicate name for this ship?"

Aragon looked at him as if baffled by the question. "Name? This is Mobile Forces Unit D-555."

"That's a designation," Michael said. "Not a name. Doesn't the ship have a name?"

"It's a piece of machinery. It has a unit designation."

"With all due respect," Lieutenant Kuei spoke up, "a ship is not just a piece of machinery. A ship is more than just metal and composites. Ships are living things. She is also her crew and... her spirit."

Aragon rolled her eyes. "More Alliance superstitions? What is this? She? Do you want a 'girl' you can order around?"

Michael frowned, shaking his head. "It's a mark of strength. This ship is a...girl...that can kick the butt of any Syndic warship we encounter. It's not proclaiming our control of the ship. It's an acknowledgement that she is a powerful entity who should be respected."

Aragon let out a heavy, exasperated sigh. "Fine, Captain Michael Geary. If your superstitions say this mobile forces unit should have a name, go ahead and give it a name. But not one of those Alliance names. None of that Spurious, Outrageous, or Irresponsible nonsense."

What name would fit? Michael wondered. A battle cruiser in the Alliance Fleet would have an inspiring name. But this wasn't an Alliance Fleet ship, and he didn't want Aragon and the other former Syndics mocking any name the Alliance personnel chose. That could lead to more friction between the groups. "Any suggestions?" he asked the others on the bridge.

After a pause, Lieutenant Kuei spoke up. "We did steal the ship, Captain. Maybe something related to that?"

"We requisitioned it," Lieutenant Law corrected, smiling. "We're not pirates."

"It was sort of an act of piracy," Geary noted. "So, like a pirate ship? Maybe…*Corsair*. That's an old term for pirates."

"I like *Corsair*," Lieutenant Kuei said. The others on the bridge nodded.

Geary looked at Aragon, who made a "who cares" gesture. "Whatever."

"Then this ship is henceforth the *Corsair*," Michael announced. An alert pinged. They were at the jump point. "Lieutenant Law, activate the jump drive and take *Corsair* into jump space for Ravana Star System."

The Alliance personnel cheered, while the former Syndics looked on with expressions of derision or incomprehension.

It had been a long time since he'd entered jump space. Michael flinched as the transition jolted his brain. The view outside, once of endless stars in endless space, was replaced by a dull, gray nothingness. "Five and a half days until we come out of jump at Ravana," Lieutenant Law reported.

"Good." That wasn't very long. The longer humans stayed in jump space, the more uncomfortable they got. It could literally drive people insane. "I'm going to finally get some sleep. Lieutenant Law, work up a watch rotation for the bridge." He touched the communications controls. "Lieutenant Bailey, you can secure fire control. Set up a watch to make sure someone is always there. Chief Taman, do the same for engineering. I want everyone to get some rest. Over the next few days we need to focus on learning as much as we can about how to operate the Syndic systems on this ship, and practice dealing with different emergencies." He paused, thinking how reassuring such routine-feeling commands were. "Well done, everyone."

He stood up, looking toward Aragon. "Are you going to stay up here?"

She nodded without saying anything, her gaze fixed on her display, her expression closed off. She was probably thinking about her comrades at Ravana, Michael thought as he headed back to the stateroom once occupied by the Syndic commanding officer of this ship.

Or thinking about how to betray him and the other Alliance personnel after they'd delivered the Tigres to Anahuac.

WAS Captain Michael Geary oblivious or just naïve? Aragon wondered as she checked on all of her subordinates and workers the next ship's day. He had seemed too relaxed when she spoke with him briefly, as if unworried about what his group of former prisoners might do with their freedom, and what the Tigres of her unit might do when confronted repeatedly by members of the Alliance they had fought and hated all of their lives.

Yet he had seemed competent enough when dealing with that Syndicate ship. Once jarred out of his imprisonment-produced moodiness, Michael Geary had performed as Black Jack's scion would be expected to do.

But he had agreed to an operation at Ravana to liberate her fellow Tigres with suspiciously little argument. Why? A small part of her wanted to believe it was because Michael Geary was Black Jack's scion, but the larger, embittered-by-experience part of her wondered what he might be planning, and how she could protect herself and her workers against whatever it was.

Walking down a passageway, Aragon saw a group of her workers watching several Alliance former prisoners who were working on some equipment while arguing among themselves and clearly trying to pretend they weren't aware of the soldiers studying them with hostile expressions.

She knew this kind of tension, when workers were winding themselves up, unable to release their stress until it blew up. "Stop thinking it," she told her workers, who stiffened to attention when they realized their commander was here. "Rein it in. Do you want to get home? We need them. Anyone who starts a fight will answer to me."

"We understand and will comply," the workers chorused.

"Go get something to eat and then get some sleep."

"We understand and will comply."

Aragon walked on past the Alliance workers, who watched her with worried gazes.

She met Sub-Executives Harbin and Nedele in a different conference room from where she'd spoken to Michael Geary. Not as nice as the CEO's conference room, but intended for executives and therefore not too basic.

"We're sitting on a bomb waiting to explode," Harbin told her. "As long as the workers were fighting the snakes, they were fine with whatever happened to the Alliance dirtballs. But now they see them moving around freely. It feels *wrong*. It feels dangerous."

"Harbin's right," Nedele said, her voice firm. "Sooner or later, someone is going to start shooting. Probably the Alliance, because they're so undisciplined. It should be us who starts it. Get it over with and make sure we lose as few of our own workers as possible."

Aragon sat down, deliberately leaning back, extending her legs, and resting her feet on the table. "That's your advice? And when we've killed the Alliance Fleet officers who know how to operate this ship, how do we get home to Anahuac, Sub-Executive Nedele?"

Nedele hesitated. "We leave a few of them alive. Make them take us home."

Aragon swung her legs down, slamming her feet to the deck, leaning forward to clench a fist that hit the table. "And how long would it be before those survivors lock this ship on a dive into the nearest star? We wouldn't even know they were doing it until it was done. If we turn this into a fight to the death between us and those Alliance prisoners, that's exactly what we'll get. Death."

A brief silence answered her.

"Executive Aragon," Harbin said heavily, "you have highlighted our problem. We need them to operate this ship. But now that we've captured this ship, they don't need us anymore. Get rid of us in a surprise attack, and they can head straight for their home without worrying about getting us to Anahuac."

Aragon nodded to him, realizing that Harbin's open statement of her secret fears had caused her own instincts to crystallize in a surprising way. "You are correct, Sub-Executive Harbin. If I had made a deal with anyone other than Black Jack's scion, that is what I would expect from these Alliance workers. Captain Michael Geary has surely realized they no longer need us. But he is Black Jack's scion. You saw him speak with those Marines. It's not just that Alliance honor thing. He intends to keep the deal. I'm staking my life on that belief, as well as your lives." She keyed a command to bring up a display of Ravana Star System. "Here is one reason I believe that. Geary has agreed to our proposed action at Ravana. He will take us to the orbital labor camp so we can free our comrades."

"Of course he will," Nedele scoffed. "He's figured out they can let us leave the ship to attack that labor camp, and then take off, abandoning us. There's no need for a stand-up fight that might cost them a lot of dead when he can stab us in the back that way."

Aragon shook her head. "He's smart enough to know we won't send all of our people off the ship. He must know we'd expect betrayal, and will keep a strong force aboard this unit to prevent that."

Harbin pointed to the display. "Executive, we've been working with that guidance from you, and there's a big problem. Nedele and I have been running attack scenarios. We've gone through every option we can think of in the simulations, and we keep coming up with the same outcome. We'll need every Tigre we've got left in the unit for the assault on the labor camp. If we send in everyone, we'll have a good chance of quickly overcoming the guard force and other defenses, and freeing our comrades before they can be massacred. If we hold back any significant number of workers, we won't have enough. Maybe Black Jack's scion has already figured that out, too."

Aragon frowned, gazing at the display, thinking. "You're saying we need more workers. How many?"

"We assumed roughly forty or fifty had to remain on the ship as the minimum to ensure the Alliance doesn't betray us," Nedele said. "So that's our deficit. We need forty or fifty more workers than we've got. And there's no way to get more. We either give the Alliance a free shot at abandoning us, or we go in with too few soldiers to have a decent chance of success."

Aragon felt herself smiling. "We need fifty more soldiers."

"We haven't got them," Harbin insisted, giving her a puzzled look.

"No," Aragon agreed. "We don't have fifty more soldiers. But I know someone who does."

The two sub-executives stared at her until sudden understanding showed.

"The Alliance prisoners?" Harbin said in disbelief.

"*Marines?*" Nedele added. "You want us to depend on Alliance *Marines?*"

Aragon grinned. "How better to ensure the Alliance doesn't try to abandon us than to have some of their own workers as part of our assault force?"

Slow smiles appeared on the faces of the sub-executives.

MICHAEL yawned and made another try at figuring out the commands on the desk in his stateroom. Syndic software programmers appeared to be just as perverse as Alliance programmers when it came to creating baffling menus, while hiding critical features behind obscure options.

He had managed to find some correspondence related to the mission this ship had been on, messages that seemed to confirm what Aragon had told him. *Upon removal of all workers from Orbital Facility PC88X, execute Operation Blind Pyotr.* There wasn't anything explaining what Operation Blind Pyotr was, but the fact that it would take place after all of the Syndic personnel were off the prison, and when no mention had been made of removing the Alliance prisoners as well, was a pretty strong hint that it would have been just what Aragon had warned of. The revolt by Aragon's unit really did seem to have saved not just her people but also all of the Alliance prisoners.

Which still made it very hard to trust a Syndic executive. Aragon seemed to be a good officer, but Syndics were famous for their ability to lie convincingly. And while he had forty-eight Marines in addition to a few hundred Fleet officers and sailors, they wouldn't stand much of a chance if Aragon's well-trained, well-equipped, and experienced "workers" launched an all-out attack.

But they'd probably wait until the ship reached Anahuac before doing that. Wait until they knew they'd reached home, and didn't need the help of the Alliance personnel anymore. How could he prepare for that likely outcome?

"Captain Geary?" Both Chief Tamans were at the door to the stateroom, both looking unhappy. "We need to speak with you."

About something so serious they hadn't called over the comm system but were here in person. "Come in," Michael said.

Chief Taman had a grim expression as he came to attention before Geary, his sister standing beside him. "Captain, we have very serious news."

Michael tried not to wince. "Something to do with the former Syndics?"

"Uh…no, sir. They helped us find this problem."

"How bad a problem are we talking about?"

"Extremely bad." Taman gestured to his sister. "Sindi actually found it."

Chief Sindi Taman pointed aft. "The automated inventory of fuel cells aboard this ship puts us at ninety-two percent of full capacity."

"Yes," Michael said. "I checked that soon after the ship was captured."

"We couldn't physically access the fuel-cell storage areas before now because of security lockouts that the…um…Tigres said might trigger lethal countermeasures if overridden," Sindi Taman explained. "But I'm old school, Captain. I was taught to always physically inventory items and not depend on automated counts, so I've been pushing to get access, and the Tigres finally managed to get those lockouts cleared."

She paused, grimacing. "Captain, I did a physical count. This ship is not at ninety-two percent capacity for fuel cells. We're at fourteen percent."

Geary couldn't move for a moment, staring at her. "Fourteen percent?" he finally managed to say. "Ancestors save us. That's dangerously low. How could the numbers be so far off?"

Chief Taman gestured around them. "The Tigres say corruption is awful in the Syndicate Worlds. Inventories are always being faked. Spares are sold for profit. Maybe the fuel cells got diverted to some black market. Or they suggested maybe it was sabotage by someone who wanted to strand those, um, snakes somewhere."

Sindi Taman nodded with a grim expression. "The automated inventories would have kept telling us we had plenty left, even after we had none. Whatever the reason for it, it was deliberate. The fuel cells we do have are stacked forward in the storage areas to hide the fact that the racks behind them are empty."

"The former Syndics know about this?" Geary asked.

"Yes, sir," Chief Taman said. "We had to have them with us when we went in to do the count, because they had to check for other dangerous security measures we might encounter. So they know."

"We have to physically inventory everything else on this ship," Geary said. "Weapons, spares, food, you name it. And I want every officer informed that we cannot trust the Syndic automated inventories. Maybe we can't trust other data we're getting, either. We have to verify we're getting accurate data from everything."

"I was going to recommend that, Captain," Chief Sindi Taman said. "It's going to be a lot of work, but it's absolutely necessary. Sir, we can't get to Anahuac on fourteen percent of our fuel cells, let alone get home."

Michael nodded, trying not to show how badly this news had rattled him. "I'll run the data to see how far we can get, but I'm sure that you're right. Which means we have to somehow get some more fuel cells."

"How are we going to do that deep in Syndic space, sir?"

"I don't know yet. Maybe there are some we can hijack at Ravana. But we will find them." He only wished he was really as confident of that as he tried to project.

Every plan had just been shredded. Worrying about what would happen when they reached Anahuac didn't make much sense when they couldn't get there with the fuel-cell reserves they had.

And the former Syndics already knew. He'd have to talk to Aragon about this.

"Captain Michael Geary. We need to talk."

He looked past the Chief Tamans, seeing Aragon at the door, her expression once again unrevealing of her emotions.

5

ARAGON waited as the two Alliance senior workers left, wondering at the somber atmosphere she had sensed the moment she reached this stateroom. Something was up. She'd have to see whether Michael Geary would tell her outright or if she would have to demand the information.

"Please have a seat," Geary said, his attitude worried.

"I'm fine standing." Aragon walked to the front of his desk, gazing down at him. "There is a problem."

He nodded. "The fuel cells."

Aragon paused, startled. "The...fuel cells?"

"I was told you'd be aware of it."

She almost snapped at him for the possibly implied rebuke. But her mind was busy trying to figure out why she wouldn't have heard about this fuel-cell thing. Geary himself had apparently just heard it from those workers, so it was a recent development. Her workers would have known to inform her, but they would have also known they should first inform their supervisors, who would have told Sub-Executive Harbin or Nedele.

Both of whom had been in a meeting with her. Workers knew not to interrupt meetings of executives unless it was critical. If the workers had been unsure, they would have waited.

Having figured out why she hadn't heard this information, and reassured that Geary was immediately telling her of it, Aragon regained her mental balance and shook her head at Geary. "Why don't you tell me, Captain Michael Geary?"

"This ship is almost out of fuel."

Whatever else could be said about Michael Geary, he was direct in delivering bad news. How had his superiors in the Alliance Fleet reacted to that? If they were anything like Syndicate CEOs and senior executives, it couldn't have endeared Michael Geary to them. "Why didn't you know this as soon as we took the ship?"

She listened as Geary explained, doing her best not to show how unhappy the news made her.

"The bottom line," Michael Geary finished, "is that our current fuel cell state is so low, we can't even reach Anahuac, let alone proceed on to try to reach Alliance space. If Chief Taman hadn't found out about the problem, our systems would have kept telling us we had plenty of fuel reserves right up until the moment the power core shut down for lack of fuel. That would have left us dependent on a limited amount of backup power and almost helpless."

"It likely was sabotage, then," Aragon said. "Whoever was outfitting this unit knew it was going to be employed by the snakes. What's the answer? How do we deal with this?"

He tapped the table between them for emphasis. "We need to find a source for more fuel cells. Without that, we can't get you to Anahuac. Even diverting to reach that labor camp at Ravana is extremely unwise while our reserves are so low."

"Really?" Aragon fixed him with a look. "Is that what this is about? Finding an excuse to go back on our agreement for Ravana?"

"*No*," Michael Geary said forcefully. "Regardless, we need to get our hands on more fuel cells. Maybe there are some we can access at Ravana."

"You haven't checked?"

It was his turn to look openly affronted at the possible reprimand. "I just found out about this."

She walked around the desk, standing close to him to call up the data on Ravana, aware of him frowning and leaning away so his head wasn't next to her chest. If it was act of pretended respect for her, it was well done. "Here. This 'mobile unit logistics facility.' Is that what we need?"

Geary leaned in, studying the data. "It shows they should have some fuel cells in stock. Maybe not enough, but anything will be better than what we've got. Damn. That facility is orbiting the primary inhabited world at Ravana, within range of surface-based aerospace fighters and orbital defenses."

"Aerospace? You mean Near-Orbit Attack Units?" Aragon tapped a command. "Sure. It says there's a unit assigned to Ravana."

Michael Geary grimaced. "You were planning on surprising the labor camp by pretending to be a CEO. We'll have to use that same idea to get to the logistics facility first."

"First?" Aragon said, letting anger show in her voice. "No. If anything went wrong, an alert would be sounded. We wouldn't have any chance of surprising the labor camp."

Geary rubbed his face, looking weary. "I know that might mean your soldiers take more losses—"

"No! Are you stupid?" Aragon pointed a rigid finger at the data on Ravana. "If the guards at the labor camp know we're coming to try to free the prisoners, they'll terminate all of them before we get there."

He stared at her. "Terminate? Kill all of them?" She watched Geary take in a long breath. "Okay. One, don't call me stupid. I'm not one of your Syndic workers. Are we clear on that? Two, are you certain of that outcome? Is it a possibility, or a certainty?"

Aragon took a step back, calming herself. He was Alliance, she reminded herself, unschooled in the ways of the Syndicate. "A certainty."

He glowered at the display. "But if we hit the labor camp first, the defenses around the planet will be alerted and we won't be able to get those fuel cells. We have to get the fuel cells first."

"It's too likely something will go wrong! We'll either have to abandon our comrades without trying to rescue them, or cause their immediate deaths!"

Geary pointed at the data. "Executive Aragon, if we don't get more fuel cells, it doesn't matter whether we rescue your comrades. We'll run out of fuel for the power core and we won't be going to Anahuac, or anywhere."

"There must be an option," Aragon said, hoping he would think of one.

"We need to be in two places at once," Michael Geary said. "But we've only got one ship." He paused, his eyes hooded. "You know, in the Alliance Fleet, we get taught to think about what Black Jack would do in any situation. But when he ended up in command at Prime, he did something none of the rest of us had thought of while we were trying to think like we thought he would."

"What does that have to do with this?" Aragon demanded.

"He looked at the situation differently than we did and saw something we hadn't. How can I look at this in a different way? Maybe…instead of focusing on trying to be in two places at once…what we need…is to get what we want at one place." He leaned forward, reading the display. "What are these, um, logistics carriers at that logistics facility?"

She bent to look. "Just dumb cargo haulers. Automated. Interplanetary capable, but not equipped for interstellar."

"Can they haul fuel cells?"

Aragon reached to get that data. "Yeah. See?" She straightened, realizing what Geary was thinking. "You want to trick the Syndicate into sending the fuel cells we need to the labor camp?"

"Would that happen?" Geary asked. "Would Syndic CEOs, like you're going to pretend to be, order that logistics facility to send fuel cells to where they were going so they wouldn't have to go out of their way to get them?"

"In a heartbeat," Aragon said, eyeing Geary with renewed respect. "It's what we under the Syndicate would *expect* a CEO to do. So it's believable. Even then, it's not guaranteed. The executive running that facility might balk, might say the fuel cells they have are earmarked for other units. Or the cargo haulers might not get to the labor camp quickly enough and be recalled when we attack. But this plan *could* work, get us what we both need."

"Hopefully," Geary said, looking relieved but still worried. "For now, we can run with that idea. I need to get with my people on running inventories of everything aboard this ship. If there's nothing else…"

Aragon shook her head at the attempted dismissal. "There's something else I need, Captain Michael Geary."

"What's that?"

"Fifty Alliance Marines."

He stared at her again, this time baffled. "I've only got forty-eight Marines among the former prisoners. Why the hell are you asking for them?"

"I need those Marines to assist in the assault on the orbital labor camp."

"You…" Michael Geary paused. "Assist in the assault? Even though my Marines and your soldiers would love any excuse to kill each other?"

"That's right. There's extra battle armor aboard this ship. We'll provide your Marines with that, and teach them how Syndicate battle armor works. Full weapons loadout for every one of them as well. Your Marines are good at assaulting orbital facilities, aren't they?"

"Yes," Michael Geary said, shaking his head, "but…your own soldiers aren't enough? I assumed you'd use your entire unit."

She gazed at him, wondering if she could concoct a plausible-enough-sounding reason, and knowing that anything she told him could be checked by those Marines for validity. If Michael Geary learned she'd lied about her reasons, he would be far less like to believe any other explanation she offered, and far less likely to ever cough up those Marines. "I'll be above the board with you on this, Captain Michael Geary. I need those Marines because I, and my subordinate executives, and my workers, do not trust you or the other Alliance officers and workers."

"That…makes no sense at all," he replied. "If you don't trust us, why do you want the Marines to be part of the attack?"

"Because if your Marines assist in the attack, I can leave some of my workers on this unit to ensure you do not abandon us on that orbiting facility, leaving us there while you depart to try to reach your homes without having to take us to Anahuac."

Michael Geary's face hardened. "I gave you my word of honor. That should be all the insurance you need."

"It's not," Aragon said flatly. "It's not enough for my workers. They don't believe in *honor*. They believe in self-interest. And they know what the Alliance is capable of. We've seen the worlds your fleet has bombarded."

"And I've seen worlds the Syndics have bombarded!" Michael Geary shot back, standing to face her. "Why should I entrust you with the lives of forty-eight Alliance Marines who you might be planning on throwing away to minimize the risk to your own soldiers?"

"I've kept my end of this deal so far! I was willing to renegotiate to arrange the operation against the labor camp!" Aragon said, leaning in toward him. "My people expect you to double-cross us! I need proof that you won't!"

"You need proof? And what do I get in return? What do you offer me in exchange for this?" He had leaned in, too, his angry face close to hers. Too close.

Aragon stepped back, her temper flaring, one hand going to the sidearm holstered at her hip. "That had better not mean what it sounds like."

Puzzlement appeared on his face along with his anger. "What are you talking about?"

"Good judgment, Captain Geary," she said, hearing the menace in her voice.

He jerked with surprise. "You think I meant sex in exchange for the deal?" Still angry, Geary held up his hands in a disarming gesture. "That was not what I meant, not a proposition or a demand. I don't play those kinds of games."

"You don't?" Aragon said, her voice challenging now. "You're a man."

He nodded. "Yeah. A man whose sister would kick his butt out of an airlock if she learned he'd tried to force a woman into a deal like that."

Aragon let her hand drift away from her sidearm. "Your sister is still alive? Lucky you."

"She was the last I heard," Michael Geary said.

"And you're afraid of her?"

"No," he said, his face still hard with anger. "I love her. She's all I've got, the last other surviving Geary." Not true anymore, not with granduncle Black Jack back, but still how he thought of things. "I don't want to do anything that would shame her. I don't want to do anything that would leave her even more alone than she is now."

He seemed sincere. Could she believe him? "How would she ever know what happened on this ship? In that bed over there? Notice it's big enough for two or three? That's one way Syndicate CEOs and senior executives get their payoffs."

He stared at the bed, then away, his revulsion clear. Either Michael Geary was a great actor, or he meant what he was saying. "I don't decide my actions, good or bad, based on whether or not anyone else will ever know what I did. I'll know. My ancestors will know. That's all there is to it."

"All right." She tried to relax and center her thoughts again. Either she believed him, and moved on, or they'd be locked in a stalemate. "If you didn't mean you wanted sexual favors from me in exchange for the agreement, what did you mean? Because I don't want any doubt what happens if you do demand that."

He looked steadily at her, his gaze unwavering. "I'm looking for some reason to agree to this. A professional reason consistent with my responsibilities to those under my command. Give me one. Why should I risk those Marines because you don't trust me?"

He'd thrown it back on her, which if she was honest was more than fair. What reason did she have beyond her own workers' distrust of the Alliance?

Distrust that ran both ways. Fate had given her the answer to this problem in the form of the other problem.

Aragon smiled slightly. "Your workers don't trust me, or my workers."

"No, they don't," Michael Geary admitted.

"If this plan goes as we hope, the fuel cells this ship needs, the fuel cells you need to get back to the Alliance, will be docked at that labor camp. Which means if we capture the camp, we'll control the fuel cells you have to have."

He watched her, nodding slowly. "Which would give you tremendous leverage over us. But if Alliance Marines are part of the assault force, they can secure the fuel cells once the garrison is defeated."

"While my workers focus on recovering our comrades." He was hesitating. She gestured aft. "Your Marines. I've been keeping an eye on them, and getting reports on them. They're…"

"Ready to explode," Michael Geary said. "I know. They've got a lot of built-up frustration and anger."

"Anger at the Syndicate," Aragon said.

He nodded again. "If I ask for volunteers to assault a Syndic base, they'll probably all jump at the chance. But how do I convince them to work with you? To participate alongside your soldiers? Under your combat command?"

Aragon shrugged. "I'm told that Alliance Marines will move mountains for beer."

"There's beer aboard this ship?" Michael Geary looked alarmed at the idea that his workers might get their hands on alcohol.

She understood that concern. "No. Not on the ship. But there will be at the labor camp. For the guards."

"Alliance Marines do have some standards, even when it comes to free beer," Geary said. "But a chance at free beer *and* the opportunity to kill Syndics might be the motivation we need."

Aragon smiled again. "You can also tell them the truth. That your Marines will be there to ensure we do not betray you."

He sat for a long moment before looking at her again. "Okay. Everything about this sucks, but we have to embrace that suck and make it work. This should work. I did think of something else. Is there any chance of Alliance prisoners at that labor camp?"

"There could be," Aragon said.

"Why didn't you dangle that possibility to get me to agree?"

"Because there's only a small chance that any Alliance people will be there. I don't promise what I can't deliver."

Geary stood up again. "All right, Executive Aragon, we have another deal."

She nodded to him, relieved to have a deal that her sub-executives and workers wouldn't have to be threatened into accepting. They'd still have to agree to work with Alliance Marines, but some simple competitive urging to use this chance to show the Marines who was best should take care of that. "You're a tough negotiator, Captain Michael Geary."

"Then let's see if I can get my Marines to buy into this, or if I'll have to negotiate with them."

HE met with Major Guerrero alone first, but before he could say anything, Commander Joe Mateo showed up. Geary would have welcomed a commander as a backup and executive officer, but Mateo was a supply officer, making him unable to help with command work, though he was valuable in different ways.

"Chief Taman let me know about the fuel cell trouble, so I jumped right on checking the food stocks," Mateo said. "The physical inventory found a food problem. Not as bad as the fuel cell problem, but it's not good."

"We don't have as much food aboard as the automated systems show?"

"Not even close to it," Commander Mateo said. "For the people we've already got on this ship, what we have will last about another week and a half to two weeks, longer if we limit consumption."

"Rationing," Michael said. "Are you counting any emergency food stocks?"

"Yes."

Michael shook his head. "Executive Aragon thinks the shortfall in fuel cells was deliberate sabotage by Syndics wanting to get back at the internal security agents they knew would be using this ship. The agents would have suddenly run out of power, likely somewhere without help nearby. And then a few days later they would have run out of food."

Major Guerrero raised his eyebrows. "Somebody not only wanted them dead, they wanted them to die slowly."

"They really hate those security agents," Geary said. "Luckily, I think we've got a food resupply opportunity coming up."

"Really?" Mateo said.

"We're going to raid a Syndic orbital labor camp at the star we're heading for, Ravana. They'll have food stocks for the garrison and the prisoners. While the Tigres rescue their comrades, we'll also haul off as much food as we can."

Mateo grinned with relief. "We're all used to Syndic prison food. It'll keep us alive."

"Better that than Danaka Yoruk ration bars," Major Guerrero commented. "Unless my memory is bad, those are worse than anything the Syndics fed us."

"Your memory is fine, Major. Unfortunately. Should I hold off on rationing, then?" Commander Mateo asked.

Michael thought for a moment. "Yes. We've got enough grounds for tension right now on this ship. I don't want people getting hangry on top of that," he added, using the old combination of 'hungry' and 'angry.'

As Commander Mateo left, Major Guerrero made a face. "I hate to admit it, but I envy these ex-Syndics getting to hit that labor camp. I wouldn't mind the chance to kill some Syndic prison guards."

"Do the other Marines feel the same way?" Geary asked.

"Pretty much, yeah."

"What if I offered you the opportunity to take part in the attack on the labor camp?"

Guerrero eyed him warily. "How would that work?"

"The Tigres have extra battle armor and weapons from the armories on this ship. They'll provide each Marine with armor, training, and full weapons loadout."

"Why?" The wariness had turned to outright suspicion.

"They don't have enough soldiers to do the job with maximum chance of saving their comrades," Michael said. "And they're afraid if they're all on the facility we might boost away and leave them."

"That's not a bad idea," Major Guerrero said.

"Except I gave my word," Michael said. "And that would mean running from a fight."

Guerrero hesitated. "It's not our fight."

"We need the food on that facility. And we think we can get the Syndics at Ravana to send the fuel cells we need there. You Marines would be responsible for securing those fuel cells in addition to helping take the facility."

"That does make it our fight.... 'We'?"

"Aragon and I. We worked up a plan. They want their comrades free; we need fuel cells and food." Michael paused. "And you get to kill Syndics, and show these Tigres what Marines can do. There's also a small possibility that other Alliance prisoners may be there."

Major Guerrero looked thoughtful. "Those are all good reasons."

"There's one more," Michael said. "There should be beer aboard the facility."

"Oh, hell. That's not fair." Guerrero paused again. "We'd have to take orders from these ex-Syndics?"

"From the Tigres. Yes. You Marines would operate as a single unit, but you'll be tied into their command net so Executive Aragon can coordinate the attack."

"Taking orders from a Syndic executive?" Major Guerrero frowned.

"She's not a Syndic anymore," Michael said.

"Sir, skunks don't change their smell just because they decide to call themselves cats."

Michael Geary crossed his arms, eyeing Guerrero. "Am I to understand that Alliance Marines will turn down the opportunity to attack a Syndic facility?"

Instead of reacting angrily to the accusation, Major Guerrero grinned. "No, sir. I'm certain every Marine aboard will volunteer. Aside from the other reasons, even if there's only a small chance other Alliance POWs might be there, we want in on freeing them." Another pause. "There's definitely beer? That the, uh, Tigres won't keep for themselves?"

"There's definitely beer," Michael said. "Hopefully you can spare one for me. Can I count on you to work directly with Aragon?"

Guerrero shrugged. "As long as she's professional, yes, sir."

"Believe me, she's professional. I'm counting on you, on all of the Marines, to show these Tigres just how lucky they'll be to have Alliance Marines fighting on their side."

"We won't let you down. Where will you be if I need to report anything?"

"Conference room Alpha," Geary said, naming the CEO

conference room with all of the bells and whistles. "I need to school myself on what my great-uncle has been doing while I was confined in that prison."

THERE was considerable irony, Michael thought, in his having to learn what Black Jack had done since *Repulse* was destroyed from secret Syndic files. Everything he'd found so far confirmed what Aragon had told him, that Black Jack had not only against all odds gotten the Alliance Fleet home after an epically long "repositioning," but had then finally forced an end to the century-long war with a Syndicate Worlds surrender.

"Why are all of these files classified?" he had asked Aragon. "I mean, not just the details, but the bare facts in them."

Aragon had given him that grim, knowing smile. "Victories are always exaggerated, while defeats are always classified. The Syndicate doesn't want its people knowing it lost any battles. It doesn't even want the people to know it lost the war. Everyone knows, everyone hears, but officially no one knows."

"But these descriptions of the battles are under the highest Syndic classification level, aren't they? How were Syndic officers supposed to learn lessons from reviewing them?"

"Don't you get it?" Aragon said. "Officially, the Syndicate never lost. Therefore, officially, there are no lessons to be learned. What really happened has to be kept very quiet."

Michael shook his head. "Officers in the Alliance Fleet have been complaining about the Alliance government. They should see this. I guess our government isn't nearly as bad as it could be." He paused, hesitant to ask the next question. "These files say that Black Jack has taken control of the Alliance government. Is that true?"

Aragon shrugged. "Maybe. That's analysis and conclusions, see?

Which means it's whatever the boss wanted to hear. You'd need to check source material for a clearer picture. Here." She opened some links. "Like this one. It says Black Jack insists he is following orders from the government. And then this comment that rejects it as disinformation. Which it probably is."

"I don't think so," Michael said, his eyes on the report. "The Black Jack I was taught about would have done that, overthrown the government, I think. But not the man I met. My great-uncle didn't seem to have that kind of arrogance."

She looked skeptical, but shrugged again. "You've talked to him, not me. All I really know is he kicked the Syndicate's butt, and he's for the people. That's all I need to know."

"I need to know more," Michael said. "I need to know *how* he kicked Syndic butt. What tactics he used to win again and again while suffering relatively few losses. Hopefully these Syndic files on the battles will give me a clue. If we encounter any more Syndic warships, I want to give us as much of an edge as possible."

Aragon nodded, her eyes on him. "The best commanders are best because they know they don't have all the answers and keep learning. Good luck with your research, Captain Michael Geary."

After she left, he called up each file in turn. Some battle descriptions had detailed information, others a lot of guesswork. Each battle was named after the star system it had taken place in. Kaliban. Sancere. Lakota. And then Lakota again, not a duplicate file but a second battle there. Ilion. Practically nothing about a fight at Kalixa except a reference to Option Omega. Omega. The end. That sounded like an ominous option. He wondered what it had involved.

He'd always been told what Black Jack would do in a fight. Charge straight in, no hesitation, fight and win or die, never give up, never retreat. Michael had never liked that way of fighting, and—even prior to his brief experience with his granduncle before *Repulse* was destroyed—had wondered how much it actually reflected the real Black Jack's thinking.

These files, in their attempts to recreate the action at battles in which the Alliance Fleet had been commanded by his granduncle, showed him something very different from that official Alliance version of Black Jack. In the 3D display above the conference table he saw complex maneuvers, maximizing firepower against portions of the enemy force. He saw multiple formations of Alliance ships moving in grand, coordinated sweeps across wide areas of space to come together at the right moments to meet and frustrate and destroy enemy forces.

What he was looking for, some standard way of fighting, didn't seem to be there. Which was baffling. How could he learn how Black Jack really fought when he couldn't see what these battles had in common? Maybe the problem was the Syndic attempts to recreate the battles. Maybe the Syndics hadn't seen, or weren't able to see, some critical elements.

But there were people aboard this ship who might be able to tell him about that.

It took some work talking to the other former prisoners to find out whom he needed to see, but eventually Michael was able to assemble a half-dozen Alliance officers in the conference room, among them Lieutenant Bailey, Lieutenant Law, and Lieutenant Kuei. "I need your help," he began as the others watched him with anticipation and curiosity. "You and I all know how the Alliance Fleet fought before Black Jack assumed command. I am trying to learn how Black Jack changed that. All of you actually got to see him in command during battles. I want to know what you saw, with all the detail that you can provide."

After a pause in which the others exchanged glances, Lieutenant

Bailey spoke up first. "Captain Geary, being in fire control meant I saw a lot of what happened in each engagement up to Lakota. Is this right? There was a second battle at Lakota soon afterward?"

"As far as I can tell," Michael said.

"At the end of Lakota, the last fight that I observed," Bailey said, "the Alliance Fleet repositioned to avoid an overwhelming Syndic attack. It looks like he came right back and hit the Syndics again. Ancestors! Look at that, William."

Lieutenant Law nodded, smiling. "Beautiful. Too bad we'd already been shipped out as prisoners."

"Nothing I'm seeing," Michael said, "matches what I was always told Black Jack would do. Are those also your impressions from seeing him command the fleet?"

Everyone nodded. "What we saw him do does not match what we were taught," Lieutenant Bailey said. "Black Jack did not follow the rules we were told to follow."

Lieutenant Voss pointed to the depiction of a battle on the display. "When he first took command, everyone was confused. He chewed out commanders for leaving formation to pursue the enemy. Remember Kaliban?"

"He raised hell at Kaliban over the way the formation fell apart as soon as we saw the enemy," Lieutenant Law agreed. "And he stayed in charge. But…I had a friend on *Dauntless*, his flagship. He said sometimes the commanding officer would argue with Black Jack, and Black Jack would listen before he decided what to do. My friend was like, senior captains and admirals don't do that. But Black Jack did. That's what I heard."

Michael Geary took that in. Captain Tanya Desjani, *Dauntless*'s captain, wasn't the sort to be intimidated by rank. It wasn't hard to believe she would have spoken up to even Black Jack. He remembered Desjani siding with him against Admiral Bloch during the debate over the planned surprise attack that turned into such a disaster. But he wouldn't have expected that Black Jack would actually take her advice into account. "I guessed from the start that Black Jack was doing something different, because as you personally experienced, he got the fleet as far back home as Lakota, and sometime after that managed to win the war we'd been fighting and dying in for a hundred years. Can any of you tell me how he did that?"

Ensign Abadi, from her age someone who'd come up through the ranks, gestured to the display. "Maybe if you show us each battle, we can key in on things, sir."

"That's a good suggestion," Geary said. "Here we go. Anyone chime in whenever you see something that triggers a thought. Don't hold back. I want to know your honest impressions and opinions."

He set the display to show battle after battle, the symbols of the ships in the opposing forces weaving above the table. The other officers watched the recreations, sometimes starting with recognition of a particular moment or flinching at the losses of Alliance ships. But no one spoke up.

The last file ended. "We were taught there was only one right way to fight a battle," Michael said. "I'm not seeing that one right way. What am I missing?"

Lieutenant Bailey shook her head. "Black Jack did things differently each time," she said, looking to the others to confirm her words. "I can't think of any pattern."

Michael stared at her. "Say that again."

"Uh…I can't think of any pattern."

Look at things differently, he thought. *Like my granduncle did at Prime.* "That's the pattern!" Geary waved at the display. "These recreations of his battles tell me that Black Jack doesn't follow some rigid rule or rules. I see him adapting to whatever the circumstances are."

"How is that a pattern, sir?" Lieutenant Voss asked.

"Black Jack doesn't fight in one right way," Michael said. "He fights in whatever way is right. Right for those particular circumstances, that situation, that composition of both friendly and enemy forces. These battle depictions don't show us Black Jack doing the same thing, don't give us a one-size-fits-all formula for winning. They show us that he wins by sizing up each individual situation and reacting as that situation requires."

Lieutenant Law stared at the display. "That's...I can't disagree, sir. In my wardroom, we kept debating how Black Jack did things. We never settled on anything. But...this is right. We couldn't settle on any one thing, because the one thing is a...lack of one way of doing things."

"So simple," Lieutenant Bailey said, "so obvious, that only another Geary could see it."

Michael looked down quickly so the others couldn't see his reaction to the well-meaning and admiring comment. "I'm more experienced than the rest of you. And it was your comments that led me to realize what we were looking for."

His expression once-more composed, he looked up to see the other officers clearly pleased by his praise for them, but also just as clearly not believing him that being a Geary had nothing to do with his insight. "Thank you. Return to your duties. Continue training on these Syndic systems. We don't know what awaits us at Ravana. We want to be at maximum readiness when we leave jump there."

He sat for a while in the conference room after everyone else had left, his eyes on the frozen image of the end of one of his granduncle's victories. It was one thing to realize how Black Jack had managed to win. It was another thing entirely to be able to do the same thing when called upon.

He'd always known he wasn't the old version of Black Jack. But he knew he wasn't this new Black Jack, either. Everyone assumed that, as a Geary, he was gifted, but he had long ago realized he was...competent.

Could he be good enough to win whatever battles awaited them?

In a few more days, depending on whether there were Syndic warships waiting at Ravana, he might learn the answer.

Chapter Six

ACCORDING to the Alliance workers, they would reach Ravana tomorrow. Aragon thought the Alliance officers were far too slack with their workers, but she couldn't deny that they seemed to be doing their jobs well.

Seated in the executive conference room, Destina Aragon gestured to Sub-Executive Harbin. "How are you and the Alliance Marines getting along?"

"I haven't killed any of them," Harbin replied.

"Good."

"Yet," Harbin added.

"We need them, Harbin. Make this work."

"I understand and will comply." Harbin made a face. "The Alliance Marines are obviously rusty. They've been locked up for varying periods in Syndicate prisons. But they're working hard to learn how our armor works. They'll be ready when we reach the labor camp. And they're very eager to kill some guards." He snorted. "I think that's helping tensions on this unit a little. Instead of focusing on our workers as possible objects of revenge, those Marines are looking forward to hammering the guards at the labor camp."

"What's special about them?" Sub-Executive Nedele asked. "I understand why the Syndicate wanted to keep Black Jack's scion under wraps in a hidden prison. Why were these others there?"

Harbin shook his head. "They don't seem to be special. Maybe they're relatives of Alliance officials. Or maybe the Syndicate wanted the prison full for efficiency reasons, so the snakes filled the quota for prisoners by grabbing whoever was handy."

"That's how the snakes usually work to fill their quotas," Nedele said with disgust.

"You don't have to tell me that." Harbin paused, his jaw tightening. "It's been a long time since I heard from my family on Anahuac."

"We won't stop fighting the Syndicate when we reach Anahuac," Aragon said. "We'll make sure everyone is found, everyone is safe."

"Do you still think these Alliance scum will go through with the deal?" Nedele asked.

"So far they're playing it as if they intend to," Aragon said. "I've got ears out, listening to what they say in private."

"Planning to hit us by surprise?"

Aragon grinned. "Mostly wondering when we'll hit *them* by surprise. And talking about seeing their families again, and doing things they miss doing. You know how that goes."

"Sure," Harbin said. "They're used to dealing with the Syndicate, aren't they? Just like us. Of course they expect us to betray them. We expected the Syndicate to betray us, didn't we?"

"That's so," Nedele conceded.

"My orders still stand," Aragon said. "No one fires the first shot at any of the Alliance workers. If I get indications betrayal is imminent, I will act on it. But until we get home to Anahuac we keep this tension short of conflict."

"Yes, Executive Aragon," Nedele said. "And after we get home? Are we really going to let them go with this mobile unit? What if they decide to bombard Anahuac from space?"

Aragon considered the question for a moment to let Nedele and Harbin see she was taking the question, and the concern, seriously. "Their commander is Black Jack's scion."

"He's not Black Jack himself, though," Harbin pointed out.

"No, he's not. But he considers himself bound by Black Jack's orders to the Alliance Fleet. And by his word. That honor thing that's so important to them. But, also," Aragon added, "he seems to see sticking to our deal as part of a commitment to his family, to not act in ways that would shame his sister or his ancestors."

"I never got their honor thing," Harbin said. "But I can understand sticking up for family. I've tried not to do anything that would harm mine. Until now."

Nedele nodded in reluctant agreement. "It's like they think their ancestors are like the snakes," she said. "Always watching them and waiting for them to make a mistake."

Aragon laughed at the comparison. "In some ways, I think you're right. But it's not just that. Listening to the Alliance workers and officers, they talk about their ancestors guiding them and protecting them as well as judging them. I never met a snake who did either of those things."

Nedele and Harbin also laughed, with a tinge of bitterness. "It must be nice to have imaginary friends who protect you," Harbin said. "Oh, speaking of seeing things that aren't there, I'm designating a few extra-reliable workers to guard the beer that'll be at the labor camp. We don't want our own workers getting into it once the garrison is wiped out."

"No," Aragon said. "We don't. Who's going to be charge of those workers?"

"Senior Worker Kat Richardson. No other worker in their right mind will mess with her, and if any lose their minds and try something, they'll be very sorry."

"Good," Aragon said. "We need to make sure we get our hands on that beer and get it back to this unit. I don't want to have to listen to those Alliance Marines complaining that we didn't hold up our end of the deal."

"They're expecting us to stick them with the most hazardous tasks," Harbin noted.

"They'll get briefed on the assault plan at the same time as you are," Aragon said. "I'm going to give them a tough assignment, but not the toughest. I want Tigres I can trust handling the really rough jobs."

Nedele made a face, her unhappiness clear to see. "Executive Aragon, I would like to participate in the assault rather than remaining on this unit in command of the backup force."

Aragon shook her head. "Sub-Executive Nedele, you will be responsible for a critical task. Not just making sure the Alliance workers don't betray us by trying to abandon us on the labor camp, but also keeping our own workers on this unit calm while the fight is going on. Overreaction, unthinking action, in response to rumors or misunderstanding of what is happening, could doom our chances of getting back to Anahuac. And I need someone I know is up to the task. Someone who is ready to, if necessary, stop any Alliance stab in the back, without provoking a fight. You're going to have the toughest job in this assault. I am certain you are the best supervisor I have for that job."

Nedele straightened, her expression smoothing out. "Thank you, Executive. I swear I will not let you down."

After Harbin and Nedele had left, Aragon sat, looking at the diagram of the orbital labor camp. But in her mind she saw a six-year-old boy. Was he still alive? Where? What did he look like now? She hadn't seen him for more than four years, had last heard about him three years ago.

She would get home. She would find him. She didn't care if she never saw her former husband again. But there was a six-year-old boy who needed her. Too many times she had not been able to protect those who depended on her. This time, she would succeed. Even if it meant working with the Alliance.

Focus. Aragon concentrated on finalizing the assault plan. Because her road home went through Ravana.

TOMORROW. Sub-Executive Harbin sat at one of the tables in the mess, shoveling down his food without tasting it, a habit born of long experience with Syndicate rations. Someday he'd be able to eat decent food again and would have to retrain himself to enjoy it. For now, it was enough to get the energy the food provided, and to have the act of eating distracting his thoughts from worries about the assault on the labor camp the next day.

There were clusters of Tigres at some of the other tables, and clusters of Alliance officers and workers at other tables. The groups didn't mix.

"Excuse me."

Harbin looked over to see the green-haired Alliance officer he'd noticed before. "What is it?" he asked, cautious.

"May I share your table? You're…Sub…Executive Harbin, right?"

"I am." Aragon had told him to always exploit any opportunity to learn what the Alliance officers were thinking. "Have a seat."

"I'm Lieutenant Bailey," she said, sitting down opposite him. "Fire Control."

It wouldn't hurt to praise her a little, perhaps get her talking freely. "Fire Control? Your shots did a number on that Syndicate heavy cruiser."

She grinned for a moment. "May I ask you something?"

"I can't stop you from asking, Lieutenant Bailey."

"That metal plate on the side of your face. It's a temporary fix. Why haven't you had a full reconstruct?"

Harbin eyed her, seeing that the question was a genuine one. "The expected life span of a sub-executive in ground combat is two weeks."

"So?" Bailey asked.

"So the Syndicate didn't see any sense in wasting time and money on reconstruction work when I'd probably die pretty soon," Harbin said, his voice sounding as matter of fact as he felt. "That's just the way the Syndicate thinks."

She stared at him, obviously shocked by his casual reply. "Why the hell did you fight for people like that?"

He might as well be candid with her and see how she reacted. "Some of us believed the lies," Harbin said. "Some of us didn't want our families punished if we failed…and all of us believed the Alliance was just like the Syndicate."

Lieutenant Bailey paused, not eating. "I…it's not. I swear it. The Alliance isn't perfect. No one thinks that. Our government… But…I lost half my face when the *Shigure* was destroyed. I can't imagine being told to live with that because my life expectancy didn't make it cost-effective."

"Half your face?" Harbin studied her. "The Alliance fixed you up nice. The Alliance also bombarded any Syndicate planet their ships could reach. We had to defend our worlds from that."

Bailey hesitated again, looking distressed. "When Black Jack came back, he couldn't believe we were doing that. We told him everyone thought we had to, in order to win the war. He asked us, if that was true, why hadn't we won yet?"

Harbin surprised himself with a laugh. "He said that? Bosses hate it when workers ask questions like that. That's the first time I ever heard of a boss thinking that way. That's why Black Jack ordered the bombardments to stop? Because he thought they weren't working?"

"No," Lieutenant Bailey said. "He told us such actions shamed our ancestors. It wasn't just that they hadn't worked, it was that we never should have started doing something so contrary to our ideals, to what our ancestors expected of us."

"Like your Marines said about not killing prisoners?" Harbin said. "No one questioned Black Jack about that?"

Bailey hesitated again. "There was some…argument, but no one disobeyed the orders. He's Black Jack. All of our lives we've been told he embodied everything that was right about the Alliance."

"And does he?" Harbin asked.

"From what I saw, yes."

"What about this Captain Michael Geary, Black Jack's scion? Is he the same?"

Bailey laughed. "That's not disrespect toward Captain Geary. He's good, from what I've seen. A Geary. But Black Jack is a category all to himself."

Harbin looked at her, thinking about having to follow in the footsteps of someone who was "in a category all to himself." It matched what Aragon had told him about Michael Geary. Capable, but with a chip on his shoulder, trying to live up to the Black Jack family name while pretending not to care about it. "Have there been arguments among you? About the wisdom of Captain Geary's actions regarding my unit?"

She didn't pause before replying. "Of course there have been. Especially at first. You're…you *were*…Syndics. Can I be honest? I doubt any of us trust you even now. But Captain Geary pointed out that we needed each other. We needed you to break us out of that prison, and you needed us to take you home. And, honestly, you don't seem to be monsters."

"There are monsters in the Syndicate," Harbin said. "We killed a bunch of them at the prison, and when we were capturing this unit."

"I've noticed you talk that way," an Alliance senior worker said as she walked up to the table and sat down next to Bailey. "I'm Chief North. I work with Lieutenant Bailey here. I mean, we'll say we're citizens of the Alliance. We're part of the Alliance. And we call you guys Syndics. But you guys talk about 'the Syndicate' as if it's something totally separate from you."

"It is," Harbin said. "It's what rules us, what controls us, what makes the rules. For anyone except CEOs, we have no say in it. We serve it, whether we want to or not. That's all."

"So we are the good guys," Bailey said. "Even if we haven't always acted like it. We were always fighting against something worse."

"Do you want me to agree with you?"

"No. I guess I just want to believe all of the sacrifices for the last century were worth it. That they had meaning."

This time, Harbin had to pause before answering. "I can understand why you want that. You can understand how hard it is for us to feel the same way."

"It looks like you guys are doing the right thing now," Chief North said. "How come we're still fighting Syndics if the war is over?"

"Because the Syndicate won't stop, Chief North. It was supposed to release all prisoners of war back to the Alliance. We, my unit, were supposed to go home when the century-long war emergency ended. But, you, us, we all have to fight to get what we were promised by the Syndicate. It never lets go. Not until you pry yourself free from its dead hand." He grinned. "What a wonderful thing to imagine. The Syndicate finally dead."

"I hope you see that happen," Lieutenant Bailey said.

Harbin smiled again. "I will not just see it. I will try to contribute to its death in any way I can." He raised his water cup. "To the death of the Syndicate!" he shouted.

Every other Tigre present scrambled to their feet, raising their own cups. "To the death of the Syndicate!"

Lieutenant Bailey and Chief North stood up, too, the rest of the Alliance workers and officers in the compartment doing the same, all of them raising their cups in support of the defiant toast.

There was, after all, common ground with these people from the Alliance. Even if that ground was only hatred of the Syndicate, that might be enough, Harbin thought.

MICHAEL had taken the primary command seat on the bridge, waiting as the final moments in jump space counted down. "Five minutes until we leave jump at Ravana, Captain," Lieutenant Kuei reported.

The five days spent in jump space hadn't been wasted. The frantic improvisation of the first fight this ship had faced was a thing of the past. The former prisoners of war had been assigned to tasks, been formed into teams, practiced operations together, gained familiarity with the Syndic controls and systems.

The Tigre soldiers who had once stood watch over the Alliance personnel on the bridge had stood down two days ago in a clear confidence-building measure by Executive Aragon.

Aragon sat in the secondary command seat, attired in a finely made suit designed for Syndicate Worlds CEOs. Ironically, she had needed the help of one of the Alliance sailors to get the tailoring done to the level of skill expected for CEO suits. Her hair had been rigidly styled to also match something a CEO would display.

She didn't look happy, shifting uncomfortably.

Michael realized he also felt unusually tense. Why? He'd done this so many times before.

"Leaving jump."

The mental jolt hit him and everyone else aboard as *Corsair* dropped back into normal space, the never-ending, featureless gray of jump space instantly replaced by the infinite stars of the space humans belonged in. For a few seconds, Michael Geary's mind was filled with fog, his thoughts unable to focus. It happened to everyone, every time they left jump space, and was especially worrisome when arriving at an enemy-controlled star. Those moments of dazed confusion could be critical if an ambush was waiting.

An ambush. That was why he was on the edge of panicking. The last time he'd arrived in a new star system in command of a ship, it had been the Syndicate Worlds capital star system of Prime, and the Alliance Fleet had run head on into an ambush that had inflicted awful losses before it could fight its way through to temporary safety. His own ship, *Repulse,* had been so badly damaged she had ended up being sacrificed as the rear guard when Black Jack led the rest of the fleet to hoped-for, temporary safety.

Small wonder he was having trouble with this.

Michael's mind finally cleared, his eyes fixing on his display to see what information the battle cruiser's sensors would show as they took in everything they could of the situation in Ravana. Nothing was close to this jump point, which wasn't surprising since it led nowhere but to the star where the prison and nothing else had been. How would the local Syndicate Worlds authorities react when they eventually saw a battle cruiser had arrived from that star? They must have seen this same ship depart for that star some time ago. How much had they known of its mission?

"No Syndic warships are present," Lieutenant Law said. "Three freighters are moving through the star system, one outbound heading for the jump point for…Cullen Star System. A second one is inbound to the primary inhabited world from that jump point, and the third freighter looks like it was about to jump for Cullen."

"Communications appear to be routine," Chief Petty Officer Okoro said from the communications station. "What we're receiving is hours old, but none show any signs of high alert."

"What about the labor camp?" Michael asked.

"Where it should be," Lieutenant Law said. "And it is definitely occupied."

"And the logistics facility?"

"Also where it should be, orbiting the primary world, Captain."

"Get us on a vector to intercept the labor camp in its orbit. Accelerate to point one light speed."

"Aye, Captain. Accelerating to point one light speed, adjusting vector. Time to reach the labor camp is forty-one hours."

Nearly two days. Michael sat back, trying to relax. "It's weird. I've operated in space for years, but I still have trouble dealing with the distances. We're about four and a half light hours from where the primary inhabited world is in its orbit, so the Syndic authorities here won't even know we've arrived for another four and a half hours. But I keep expecting them to have immediately seen us."

"I need to send my messages now, don't I?" Aragon asked, sounding abrupt.

"Yes. That's routine, to send any necessary messages as soon as you arrive at a star," Michael said. "Are you okay?"

She bent a glare his way. "I need to get in character. A Syndicate CEO. The more important they are, the meaner they are to anyone less important. I don't want anyone asking questions. The Syndicate authorities here know something was at Ravana, but they're unlikely to know just what it was or who was there. That gives me a chance to pretend to be someone very important. Speaking of that, we need to switch seats. Anyone seeing my transmission might notice I'm not in the primary command seat and wonder why."

"Understood," Geary said, standing up and moving away.

Aragon moved a little stiffly in the tight suit, sitting down and checking the feedback image. "That officer," she said, pointing, "has to move. She might show in my message."

Michael gestured to Lieutenant Kuei, who hastily moved a few meters to one side.

He watched Aragon inhale slowly, her eyes closed, her expression hardening even more. When her eyes snapped open, Geary almost jerked with surprise at the furious intensity in them.

Aragon stabbed the comm controls. "Syndicate Labor Camp 660, this is CEO Pavia on Mobile Forces Unit D-555. I am en route to your facility to deliver a new consignment of prisoners. Expect my arrival in forty-one hours. Forthepeople, Pavia, out."

Executive Aragon paused just a moment before hammering the controls again. "Mobile Unit Logistics Facility Ravana, this is CEO Pavia on Mobile Unit D-555. My unit requires fuel cell replenishment. I expect every available fuel cell to be delivered to Labor Camp 660. The fuel cells are to be at the camp before my unit reaches it so this unit can resupply without delay. Forthepeople, Pavia, out." She nearly spat the last words.

Michael saw the other Alliance personnel on the bridge staring at Aragon in mingled horror and worry, startled by her transformation. He walked back to the primary command seat as Aragon stood up. "You were...very believable."

She shot a glance at him. "That had better be a compliment. I've had a lot of unpleasant experiences with CEOs to draw on."

"I was expecting the messages to be longer," Geary said. "Giving them the reasons why you needed the fuel cells and why you were delivering prisoners."

Aragon shook her head as she loosened the collar of her suit. "If I had done that, they would have known I was a fake. Syndicate CEOs never explain, and never provide any information they don't have to. You do what they say because they said it. If I did my impersonation right, the executives in this star system will be too scared to ask any questions."

"What happens to someone who does ask questions?"

"They end up at Syndicate Labor Camp 660 or another like it, or they just…disappear. Unless they're publicly executed as an example to others to do as they're told and not waste time with questions."

Geary blinked. He'd known the Syndic system was brutal, but seeing it in action was still hard to grasp. "What about the CEO running this star system? Aren't you supposed to check in with them?"

Aragon grinned humorlessly. "Only if you are junior to them. Waiting for that CEO to call me first is what a senior and more powerful CEO would do. A more junior CEO wouldn't risk offending the star system CEO and would call first. It's all about power games, Captain Michael Geary." She yanked at a seal on the suit. "If you'll excuse me, I need to get out of this Syndicate boss suit before I throw up on it. I'm probably going to need it again."

She paused before leaving, though, looking at him for a moment as if deciding whether to say more. "Captain Michael Geary, there's something wrong in this star system. There aren't any Syndicate mobile forces here. Not even minor ones. What about the Near-Orbit Units?"

Michael looked toward his watchstanders. "Have we seen any signs of Syndic aerospace activity?"

"No, Captain," Lieutenant Kuei said.

"There aren't any signs of military aerospace forces active in communications," Chief Okoro added.

Aragon nodded, her expression bleak. "It looks like the system defense forces and the mobile planetary defense forces have been stripped from this star system."

"You're sure there would be such forces here?" Michael asked. "I know they were listed in the data for the star system, but Alliance information like that is often outdated."

Aragon gave him one of those looks that meant she couldn't believe he would ask such a question. "Those 'defense' forces help keep the local population in line. They should be here. They're not. The Syndicate sent them somewhere else."

"If they're important to maintain control of this star system, why would the Syndics do that?" Michael asked.

"The most likely reason is that they've been sent somewhere for a higher priority mission, in the expectation they'll return once that mission is completed. The Syndicate is up to something. My best guess would be rebellion suppression somewhere." Aragon looked at the display showing the view outside the ship, numberless stars piercing the dark. "Someone at another star is probably either catching hell, or about to catch hell."

Geary followed her gaze. "And there's nothing we can do about it." He wanted to do something, instinctively desiring to stop whatever the Syndics were doing.

Aragon's smile this time was unpleasant, promising the worst for her targets. "We are doing something. This may seem like a small sting in the side of the Syndicate, but every action that makes them look weak, that requires them to keep more forces in every star system to maintain control, works to end their domination."

He frowned. "That would be small comfort to whoever is catching hell."

Her smile shifted, becoming that of someone sharing a task. "Those who have been ruled by the Syndicate will take whatever we can get, Captain Michael Geary."

"Then I'll give them whatever I can."

"You mean that." It was a statement, not a question. Aragon studied him. "You *are* Black Jack's scion." She turned and left without saying anything else, leaving him uncomfortably aware of the approving expressions on the faces of the other Alliance personnel on the bridge.

THE labor camp orbiting the gas giant was a bit closer to *Corsair*, so their reply arrived first, more than eight hours after Aragon had sent her demands. Since the message, traveling at the speed of light, had required more than four hours to reach the labor camp, and the reply almost as long to cover the distance to the battle cruiser that was coming closer all the time, that meant the reply had been sent without any delay. "Thank you for gracing our star system with your supervision. Everything will be in readiness for your arrival, Esteemed CEO Pavia," a stern-looking man replied. "Please advise me if there is any other way in which I may serve you. Forthepeople, Renaud, out."

Aragon, who had come back to the bridge to view the reply, and was now wearing her customary skin-suit working uniform, laughed, surprised to be able to be amused by the Syndicate politics that had enraged her for so long. "An executive second class, getting on in years, in a backwater star system, assigned to control of a labor camp. He's hoping this powerful CEO Pavia might be his ticket out of here."

"You can read all of that in him?" Captain Michael Geary asked.

"If you received a message from another Alliance captain, you could see a lot in it that wasn't said, couldn't you?"

"Probably," he admitted.

Aragon sat back in her seat, waiting, trying not to get tense with worry. "We should hear from the logistics facility soon." If that executive didn't crawl as well, didn't offer up the necessary fuel cells, she and Michael Geary might be having a very intense argument in which both would be right but only one could get what they needed.

It took another half hour before that reply showed up. A woman, older, rigidly correct, speaking with the proper amount of respect but no more. "CEO Pavia, the necessary steps are being taken to deliver the requested fuel cells. Unfortunately, spare fuel cell stocks at this facility have been recently drawn down in support of the Special Military Operation at Kane. I am sending you all that remain, per the attached specifications and loading documents. They should arrive at the labor camp shortly before your mobile unit. I remain at your service. Forthepeople, Kwan, out."

Michael Geary tabbed the attachment. "Chief Taman, let me know how well this meets our needs." He turned an inquisitive look on Aragon.

She nodded to him. "An executive first class, nearing retirement. I'd guess she's been at this job for some time and has put down local roots on the planet. She doesn't want to offend the powerful CEO, but also doesn't want to attract too much notice."

"A content bureaucrat?" Michael Geary said.

"Essentially," Aragon said. "It's harder to hate them, but without people like that keeping things working, the Syndicate couldn't survive. Did you notice? Kane. That's the star where that rebellion suppression mission is going."

He nodded. "That's where the Syndics were going to send your unit, isn't it?"

"Sure. Earlier I took a look at the snake files on Kane. Just to see what sort of hellhole we were going to be sent to." She shook her head. "The primary world has been previously heavily bombarded from orbit. Our orders aren't in the files we've been able to access so far, but since they've already trashed the planet from orbit and it hasn't surrendered, any follow-on mission would have to involve ground forces."

"How tough would that have been? If you'd gone?" Michael Geary asked her.

Aragon shook her head again, letting him see her feelings. "The snake files confirm that Kane is associated with Midway. That means Drakon may be defending the planet. Even if Drakon's not there, the snake files call Kane's defenders 'fanatical.' I've had my fill of that kind of fight."

He looked back at her, apparently realizing that she was referring to fights against the Alliance, and apparently deciding not to pursue that. "Then it's a good thing we're going to Anahuac instead of Kane," Michael Geary finally said.

Later, she would wonder if that statement had led his ancestors to mess with both of their plans.

At the moment, though, Michael Geary answered a call from engineering. "Chief Taman?"

Aragon heard the senior worker speaking to Geary.

"Captain, what's on that manifest isn't nearly enough to top us off. If we get all of those fuel cells, we'll be up to forty-three percent reserves. That's not great, but it's a lot better than fourteen percent." A pause. "Actually, we'll be just under thirteen percent if we execute an efficient braking maneuver to match orbits with that labor camp."

"We can't do efficient," Aragon said. "I'm a powerful CEO who's flaunting her status. We need to do a dramatic braking to the labor camp."

Michael Geary gave her an amused look. "We can do dramatic braking. Thanks, Chief." He studied her for a moment. "Those extra fuel cells will get you and us to Anahuac, but there's no way they'd get *us* home."

"What are you asking?" she said.

"That IOU outstanding between us. Will you commit to trying to help us top off on fuel cells somewhere else before we drop you at Anahuac? We could raid another of those logistics facilities, but that might involve a tough fight. Having you act as a Syndic CEO seems to be the play we need to get more fuel cells without risking major damage."

She could argue the fine points of their earlier agreement, but why do that when so far the Alliance side had kept up their end of the agreement? And getting that IOU out of the way would leave their accounts balanced again. Aragon nodded to him. "Yes, Captain Michael Geary. Anything we steal from the Syndicate weakens it. And we did make a deal that you would have a chance to reach your home. Do you agree that this resolves the IOU?"

"Yes." He looked at his display, then bent a smile her way. "Dramatic, huh?"

"As much drama as possible."

He smiled again. "In case you were not aware, Executive Aragon, in the Alliance Fleet, battle cruiser commanders are considered to be the drama queens, always putting on shows of how fast and maneuverable their ships are."

She couldn't help smiling in return. "So, you've got this?"

"Born to it," Michael Geary said with a laugh.

"Captain, we're receiving a message sent from the primary inhabited world," the Alliance senior worker named Okoro said. "It's marked for CEO Pavia."

"Route it to us," Geary ordered.

Aragon watched the communications window appear before her. A man this time, his attitude respectful but not subservient. "CEO Pavia, this is CEO Cunha. Welcome to Ravana Star System. My subordinates are acting to meet your requirements. If you require further support, please do not hesitate to inform me. My respects to CEO Bezrukof in the event she is also on your unit. Forthepeople, Cunha, out."

"Who is Bezrukof?" Michael Geary asked her.

Aragon smiled slightly. "The CEO in charge of the prison where you were held."

"She's dead, then."

"Most sincerely dead," Aragon said, "as my grandmother would say. I won't inform CEO Cunha of that."

"Is Cunha going to be a problem?" Geary said.

"No. He clearly knows something about the facility that was at Augusta, but he's just as clearly trying to avoid trouble with me or anyone else who comes through."

"Captain?" This call once again was from the senior worker known as Taman. "There's something about this manifest for the fuel cells that's screwy."

"What's that, Chief?" Michael Geary asked.

"It's in Annex C to the manifest, a listing of, uh, 'anticipated life support and ration expenditure,' along with what looks like an accounting code. Aren't those cargo haulers bringing the fuel cells to the labor camp supposed to be fully automated?"

"They're supposed to be," Geary said, shooting a worried look at Aragon.

"Send me the manifest," Aragon said, scanning through it rapidly as soon as it appeared. "Your senior worker is right. That means there should be...here. Sub-section four. Passenger manifest. This code means they're returning to the camp from leave on the planet. And this…damn."

"What?" Michael Geary's voice was calm as he watched her.

"This other code. They're returning in active status, and here's the weapons manifest." Aragon punched the arm of her seat. "Those fuel cells are going to be accompanied by an armed guard force of twenty workers. How soon before we arrive are the fuel cells supposed to get the labor camp?"

She saw Geary look to one of the junior officers. "They're slow, Captain," the lieutenant replied. "If they leave the logistics facility within the hour, they'll reach the labor camp less than two hours before we get there."

Aragon shook her head angrily. "They'll have to go through quarantine and contraband screening. That's usually a four- to five-hour ordeal. Those guards will still be with those fuel cells when we reach that camp." She raised her comm link. "Sub-Executive Harbin, Sub-Executive Nedele, meet me in the conference room. We need to modify our assault plan." She paused. "Harbin, bring that Alliance Marine. The one in charge of them."

"Major Guerrero?" Harbin replied in surprise.

"Yes. I'll see you there in ten minutes." Aragon looked at Michael Geary, who had been listening. "We can still make this work, but it's going to require me to do something I do not want to do."

"What is that?" Geary asked.

"I'm going to have to trust you."

7

WHEN Aragon reached the conference room, Harbin and Nedele were already there, as well as Major Guerrero, who was watching her with open suspicion. "We have a problem," Aragon said, calling up the diagram of the labor camp. "Those fuel cells this mobile unit needs will be accompanied by a guard force of twenty workers with arms and armor. They won't be expecting trouble, but if they fort up inside those cargo haulers we'll have a serious problem."

She pointed to Nedele. "There's only one way to ensure those guards don't use their control of the fuel cells to hold all of us hostage. The workers you were going to command aboard this unit will instead have to surprise and defeat that guard force and take possession of the fuel cells."

"How do we prevent the Alliance prisoners from taking their ship away and leaving us stranded?" Nedele protested.

"Their Marines will still be with us. They won't abandon them. And they need those fuel cells to get anywhere."

Major Guerrero frowned. "My Marines were supposed to take control of the fuel cells once the garrison was defeated. Instead, you'll have control of them?"

"Sub-Executive Nedele will transfer control to you once the guards with the fuel cells and the garrison are eliminated," Aragon said.

"How do we know you'll do that?" Guerrero asked.

Aragon held out a hand to silence Harbin and Nedele before they berated Guerrero for the insubordinate question. "Because we need Captain Michael Geary to be able to take us home to Anahuac. We need you to have those fuel cells. We don't trust each other, and this plan leaves both sides in a position where, for brief periods, they'll have to give the other side considerable leverage over them. But the basics of the deal haven't changed. You need us to get those fuel cells. We need you to get us home."

Major Guerrero nodded. "If Captain Geary agrees to it, I won't object. It's going to be tricky, though."

"The hand-off between forces will be," Aragon acknowledged.

"No. I mean eliminating guards stationed with the fuel cells," Guerrero said. "Marines are trained in ship-boarding operations, and one of the strongest lessons we get imprinted on us is to never fire anything in any direction where it might end up hitting a fuel cell. The results can be very, very unpleasant for anyone within a large radius." He paused, watching them to see how they were taking his statement. "Maybe, since we're trained in this, my Marines should take the fuel cells. Not because of distrust, but because I don't want to be blown to hell."

Nedele spoke up. "What are the approved tactics for taking out opponents near fuel cells?"

Guerrero paused to think. "The short version is get as close as possible, hand to hand ideally, and take them out with knives or other weapons that don't pose a danger of setting off the fuel cells with a stray shot."

"Can you do that?" Sub-Executive Nedele pressed him. "Can you get that close before they realize you are hostile?"

This time Guerrero frowned, leaning in to study the diagram. "We'd have to approach across this landing platform? That's a wide, open area. We'll be in Syndic armor, but if there are any communications required, it might be very hard not to tip them off that we're not what we seem."

"You will be challenged when you start to approach them," Aragon said. "That's a certainty. If they seal those cargo haulers before you reach them, getting them out without a lot of firepower might be impossible."

Guerrero sat gazing at the display. She let him think, waiting. It would be better if this Alliance officer came to the necessary conclusions without feeling pressured.

The Marine major finally shook his head. "What you said earlier, uh, Colonel, is true. We both need this to work. And I'm experienced enough to know your people have a lot better chance of getting it done than mine do. Except for the special tactics to be used around fuel cells."

Colonel? The Marine was calling her by an Alliance military rank, but one she knew was senior to his own rank. So he was showing respect. She decided to let it slide. "Can you train Sub-Executive Nedele's workers in those tactics in the time we have left?"

"How much time have we got?"

"About thirty hours as of now."

"A bit more than a day." Major Guerrero nodded. "If Nedele's soldiers are anything like Harbin's that we've worked with, yes, we can do that. Mind you, I'm not promising to turn them into Marines in that length of time."

"Why would we want to be Marines?" Nedele demanded.

Guerrero's smile was fierce, exposing his canines. "Watch us fight on that labor camp and you'll see why you'd want to be one of us."

"Challenge accepted," Nedele told him.

"You accept this plan?" Aragon asked Guerrero. "It is critical that I know you will carry out orders, especially if the situation once we make contact requires rapid changes to the plan."

He eyed her before nodding again. "Colonel Aragon, I couldn't take orders from a Syndic. But, as Sub-Executive Harbin has made clear to me, you guys are Tigres. I want to get my people home. We have to fight this battle with what we've got. Yes, I will carry out orders. But there will be a high potential for accidental engagement of friendlies in this situation. We're all in the same armor, we're all heavily armed, and we all don't feel comfortable knowing the other has a clean shot at us."

"Fair enough," Aragon said. "I will instruct all of my workers that anyone who fires on one of yours will be terminated immediately. No investigation, no excuses. Will you do the same?"

Major Guerrero hesitated before finally nodding. "Yes. If it's an individual action. If a whole bunch of yours come at us, all firing, and ignoring our calls to hold fire, that'll be different."

"That won't happen," Aragon said. "I will be in charge, making sure you all engage the Syndicate workers, not any of our own. Thirty hours, everyone. Let's be ready. Unless otherwise notified, I want everyone in armor and ready to go an hour before arrival at the labor camp. Captain Michael Geary says this mobile unit will brake hard on approach, so movement may be difficult in the final period leading up to the attack."

"I have one remaining question," Guerrero said.

She fought down a burst of irritation. "What is it?"

"Prisoners. I know Captain Geary's policy regarding them. What is yours?"

That was easy. "We intend to wipe out the garrison, Major Guerrero."

"What if some of them surrender to us?" he asked. "Turning

them over to you to be killed would violate the spirit of our orders."

"If they're snakes, they're going to die," Aragon said. "But the odds of snakes surrendering is very low, because they know what their fates would be, and that death might be a welcome release after the workers have had their way. If you capture any normal workers, I'll agree to put them on one of those cargo haulers that can take them back to the logistics facility. If any of those surrender to your forces."

"I'll let Captain Geary know," Guerrero said, but he didn't make further protest.

Aragon glanced at Harbin and Nedele, who looked back in ways that showed they realized she hadn't promised those workers would be alive when they were put on the cargo hauler. Living in the Syndicate taught everyone to be wary of every word that was used, and not used.

It probably wouldn't matter, since the odds were small that any regular workers were at the labor camp. Tasks suited to that kind of worker were usually assigned to some of the prisoners so the Syndicate didn't have to worry about filling those positions. And if the camp got off a message about being attacked, it wouldn't matter if such workers survived.

But if she had to keep what had happened at the camp a secret from the Syndicate, she would do what she had to do.

ARAGON felt the structure of the mobile unit tremble under the strain as the main propulsion roared to reduce velocity quickly. The forces unleashed by the braking move were leaking past the inertial dampers, forcing her and the other waiting Tigres to brace themselves even though they were in battle armor. As the mobile unit let out a prolonged groan from the stress on its structure,

Aragon wondered whether she really should have asked Captain Michael Geary for a dramatic approach to the labor camp.

On her link to an external view, the gas giant loomed large, the multicolored bands of clouds adorning it creating an image of strange beauty. The dot marking the labor camp mining facility orbiting the gas giant was visible, growing in size faster as the battle cruiser swooped along a vector that would end with it exactly matching the movement of the orbital facility.

She checked her workers' status again on her armor display. This would be a particularly complex operation, and not just because of the Alliance Marines who would be fulfilling a critical role. Her Tigres and the Marines were spread out through the cargo compartments whose large hatches would offer direct access to the labor camp when the mobile unit came to a halt.

A small image of Michael Geary's face appeared on her display. "Ten minutes until we match vector with the orbital facility. We should be within one meter of contact. The cargo carriers are already docked, and from the sensor readings still have life support active, so those guards are still on them. You have a reception committee waiting on the loading dock. I'll route any messages I receive from the facility directly to you."

"I understand," Aragon replied. "Give me a look at the reception committee." As Geary's image vanished, she shifted channels to speak with all of the attackers. "Ten minutes. Our comrades, our fellow Tigres, await rescue. We will not let them down!"

Another small window appeared on her faceplate display. Aragon studied it, seeing someone in the specially adorned space suit of a senior executive standing at the end of ten guards in full armor, five on each side of an actual red carpet tacked to the loading dock surface. Executive Second Class Renaud was going out of his way to try to impress CEO Pavia. "Plan change," Aragon said over the command circuit. "When the mobile unit stops, everyone wait. Do not open the cargo hatches until I order it. Harbin, I'm going to walk out like a CEO on an inspection. Have a dozen of your workers follow me in a double column. When I give the word, I want those workers to take out the honor guard while I handle the executive. Everyone else will begin the assault at that time. Understood?"

"I understand and will comply," Harbin and Nedele chorused.

"Understood," Major Guerrero said.

Aragon took a moment to feel pride that she could change a plan on the fly, at the last moment, and her sub-executives and workers would adapt and follow the new plan without flailing in confusion. The Syndicate didn't like having workers who could think, and barely tolerated sub-executives who could manage independent thought. But she had encouraged and trained her people to be able to handle situations like this. It had saved their lives, and hers, more than once.

There was an additional wild card this time, though. The Alliance Marines. Guerrero had acknowledged her order. Would he obey it? She could only hope he would, and promise herself to exact vengeance if Guerrero went wobbly on her and cost the lives of some of her workers as a result.

The force of the main propulsion altered slightly as the unit's maneuvering systems made a minor adjustment. A minute later the main propulsion cut off. On her external view, Aragon could see the labor camp loading platform.

Instead of triggering the big cargo hatch to open, she hit the control to open a small hatch just to one side.

The gap between the mobile unit and the landing platform was perhaps half a meter. Michael Geary really was good at driving a unit like this.

She took a long step out, one armored boot landing on the platform, her display telling her that Harbin's dozen soldiers were following in two lines. Executive Renaud was waiting, doubtless torn between hopeful anticipation and fear of what a powerful CEO could do. As she took the several steps to reach him, Aragon thought about what measures that executive had probably taken against her fellow Tigres imprisoned here. No one got assigned to a labor camp command because they had a soft heart, and anyone trying to impress their superiors like Renaud clearly hoped to do was certain to be particularly hard on their prisoners.

Which was why she felt neither pity nor hesitation as she reached the end of the honor guard, facing Renaud in his unarmored suit, and drew her sidearm with a smooth motion. "Go!" Aragon shouted as she fired twice into Executive Renaud's face shield.

A flurry of shots behind her marked her escort wiping out the honor guard as the cargo hatches sprang open and the rest of the Tigres along with the Alliance Marines swarmed out, the mass of attackers rapidly dividing into three primary groups as they headed for their objectives.

There were times to lead, and times to hold back a little to concentrate on the overall battle. Aragon let herself fall behind, most of her attention on her helmet display as it showed her forces charging toward their objectives.

An alarm finally began sounding. Someone must have been monitoring the landing platform, and been shocked into inaction for a few precious seconds as the surprise attack erupted.

Harbin's force, the largest, was driving forward to penetrate the prisoner areas and gain control of the prison systems so no one could order the prisoners killed.

Off to the side, the Alliance Marines had reached a critical juncture where the passage from the guard barracks came out, as well as a side passage that would allow bypassing a block at the main passage if it wasn't also secured, and beneath them a maintenance tunnel that had to be sealed off. She'd worried that the Marines would charge onward, trying to assault the guard barracks, rather than setting up the defensive blocks she had ordered, and waited, tense, to see if they followed the plan. As the Marines halted and took up positions, Aragon breathed a sigh of relief and shifted her primary attention elsewhere for a moment.

Nedele's force had rounded some structures and headed across a wide stretch of open platform for the cargo haulers. Monitoring the feed from Nedele's armor, Aragon could see two guards standing at the hatches to each of the haulers, gazing in surprise at the troops in Syndicate armor headed their way, doubtless trying to figure out who was attacking and whether the alarm was even real.

Ten of Nedele's workers were well in front of the others, running as if their lives depended on it. Aragon heard the senior worker with that group shouting into the common command frequency. "Rebels! Right behind us! Let us in and we'll help you hold them off!"

Steadier, more prepared troops probably would have also hesitated as the first ten of Nedele's troops reached them. One pair had belatedly begun trying to seal their hatch as the senior worker bulldozed her way through in her armor and buried a force knife in one of the cargo-hauler guards. The other nine swarmed the additional guards at the hatches, keeping access open for the rest of Nedele's workers, who stormed in, knives slicing into the remaining guards as they frantically tried to armor up. A couple of them got off shots, causing Aragon to curse at the possibility of an accident involving the fuel cells, but quickly died.

The labor camp's ready response force had charged out and run straight into the Alliance Marines, who wiped them out with a merciless barrage. Behind them, though, came the rest of the guards who hadn't been on duty, charging ahead repeatedly in desperate attempts to break out. "Hold your ground!" Major Guerrero ordered. "We don't give up one centimeter! Show these Tigres how Marines fight!"

Harbin's force had already broken into the main command structure as well as the prisoner barracks. Aragon followed, heading for the office where the executive controls would be.

A unit of snake vipers charged down the side passage guarded by the Marines, trying to take the main blocking force in the flank. Despite a fanatical effort driven by knowledge they would certainly die at the hands of whoever was attacking, the vipers failed to push back the Marines even though a couple of them closed to hand-to-hand range before dying.

"Cargo haulers are secured," Sub-Executive Nedele reported. "Taking up guard positions around them."

On the feeds from Harbin's force, Aragon saw her workers charging through empty barracks, no sign of prisoners. Reaching the last building, they found a group of about a dozen men and women in Alliance uniforms, their hands raised in surrender. "Where are they?" a senior worker shouted at the Alliance POWs. "The Tigres. Where are they?"

An Alliance woman officer shook her head. "You mean the other prisoners who were here? They're gone."

"Gone? You mean they were terminated?"

"No! Not that we saw!"

"Three weeks ago," a man added. "They were marched out about three weeks ago. All of them."

"Where? Where were they marched to?"

"There were freighters docked here. That's all we know." The Alliance prisoners looked haggard and thin, fear in their eyes as weapons were leveled at them. But they stood steady, facing what might be their ends.

The senior worker stepped back. "We're here to free prisoners. You're prisoners. That means you're safe with us."

The Alliance POWs stared at him in disbelief.

Harbin called her. "Executive Aragon, our fellow Tigres are gone. What we can see matches what the Alliance prisoners are telling us. They were taken away weeks ago."

"Have a squad escort those Alliance prisoners safely to the mobile unit," Aragon ordered. "I'm almost to the executive's office."

"Colonel Aragon," Major Guerrero called. "Request permission to go over to the attack and clean out the guard barracks. The attacks on us have stopped but there are some holdouts still in there."

That attack made sense now. "Go get them, Major," Aragon said. She was at the door to the executive's office and barreled through, her weapon raised.

A sub-executive was at the desk, frantically trying to enter commands. He scooped up a pistol as she entered, but before he could fire, Aragon's shot knocked him down.

She came around the desk, her weapon aimed at the sub-executive, who was sprawled with his back against the wall, blood spreading over one side of his suit where Aragon's shot had gone home. "Where are they?" she demanded, her pistol aimed straight at his face. "Where are our comrades from the 1234th Regiment?"

"Comrades?" The sub-executive, his face twisted with pain, stared at her. "You're Aragon. I saw your files."

"Where are they?" Aragon repeated, kicking him with carefully measured force where he'd been wounded and hearing one of his ribs snap.

The sub-executive gasped, his breathing ragged. "The same place you're going. Why the hell...you're supposed to be going there."

"*Where?!!*"

"Kane." To her surprise, the sub-executive began laughing even though the motion seemed to cause him agony.

"Why is that funny?" Aragon asked.

"Because the families of the 1234th were sent to Kane, too. To motivate them. Your families also. All the way from Anahuac. They'll be there. And when the Syndicate learns you've gone rogue, they'll die. Your families will all die the deaths of traitors."

Aragon aimed carefully at his head, then remembering his cruel laughter changed her mind, instead putting a second shot into the sub-executive's throat. Stepping back as the sub-executive choked on his own blood, she gestured to Harbin. "Post two guards on him to watch him until he dies."

"I understand and will comply." Harbin's anger was easy to hear. "Our families are at Kane? Did I hear right?"

"Yes," Aragon said. "Supervise the requisitioning of supplies from this camp. I want everything that might be useful, including all weapons and all of the food. The Alliance workers will be ready to receive it."

She walked away, trying to control her own rage. "Major Guerrero, status."

"We've just finished cleaning out the barracks," Guerrero reported. "No prisoners. They all fought to the death."

"I told you prisoners were unlikely to be a problem. Major Guerrero, if you've confirmed the barracks are clear, you can take your Marines to the cargo haulers. Sub-Executive Nedele, the Alliance Marines will be coming your way. I want a clean hand-off of those fuel cells."

"Roger, Colonel," Guerrero replied.

"I understand and will comply," Nedele said.

Aragon switched channels again as she paced in the hallway outside the executive's office. "Captain Michael Geary, we have a problem."

"How serious?" Geary answered at once.

"Not immediate, but serious. We have taken the camp. The garrison is dead. Your Marines will soon have possession of the fuel cells. There were about a dozen Alliance POWs here. They are being escorted to the mobile unit. My workers will be bringing food pallets out as soon and as fast as they can."

"Those don't sound like problems," Michael Geary said.

"We need to go to Kane."

"Kane? Why—? Oh, hell. Executive Aragon, we just saw four Syndic warships that arrived several hours ago at the jump point from…Fusang. Two heavy cruisers and two light cruisers. We need to get those fuel cells and the food loaded and get moving."

"We're on it. Get your own workers going, Captain," Aragon said.

She walked back into the office, ignoring the sub-executive twitching out the last remnants of his life on the floor. Checking the controls confirmed that he had been trying to send out an alert, but had failed because he lacked one of the dead executive's access codes. The rest of the star system should be oblivious to what had just happened here.

"Get your hackers on this," Aragon told Harbin. "Make sure routine status reports keep going out. I want to be able to over-load the camp power core after we leave. Let me know when that's ready." She paused before leaving. "And make sure the damned beer gets loaded on the mobile unit, too. Those Alliance Marines earned it."

MICHAEL sat on the bridge of the *Corsair*, monitoring the resupply efforts and watching the activity of the Tigres and the Alliance Marines. He'd sent Commander Mateo to greet the newly released Alliance prisoners and get them taken care of until he could spare the time. For now, he needed to be watching those fuel cells come aboard, and the pallets of food being piled on the loading platform.

Chief Taman had gotten the Syndic engineering support drones working, the chunky devices trundling on their own across the loading platform to the cargo haulers, where Chief Sindi Taman was overseeing the drones removing fuel cells from the hauler racks and starting back to the ship. "Captain Geary," Sindi Taman reported, "I have physically checked the number of fuel cells on these haulers. It matches the manifest we were sent. Apparently there are some honest Syndics here!"

"Or the Syndics here were too scared of our pretend CEO to play games," her brother replied.

As if summoned by Chief Taman's reference to her, the heavy clomp of battle armor boots on the deck warned Michael that Aragon had returned and was entering *Corsair*'s bridge. She had raised her faceplate, revealing an impassive expression rather than the joy of victory. "We have a serious problem," she repeated.

"The Tigre prisoners aren't here," Michael said. "I heard."

"They were taken to Kane, forced to participate in the rebellion suppression mission there."

"That's…unfortunate," Geary said, not sure what else to say. "Wait. You said *you* want to go to Kane? Before going to Anahuac?"

She grimaced, removing her helmet. "Can we speak in private? For just a few minutes?"

"All right, if it's only a few minutes." The commanding officer's stateroom wasn't far from the bridge. He went in first, waiting while Aragon came carefully through the door, still bulky in her battle armor.

"You have kept your end of our deal," Aragon said. "But I must ask more of you."

"Renegotiating again?" Geary asked.

"Yes. Take us to Kane."

"Kane is about as far from Alliance-controlled space as it is possible to get. That's going to make our trip home a lot harder."

She didn't answer for a moment. "Please, Captain Michael Geary."

He stared at her in disbelief. Aragon was pleading with him? "Why do you want this so badly?"

"Because the Syndicate didn't just send our comrades from the 1234th to Kane. They also sent their families there, from Anahuac. Our families, too, those of the workers in my unit. As hostages, to force us to fight for the Syndicate."

Michael took a deep breath. "Syndics. How can anyone...? Executive Aragon, you told me you don't have anyone left. Just your son, and you don't know where he is."

"He probably wasn't taken," Aragon said.

"So this is about your people. Your workers. Their families."

"Of course it is. This isn't about me." She paused, her eyes dark. "I have too much blood on my hands, Captain Michael Geary. If there is some power far greater than the Syndicate watching and judging us, I know what my fate will be. But these workers of mine have suffered and died and stayed loyal to me. I will return that to them."

That explained why Aragon felt this so deeply. But it was also a major change in plans. "Executive Aragon, I have to think of the others on this ship. I promised to bring them home."

"You want to get home? Help Kane. Kane is associated with Midway. Have you read the snake files? Drakon has helped Kane. And your Black Jack has helped Drakon in his rebellion. They have a much bigger deal going than the one between us."

"How does that get us home?"

"Midway has a hypernet gate. You could use that to get back to somewhere close to the Alliance, then jump the rest of the way."

He studied her, knowing how badly Aragon wanted this. She would tell him anything she thought might sway him. "Why would Midway let us use their gate?"

"Read those files, Captain Michael Geary! Black Jack has helped defend Midway. Midway has allowed your Alliance Fleet to use their hypernet gate. Black Jack has a deal with Drakon and his co-ruler Iceni," Aragon repeated. "They will help Black Jack's scion."

It was a convincing argument. "Executive Aragon, I can't decide this on the fly. We've got four Syndic warships to deal with, and whether we aim for Anahuac or Kane, we have to jump for Cullen from here, so we may not be able to avoid them if they try to intercept us. If there's another fight, we might take damage that limits our options. That's after we get everything we can loaded onto this ship." Geary eyed her, deciding to be fully candid with her. "And my people, my officers and sailors, are going to wonder if this is a trick."

"Captain Michael Geary, once the Syndicate hears we have rebelled, it will order those families to be killed. As punishment for our actions, and as an example to warn anyone else who considers rebellion."

He paused, horrified. "Why didn't you tell me that up front? That's your strongest argument."

Aragon looked steadily at him. "Because it lets you know how badly I need this. It gives you tremendous leverage over me in our negotiation."

"Leverage? You really think I'd use my knowledge of the danger to your families against you?"

It was her turn to hesitate. "That has been my experience."

"With me?" Michael demanded.

"No," Aragon said.

"I'm not a Syndic," he said, trying not to get angry when this shouldn't be about him. "You're certain the Syndics would do that to your families? This isn't a worst-case guess?"

"I know of similar cases," Aragon said. "It's not a guess." She must have seen his struggle to accept her words. "I'm not lying. Not about this."

"I don't think you are," Michael said, realizing something about Aragon that he had already suspected. "You have honor."

She glared at him. "Honor? What is that? I'm not obsessed with my 'honor' like you Alliance fools."

"No, you're not, not in that way," Geary said. "I used to be like a lot of others in the Fleet, thinking that honor was about how others saw me, how others treated me. But I've been talking to the officers who spent more time with my great-uncle, Black Jack. He remembers the truth. Honor isn't about me. Honor is about how I treat others. How I act and what I do and why I do it. Like it or not, Executive Destina Aragon, you do have honor. The kind of honor that matters."

It was her turn to stare at him in disbelief. "Is this some weird kind of come-on? Because it's a bad time for that—and if it is a come-on, thank you for being what you think is nice about it, but no. You're not my type."

He grinned. "No offense, but also no. It was a sincere compliment."

"I don't need compliments, Captain Michael Geary," Aragon said. "I need to get my workers to Kane so we can free our families, *save* our families."

"I can't make any promises yet. I do need to get the other Alliance personnel on board with this. But, for the sake of your honor and mine, I intend to try to convince them we should take this ship to Kane and deliver you there. Can you wait for an answer until we know the outcome of dealing with those four Syndicate warships?"

She hesitated. "That's—what? Another day?"

"Roughly. It'll depend on what they do and what we do."

"My workers are going to be hearing about Kane. What do I tell them?"

It was his turn to hesitate, not wanting to make a commitment yet, but knowing how those 'workers' would be feeling. "You can tell them Black Jack's scion is also for the people."

All of those years fighting against the legacy of Black Jack, and now he was embracing it. Because other people needed to see that in him. Remembering his brief interactions with his great-uncle, Michael once again thought he might have gained some insight into the man he had once hated.

AS usual when time was critical, everything took longer than hoped, especially loading the fuel cells.

On the plus side, there was more food than expected. "The Tigres think when the Tigre prisoners were taken from the camp, no one ordered that any rations be taken as well," Commander Mateo said, "so the camp had all that excess food they weren't around to eat in the last three weeks. It's basic stuff, but so far it's all testing safe."

"And it's not Danaka Yoruk bars," Michael noted.

"No, thank our ancestors for that." Mateo made an angry face. "The camp had plenty of food on hand, but the Alliance prisoners here are all malnourished, and they say they've been worked to exhaustion, especially in the last three weeks. One of the prisoners died a week ago, too worn out to keep going."

A week ago. If only they could have been here sooner. "What happened to the remains of the prisoner?"

Mateo looked even angrier. "According to the people we liberated, the Syndics tossed the bodies of dead prisoners off the camp, down toward the gas giant to be incinerated on entry into atmosphere."

It wasn't an honorable burial by anyone's standards. "The Syndic in charge of this camp was killed by Executive Aragon."

"Good! These Tigres…they're a bit scary, but they're that not bad, are they?"

"I guess not," Michael said. "I wouldn't have wanted to tangle with them before they revolted against the Syndicate Worlds, though. How long will the new food stocks last us?"

"I haven't run the numbers yet because we're still inventorying, but easily more than a month. It'll take less than that to reach Anahuac, right? After that we'll have a lot fewer mouths to feed."

"Yes," Michael said, thinking that he couldn't bring up Kane just yet.

Aragon came back onto the bridge, wearing the Syndic CEO suit. "I need to sow some confusion. Captain Michael Geary, what are the Syndicate mobile forces doing?"

"They're heading in-system," Geary said. "So, in our general direction, but not yet on intercept. It looks like they're cutting through the star system on the way to the jump point for Cullen."

"They must have checked in with the star system CEO," Aragon said, frowning. "What they'll do depends on their orders. Can you clear the command seat and the area behind it?"

"Sure," Geary said, getting up and gesturing to the Alliance personnel who would be in line of sight behind the seat.

Aragon sat down, her attitude shifting as she took on her mock CEO persona. As hard as the real Aragon could be, Michael had been startled to see how much harder a CEO Aragon might have been.

She touched the comm controls. "Eyes only for CEO Cunha. I have been distressed by what I found at this facility. The executive in charge does not appear to be stable. The guard force is borderline insubordinate, their continued loyalty to the Syndicate questionable. If I were not in a hurry I would stay and clean up this mess. You would be wise to take action before serious consequences occur on this facility. Forthepeople, Pavia, out."

"What's going to happen to the labor camp once we leave?" Michael asked her as Aragon relaxed a bit.

She shrugged, the motion constricted by her tight suit. "A while after we leave, a message apparently from Executive Renaud will be sent saying some of his guards are refusing orders and he will restore order by any means necessary. Followed by a garbled transmission. Followed by the power core on the labor camp overloading and blowing everything to hell."

"Making it look like we did nothing," Michael said. "And destroying all the evidence of what did happen here. Just like at the prison we were held at."

Aragon shrugged again. "I like blowing things up. Especially when the things belong to the Syndicate."

Sometimes it was very hard to tell whether or not Aragon was joking.

"Captain?" Chief Okoro called. "We have a message coming in, apparently from those Syndic warships."

"Accept it, Chief," Geary told Okoro.

A virtual window appeared, showing a woman in a Syndic suit. "CEO Pavia, this is Executive First Class Lim. The mobile forces under my command are heading to Kane Star System. I was directed by CEO Cunha to contact you to determine if that is also your destination so I could place myself and my units under your command. I await your orders. Forthepeople, Lim, out."

Aragon directed a sharp look at him. "We should stop them. If they reach Kane, we would have to fight them there."

She was assuming Kane would be their destination, drawing surprised looks from the Alliance personnel within earshot. Michael decided to avoid directly dealing with that issue. "We have a chance to take out those Syndic warships. If they think we're friendly, we could hit them by surprise when they join up with us under orders from CEO Pavia."

"By surprise?" Aragon asked, sounding a bit sarcastic. "Would that be *honorable?*"

"Deception is permitted in warfare," Michael said.

"Technically, you're not supposed to be at war with the Syndicate anymore," she pointed out.

It was his turn to shrug. "The Syndicate Worlds isn't abiding by the peace treaty when it comes to us, and we've never been officially told hostilities have ended. In fact, we have already been attacked by a Syndic warship back where our prison was." He wasn't surprised to see his fellow Alliance officers and sailors nodding in vigorous agreement. "The Alliance POWs we liberated here are further proof that the Syndicate Worlds considers us to still be active enemies. We have to consider those Syndic warships to be threats to us."

"Sure. They're threats. But there are four," Aragon said. "Can you take them with one ship?"

"Our battle cruiser has the same firepower as those four Syndic warships combined," Geary told her. "And we're able to accelerate and maneuver better than even cruisers." A thought came to him. "*And* if CEO Pavia orders them into the right positions relative to us, we can hit them hard with our first volley while they're unprepared."

"CEO Pavia will consider your request," Aragon said dryly. "What do I tell them?"

"Order them to join up with us before reach the jump point for Cullen, at…uh…ten light minutes from the jump point. They'll have to push a little to make that, but that's what a Syndic CEO would demand, right?"

"Yes," Aragon said. "Should I tell them which relative positions to take up?"

"Not yet," Michael said. "Just before they meet up with us. I don't want them to have a lot of time to wonder why they're being staged like sitting ducks."

Aragon shifted her persona again. "Executive Lim, your service is accepted. Rendezvous with my mobile forces unit ten light minutes from the jump point for Cullen. Forthepeople, Pavia, out."

As she stood up, loosening her CEO suit with a sigh of relief, Michael gestured toward the labor camp. "How long until your people are done out there?"

"We've searched everything and collected everything we need. Including the beer for your Marines. Make sure they get clearance before they try to collect it, by the way. Harbin put a senior worker named Kat on guard to make sure no one else gets to the beer, and messing with Kat is a bad idea. She's a very good shot. Aside from that, maybe ten or fifteen minutes for my hackers to finish their sabotage work."

"Good." Michael made another call. "Chief Taman, how much longer to get those fuel cells aboard and locked down in their racks?"

"I think half an hour, Captain. Sindi?"

"Half an hour max, Captain," she confirmed.

"Good," Michael repeated. "See if you can safely beat that time. Commander Mateo, how much do we have left to bring on board? I want to get moving in half an hour."

"We can make that, Captain," Mateo said. "We'll have plenty of time to sort out the food storage once it's aboard."

Michael shifted channels. "All hands, this is the captain. We intend to get underway again in half an hour. Make sure you're ready. We've got a rendezvous with four Syndic warships and we don't want to be late."

8

"**ACCELERATE** to point one light speed. Come port zero three zero degrees, up one four degrees." *Corsair's* main propulsion kicked in with more force at the same time as thrusters fired to alter her heading, pushing the battle cruiser onto a new vector while velocity built rapidly.

In the primary command seat on the bridge, Michael smiled, enjoying the feel of once more driving a fast, nimble, and deadly battle cruiser. He realized he had begun thinking of *Corsair* not as a captured enemy ship, but as *his* ship, the Alliance personnel aboard his crew, and even the Tigres as sort of a strange ground forces detachment temporarily assigned to the ship.

"Captain," Lieutenant Kuei reported, "if the Syndic warships react as expected to our new vector to meet us ten light minutes short of the jump point for Cullen, intercept should occur in twenty hours."

Twenty hours. Michael touched the internal comm command to broadcast his words throughout the ship. "This is the captain. Projected time to intercept of the Syndic flotilla is twenty hours. I will bring the ship to full battle readiness in eighteen hours. Make sure you're ready. For now, get rest, and make sure your equipment is in top shape."

He had time to tour the ship, walking around to speak to the Alliance personnel so he could personally gauge their morale. As he walked, he passed or saw groups of Tigres, all of whom watched him with intense gazes that held varying degrees of worry and curiosity and even pleading.

They knew about their families. They probably knew he would be deciding not just their fates, but those of their loved ones.

It wasn't the sort of decision he was ever comfortable making. But there was no way to avoid his responsibility for making it. No honorable way.

The newly liberated prisoners were gathered together in a rather Spartan compartment that would have served as a rec room for Syndic workers. He went in, gesturing them to stay seated as some began to scramble to their feet when they saw his rank. Their uniforms were ragged, their frames too lean, reflecting the hard conditions that they had labored under for too long. "Relax. I wanted to check on you all personally. I'm Captain Michael Geary."

The woman officer who seemed to be the most senior in rank among the newly freed prisoners smiled. "It still feels like a dream, or something out of a legend. A Geary coming to rescue us. Black Jack returned. Supposedly the war won. I think we're all a bit worried about waking up and finding we're facing our next shift at that labor camp."

"I've woken up a few times in the last couple of days worried about the same thing," Michael admitted. "Afraid to open my eyes and see the walls of that cell still around me."

"The Syndics should have known they couldn't hold onto a Geary!" a man among the former prisoners said with a laugh that the others joined in on.

He was about to object that him being a Geary had nothing to do with it, his old rejection of his legacy as a Geary coming to the fore, when he remembered what Aragon had told him. She'd only offered him that deal because, as "Black Jack's scion," he was regarded as someone who might keep up his end of the bargain.

The old, old bitterness rose in him, the denial of anything special about being a Geary, tied to the refusal to accept that his granduncle had ever been the mythical hero the government and the Fleet had built him into after his supposed death. All of his life he had known that being a Geary did not bring him anything except impossible expectations from others, unwelcome and impossible-to-meet comparisons with Black Jack, and a future that demanded sacrifices while offering no choices.

Balanced against that for the first time was the realization that his status had worked to save every other prisoner from the Alliance currently on board this ship. And it had given impetus to the deal that had also saved Aragon and her Tigres from being ground down by the Syndicate Worlds on another hopeless mission. He'd never been given independent command operating on his own, instead always being under the eyes of superiors. But he had done that, now, maintained discipline and organized the mass of prisoners into a crew and successfully engaged a Syndic warship under extremely difficult circumstances.

Most of all, perhaps, was the fact that embittered, worn-down Executive Aragon and the rest of her Tigres had looked at him and seen hope. Not because they'd always been told to believe in Gearys, but because of the actual things his granduncle had done. And while he, Michael Geary, hadn't won the war, he had not failed these people. Not yet, anyway.

So, this time, instead of angrily rejecting the comparison, he merely gestured around him. "We all got to this point together, both us and the Tigres."

"These Syndics?"

"They were Syndics once," Geary said. "They haven't acted contrary to our deal, and they hate the rulers of the Syndicate Worlds."

"They killed the Beast," another woman said. "When they wiped out the guards at the labor camp. I saw him dead. He's in hell where he belongs thanks to them. That's enough for me."

"We're ready to join the crew, Captain," the senior former prisoner said, drawing quick nods of agreement from the others. "Just tell us where we're needed."

He looked at the earnest faces, thin, drawn by the ordeals they'd just been rescued from, but ready to fight. Ready to trust him. A burden, but also a pretty amazing thing for a man who'd always felt himself a condemned imposter. "You need to be medically cleared first. Our only doctor aboard is a combat medic with the Tigres. She'll be checking you out. Don't worry about her being a Tigre. She's been working herself hard looking after everyone on this ship. When you're cleared, Commander Mateo will enter your experience and specialties into the database he's maintaining."

"We've got a fight coming up, Captain, don't we?" another man asked. "We want to help hit the Syndics again."

"I understand," Michael said. "Get yourselves rested, get something to eat, and be ready when you're called on."

Ready to hit the Syndics again. As Michael walked down the corridor, he suddenly wondered what would happen to such fighters if the war really was over, if the Syndics were eventually going to abide by the peace treaty. Everyone he knew, including himself, had assumed the war would just keep going on, endless and inevitable. And wars needed sailors and Marines and soldiers and aerospace specialists. What happened to all of them if the war really did end?

What would happen to him, if he got home and discovered the Alliance no longer demanded the blood of Gearys?

A future he had never dreamt of suddenly gaped before him.

He reined in his imagination, telling himself that there wouldn't be any future if he didn't get everyone home first.

And the first step in accomplishing that would be winning another fight.

TWO hours after they'd left the orbital labor camp, the facility, apparent now only as a tiny black dot against the majestic span of the gas giant, suddenly flared into an intense spot of light that quickly faded.

Michael listened as Aragon/CEO Pavia sent a message lambasting the star system CEO for not taking action sooner. "What if the workers on that facility have sympathizers elsewhere in this star system? Check everywhere and everyone! Forthepeople, Pavia, out!"

She grinned after the transmission ended. "Everyone is going to be busy covering their butts from any potential blame for the loss of that labor camp, and looking for more worker saboteurs. By the time they start asking whether CEO Pavia and her unit could have had anything to do with it, we should be leaving this star."

"THIRTY minutes to intercept," Lieutenant Law announced.

"Very well," Michael said, seated once again on the bridge of *Corsair*.

Next to him, Executive Aragon was in her CEO suit once more, listening without visible emotion to something on her communications link. "We have a problem, Captain Michael Geary. My workers keeping an eye on the snake comm channels tell me the senior snake aboard one of those Syndicate mobile units is trying to contact the senior snake aboard this unit."

"Your workers can't fake being internal security agents?" he asked.

"No. There are verbal recognition codes. The snakes memorize them and they change frequently."

"What happens if a snake forgets the code for that day?" Geary asked.

"They die," Aragon said.

He waited, expecting more, then realizing that Aragon had said all that she thought needed to be said. "All right. What can we do?"

"I've directed my workers to stall, having them respond by saying the senior snake aboard this unit is checking on our weapons crews. That should be believable. But it won't work forever."

"Can it work for another half hour?" Michael said.

"Maybe. Maybe not. I would recommend being ready for when it stops working."

Michael sat back, thinking. "The moment we start powering up weapons, it will set off alarms on those Syndic ships. The same if we strengthen shields. Ideally, we want them positioned before we do those things."

"This formation?" Aragon pointed to her display.

"Yes. Both heavy cruisers just off our bow, one a bit to starboard, the other a bit to port, well within range of our hell lances."

"Explain," Aragon said.

"Warships are designed around engagements where they face the enemy bow on. In space a ship can be going in a different direction but pivot to face the enemy. So the bows have the strongest shields, the most weapons, and the most armor. The sides of the ships aren't as well protected or armed. The sterns have the weakest shields, and because the main propulsion is there armor can't help much."

Aragon nodded. "You intend kicking both of those heavy cruisers in the butt before they realize we're hostile."

"We can knock out or severely degrade their main propulsion, after which they'll be easy for us to pick off at our leisure. If we can get them where we want them to be before we open fire."

"CEO Pavia will do her best. When?"

"Send them the formation instructions twenty minutes before they intercept us," Michael said. "I'm going to play it by ear on when to power up our weapons."

It was perhaps to be expected that his plans would go awry before then.

"We're receiving a call from one of the Syndic heavy cruisers, Captain," Chief Okoro called out.

Michael checked the time. Twenty-two minutes before intercept. The two groups of ships were fairly close together now, the four Syndic cruisers off the port side of *Corsair* and slightly above, their relative positions only very slowly changing as the distance rapidly grew less.

Aragon took over the primary command seat again.

They were close enough for real-time conversation. Michael, watching on a receive-only virtual comm window, saw Executive Lim looking considerably more nervous than in her earlier message. "Esteemed CEO Pavia, I have been instructed by the senior Internal Security Service agent aboard my unit to inform you that he has been unable to contact his counterpart on your unit."

Aragon looked almost bored. "How is this *my* problem?"

"The senior Internal Security Service agent on my unit is… concerned that something may…be amiss on your unit."

Aragon's bored attitude shifted to a menacing stare. "Are you implying that I am unaware of the status of a unit under my direct control, Executive Lim?"

Michael could almost feel sympathy for the Syndic executive, caught between a suspicious security agent and an imperious CEO.

"I would never imply such a thing, Esteemed CEO Pavia," Lim said, every word coming out carefully. "I merely wished to pass on my message as I was instructed to do, knowing that you would be able to satisfy the concerns of my senior Internal Security Service agent."

"Is that so?" Aragon gave Lim the narrow-eyed look of someone deciding whether or not to unleash their fury. "You may inform your senior agent that the senior agent on this unit, indeed all agents on this unit, are carrying out their duties. I was informed there is concern regarding the workers who operate some of the weaponry onboard, including possible sabotage. This is being fully investigated as we speak to ensure there is no possibility of hindrance to the mission I have been ordered to carry out."

Executive Lim glanced sideways, probably trying to see if the senior agent on her ship had heard and was satisfied with the reply. A drop of nervous sweat appearing on one side of her forehead, Lim returned her focus to Aragon. "Esteemed CEO Pavia, the senior agent wishes you to inform his counterpart immediately that he requires confirmation of the security status on your unit."

Aragon looked seriously put out, but finally nodded. "Fine. You may inform your agent that the senior agent on my unit will be told." She looked to the side as if receiving a report. "I have just been informed some or all of my unit's weapons will be powering up to check for sabotage and functionality. You should inform your senior Internal Security Service agent that this is at the direction of his counterpart. Is there anything else, Executive Lim?"

"No, Esteemed CEO Pavia."

"I am sending you the positions your units will take up. I want you to proceed directly to them," Aragon added.

"Yes, Esteemed CEO Pavia." Executive Lim hesitated, her eyes on something close to her. "Esteemed CEO Pavia, these positions will be very close to your unit."

"Do you think I am unaware of that?" Aragon asked, her voice

suddenly much softer but somehow much, much more intimidating.

Lim nodded quickly. "I understand and will comply, Esteemed
CEO Pavia."

"See that you do," Aragon said, reaching to end the transmission without any polite sign-off. As the virtual comm window
and the image of Executive Lim vanished, Aragon nodded to
Geary. "Captain Michael Geary, you may power up your weapons."

He shook his head at her, smiling. "That cover story for powering up our weapons was brilliant. You would be a very dangerous
opponent, Executive Aragon."

This time her disconcerting gaze was aimed at him. "You just
realized that?"

He was still trying to decide whether and how to answer her
when Lieutenant Law called out. "Captain, the Syndic warships
are altering vectors slightly. It appears they are heading for their
assigned positions."

Michael dropped into the secondary command seat and studied the display before calling fire control. "Lieutenant Bailey,
begin powering up the hell lances in five minutes."

"Five minutes," Bailey confirmed. "How about grapeshot?"

"Three minutes after you start powering up the hell lances."

"What about shields, sir?"

Michael considered that, hating the idea of deliberately initiat-
ing combat with shields at standard strength. But it was hard to
believe the Syndic warships would accept *Corsair* strengthening
shields and powering up weapons. If they shied off, it would ruin
the planned ambush. "Leave them. The moment we fire I want
the shields to start powering up to maximum. When I give the
order, I want a full volley into the first Syndic heavy cruiser, the

one with Executive Lim aboard, then as quickly as possible a second volley into the stern of the second heavy cruiser."

"Got it, Captain." Lieutenant Bailey grinned. "Nearly zero relative speed, and close targets with their sterns pointed at us. I could aim and fire manually and we still couldn't miss."

"But you'll still use the fire control systems," Michael said, making sure it sounded like an order.

"Yes, sir." Bailey seemed a little abashed, confirming his suspicion that she might have really intended trying manually aimed shots. When it came to their weapons, gunners would sometimes attempt things no other type of sailor would dream up.

The minutes crawled by while Michael wondered how much longer the Syndics would keep following the directions of "CEO Pavia." "How patient are Syndic snakes?" he asked Aragon.

"They're not," she replied.

"Any guesses why we haven't already gotten an ultimatum?"

"Guesses? Sure. The senior snake on a unit of this size would probably outrank the senior snake on Executive Lim's smaller unit. The snake on Lim's unit must be extremely angry at the delay in communicating with his counterpart, but also worried about interrupting a security dragnet operation being carried out by a snake who outranks him." Aragon smiled. "Right now, Lim and everyone else on her unit are probably sweating buckets because their snakes are ticked off and looking for someone to vent their frustration on."

Michael tried and failed to summon any sympathy for Executive Lim. "Will they reach a point where they order Lim to stop following Pavia's orders?"

"Yes." Aragon shrugged. "I can't guess when that point will be. Maybe in the next second, maybe in ten minutes."

Right on time the hell lances began powering up. Michael

watched the Syndic formation moving slowly across the top and front of *Corsair*, heading for the assigned stations just off *Corsair*'s bow. The heavy cruisers were so close they could easily be seen by the unaided human eye.

"I've never been this close to an undamaged Syndic warship," Lieutenant Law commented.

"Neither have I," Michael said.

One minute passed. Two minutes.

Three.

"Captain, the Syndic warships have begun strengthening their shields," Lieutenant Kuei said.

They weren't in position. But they were still close. Geary checked the status of his hell lances, seeing that the grapeshot launchers had also begun powering up.

"Incoming message," Chief Okoro said.

This time they saw not Executive Lim, but a man with a ferocious glower. "CEO Pavia, I demand to speak immediately to an Internal Security Service agent on your unit."

Aragon glanced at Michael, who nodded. "Certainly," she said. "I'll get one."

"I will wait," the snake announced, his words dripping with threat.

Michael already had a link up to fire control. "Lieutenant Bailey, we're out of time. I'm going to use the thrusters to bump our bow up and slightly to port. As soon as every bow hell-lance battery and grapeshot launcher bears, let the Syndics have it."

"I understand weapons free as soon as our batteries will bear on the targets," Bailey answered. "Chief North is standing by to lock fire control on the Syndics just before we shoot."

"CEO Pavia! Where is an Internal Security Service agent? Do not think yourself safe from Internal Security!"

Seeing how close the hell lances were to being ready to fire,

Michael fired some of the thrusters on *Corsair*, pushing her bow up and a bit to port.

"You will—" The snake somehow looked even more enraged. "Your unit is moving. What are you doing?"

Aragon smiled. "Giving you your answer…snake."

"Fire control is locking on the heavy cruisers," Lieutenant Law called out.

Corsair trembled as every hell-lance battery and every grape-shot launcher that could bear unleashed their fire on the first Syndic heavy cruiser, the heavy barrage at close range slamming into the weak rear shields, collapsing them, and leaving the ship unprotected against the rest of the shots.

The image of the snake on the comm window, his shock just becoming apparent, disappeared as the heavy cruiser exploded, so close that *Corsair*'s strengthening bow shields barely held off the shock wave.

Lieutenant Bailey had already shifted targets, pouring another massed salvo into the stern of the second heavy cruiser just as its main propulsion started to flare in an escape attempt. The heavy cruiser's stern shields collapsed, allowing hell lances and grapeshot to penetrate its hull and tear through everything in their path.

"Accelerate to point one three light," Michael ordered. "Come starboard zero zero two degrees. Target first light cruiser."

Corsair leapt forward as her main propulsion flared at nearly full power, racing past the tumbling wreckage of the second heavy cruiser. Explosions rippled through the heavy cruiser as *Corsair* accelerated past it, the badly damaged warship finally exploding in *Corsair*'s wake.

The two light cruisers, after wasting a precious few seconds while their commanders tried to absorb the sudden attack, started accelerating as well, one angling starboard and "climbing" relative to *Corsair*, while the other veered to port and "dove" away from the battle cruiser.

"Can you catch both of them?" Aragon asked Michael, loosening her CEO suit.

"Yes," he replied. "That's what battle cruisers are for. Able to accelerate fast enough to catch anything they want to catch, or avoid anything they don't want to catch them. And this time my crew is familiar enough with the systems on this ship to use them to maximum advantage." He had angled *Corsair* to starboard and up, the battle cruiser quickly closing the distance on the Syndic light cruiser. On his display, he saw *Corsair*'s projected track sweeping under and past the light cruiser's path.

Corsair tore past the light cruiser, the much smaller warship's main propulsion at full as it strained to escape. The relative speed was still fairly slow, making targeting easy. *Corsair*'s hell lances walked down the length of the light cruiser's hull, tearing through the midships shields and then through the ship itself. As *Corsair* passed the light cruiser's bow, her grapeshot launchers hurled out their ball bearings, ripping apart the forward part of the light cruiser and leaving the stern section tumbling helplessly.

Michael barely noticed his crew cheering as he angled *Corsair* back toward the last light cruiser, the battle cruiser whipping through a vast turn and "down," heading for the fleeing enemy. They were going into a stern chase, slowly overtaking the Syndic light cruiser. "We'll reach weapons' range in twenty-five minutes," Lieutenant Law reported.

The outcome would take a while, but once the battle cruiser could start hitting the light cruiser, there was no doubt who would win.

The light cruiser's commander must have realized that as well.

The Syndic light cruiser abruptly began another turn and climb, shifting vector as rapidly as possible. "It looks like he's going to make a firing run on us," Lieutenant Law said.

Michael watched the light cruiser, thinking that it was a heroic but futile gesture. Or perhaps simply a desperate but still meaningless action. One way or another, the light cruiser was doomed, but the only way that light cruiser had a chance of hurting *Corsair* was if a piece of its broken hull struck the battle cruiser.

Or if the entire ship hit *Corsair* head on, he suddenly realized. The Syndic commander knew they were going to die, either in battle or at the hands of the snakes on their ship. Why not go out in a way that would destroy both *Corsair* and those snakes? There'd be nothing left of both ships and all of those aboard them but fine dust. "He's going to try to ram," Michael said.

Everyone else on the bridge stared at him, but Aragon simply nodded. "The snakes aboard that unit might have ordered that action. Or it might be a last attempt by the commanding officer to ensure their death will be seen as heroic by the Syndicate so their family will be safe."

This was on him. He'd have to make the necessary maneuvers. Michael did his best to sound cool and confident. "We're going to dodge, late enough that he can't manage an intercept anyway, but soon enough that we can still hit him as we pass each other. Lieutenant Bailey, make sure we nail this guy."

But it would be his maneuvering that would decide things. If he gave in to fear and moved too much, the light cruiser would miss a collision, but *Corsair* would also not be able to score hits on the Syndic. That would mean he'd have to do it again, setting up another head-to-head firing run with the risk of collision. If he didn't move enough, though, trying to ensure good hits on the light cruiser, the Syndics might still manage their hoped-for mutual annihilation. Even a glancing blow at such speeds would totally annihilate both ships.

The two ships had settled out on their vectors, the projected courses curving through space until they met.

Michael kept his eyes on his display, trying not to think about the other Alliance personnel on the bridge watching him. One of his hands rested on the maneuvering controls, ready to activate thrusters. He tried to breathe slowly, calming his body and mind.

He knew he wasn't the best battle cruiser driver in the Alliance Fleet, not even before he had been captured and spent a long time in a cell, his skills getting rusty from disuse. If the person in this command seat had been Tanya Desjani, he doubted she would feel any worries, instead smiling with anticipation of the test of her skill.

As the minutes spiraled downward toward the moment of intercept, the old, old fears came to stab at his confidence. Had he ever really earned his promotions, or had they only come because he was a Geary? Had his skills warranted command of a battle cruiser, or had that only happened because he was a Geary?

Had he ever really earned anything?

He felt eyes on him and glanced to see Aragon watching him for a moment before looking away. Her expression was as usual hard to read, but she didn't look nervous. Then again, did Destina Aragon ever look nervous?

He'd been trapped growing up a Geary. She'd been trapped by being born in the Syndicate Worlds. Neither of them had made the choices that brought them to that orbital prison where he had been held for so long. But everything since then had been the result of their choices.

They'd made it this far. He could make it the rest of the way as long as he didn't freeze or overreact. This was his chance to prove he was a decent fleet officer, and not simply someone being propelled ever upward because of his name and heritage.

"One minute to intercept," Lieutenant Law said, his voice sounding unnaturally loud on the otherwise silent bridge.

The seconds to intercept scrolling down rapidly, the Syndic light cruiser thousands of kilometers away but coming toward them at tremendous velocity, their own speed also devouring the distance, so far away, but suddenly there…

Michael's hands hit the controls without conscious thought, more of a reflex, thrusters firing, *Corsair* bending away from her projected track, the light cruiser here and also firing thrusters to try to compensate for Corsair's move and—

Past.

Corsair had trembled as she unleashed her full armament on the light cruiser, a wall of energy and matter that the light cruiser ran into, shredding the Syndic ship from end to end.

Michael took a deep breath, trying to slow his heart, which was beating far too fast, as if he'd just run a hundred-meter dash.

"Closest point of approach was one hundred meters," Lieutenant Kuei said, awe in her voice.

At the speed they'd been moving, that was practically touching distance, impossibly, dangerously close.

A belated cheer sounded, the others on the bridge celebrating the victory.

"Bring us—" Michael paused to swallow and steady his voice. "Bring us back around to a vector aimed at the jump point for Cullen, Lieutenant Law."

"Yes, sir!"

They were all looking at him, admiration clear, sure that his special skills as a Geary had been the key to succeeding at such a dangerous maneuver.

He looked over at Aragon, who nodded to him, also looking impressed. "Good job, Captain Michael Geary," she said.

"I was lucky," he said, so low only she could hear.

Aragon just nodded once more. "Sometimes we make our own luck by not giving up, or not simply accepting the hand that fate has dealt us. Sometimes, luck comes to those who earn it."

"Sometimes," Michael agreed.

THIS was one of the largest compartments on the ship, large enough to gather almost every Alliance officer, sailor, and Marine in one place. Michael strode in, hearing Commander Mateo shout "attention on deck" and seeing everyone come to attention, the drone of conversation instantly halting.

He walked until he reached one bulkhead and turned to face them all. "There's a matter that requires your input," he said, his voice carrying in the expectant silence. "My agreement with Executive Aragon was that her soldiers would free us from the prison, and in exchange we would take her and her soldiers home to the star system of Anahuac. After that, we could use this ship to fight our way back to Alliance-controlled space. Some of you may have already heard that Aragon wants to modify that deal. Instead, she wants us to take her and her soldiers to Kane Star System, where the Syndics are currently attacking the primary world for having rebelled against the Syndicate Worlds."

"Sir, where is Kane?" a sailor asked.

"Nearly as far from the Alliance as you can get and still be in human-occupied space," Michael said.

"Then how does going to Kane get us home?" Lieutenant Pradeesh asked.

"We go from Kane to Midway," Michael said. "It's one jump. The Syndic files on this ship confirm that Midway is not only also in rebellion against the Syndicate Worlds, its current rulers have reached some kind of accommodation with Admiral Geary. My great-uncle has apparently been promoted. According to the Syndic files, the Alliance Fleet has helped defend Midway against attacks, something that really makes the Syndics unhappy."

He didn't mention a puzzle in those files, that some of those attacks on Midway had apparently involved a mysterious enemy identified only by a code word. If the attacks hadn't been by the Syndicate Worlds or the Alliance, who else could have carried them out? Kane was very, very far from other human stars independent of either the Alliance or the Syndicate Worlds.

But that probably didn't matter in terms of making this decision. Michael waited for a moment as smiles broke out among the Alliance personnel at news that the Alliance Fleet had been in action at Midway and the Syndics didn't like it. "Midway has a hypernet gate. Going home by jumps would take us dozens of jumps and a long time. If we can use the Syndic hypernet, we can quickly reach a star system that's only two or three jumps from Alliance space."

"Captain?" Lieutenant Kuei had a skeptical expression. "Wouldn't that depend on the Syndic files being true and not disinformation to fool even their own people? Black Jack apparently got the Alliance Fleet home by making jumps."

"He had a lot more ships," Lieutenant Bailey said, her green hair standing out more clearly than usual in the crowd. "All of them fully crewed. And fast fleet auxiliaries to manufacture more fuel cells and spare parts."

"We'd have to refuel repeatedly to get home by jumps," Chief Taman said. "Getting more fuel cells would be really challenging, and we'd have to do it again and again. Speaking from an engineer's perspective, we can make it to Kane and Midway on our current fuel-cell status. Getting home? At least three, probably four, complete top-offs of our fuel cells."

"That sounds nearly impossible," Lieutenant Bailey said.

"It'd be really hard," Chief Sindi Taman said.

Chief North looked puzzled. "That sounds like the Tigres suggesting we go to Kane and Midway is pointing us where we'd want to go. But why do *they* want to go to Kane, Captain? Just to make it easier for us? A lot of these Tigres seem okay, but you know what they say about Syndics bearing gifts."

"It's because their fellow Tigres were taken to Kane," Lieutenant Bailey said. "And their own families. Sub-Executive Harbin told me. The Syndicate Worlds took their families to Kane as hostages."

An angry murmur arose from the group.

"That is correct to the best of our knowledge," Michael said, his voice once more quieting the discussion. "Executive Aragon, her entire unit, wants to go to Kane to rescue their own families as well as their comrades, and in the process fight the Syndicate Worlds. So, yes, going to Kane looks like it benefits us a lot, but it's even more important to them. It's not a gift. They're asking us for this."

Commander Mateo spoke up. "These people with us call themselves Tigres now. Taking them to Kane will hurt the Syndics, and give us a lot better chance of getting home. Isn't this an example of that old saying that the enemy of my enemy is my friend?"

"Maybe not friends, but Colonel Aragon has played straight with us," Major Guerrero said. "We're still alive because of the deal she made with you, right, Captain? And we're able to discuss and make this decision because we're free, not still prisoners working under threat. Hell, they armed and equipped us as well as themselves for that labor camp fight, and they haven't asked for that armament back. I'll defer to you fleet officers on the merits of going to Kane as a way of getting home, but as a Marine I think we owe these Tigres. And since they want to go kill more Syndics, we should help them with that."

"We don't know what we'd encounter at Kane," Michael cautioned. "We know the Syndics are staging an offensive there, so we're likely to meet hostile forces that outnumber us. We have to assume a tough fight will await us."

Lieutenant Law grinned. "We're Alliance Fleet, aren't we? So there's a tough fight. What would Black Jack do? Let's go get them! Not just drop off the Tigres, but see how many more Syndic warships we can take out to help the Tigres and hurt the Syndicate Worlds!"

A rumble of agreement ran through the crowd.

"Does anyone else want to say anything?" Michael asked.

An older man spoke up. "From Kane, we'll go to Midway? And from Midway, we go home?"

"From Midway, we go home," Michael said.

He saw the reaction to those words ripple through his audience. Home. Some of them had been prisoners of war for a long time. All of them, himself included, had expected to spend the rest of their lives as prisoners. The idea that they might actually, finally, return home had been hard to believe at first. But now, they could believe that he would get them home.

And, to his own surprise, he could believe it, too.

ARAGON was seated at the desk in her stateroom, gazing at the display with the look of someone who wasn't really focused on whatever it showed. "Executive Aragon," Michael said from the doorway.

She looked at him and stood up, her expression guarded. "What is it, Captain Michael Geary? A decision?"

"Yes. We're going to Kane. We'll not only get you to the planet, we'll do what we can to deal with Syndic warships certain to be there. No guarantees, because we might face really bad odds. But we'll do what we can to clear space of hostile forces for you."

Aragon took a deep breath. "I'm in your debt."

"Not just mine," he said. "No one dissented. Every Alliance officer, sailor, and Marine agreed we should do this."

"And…the price?"

"It's part of the deal," Michael said. "Obviously, if you can help us acquire more fuel cells and other supplies on the way to Kane, we'd like that to happen. And if there's any way to put in a good word for us with that Drakon guy at Midway, we'd want to see that."

"Done," Aragon said. "That's it?" she asked, clearly skeptical.

"That's it."

"Why? You know how much leverage you have over us. You don't trust us, and the feeling is shared. I can't hear you without wondering if you're lying, setting up me and my workers for a betrayal."

"My people are thinking of you as Tigres. No, they don't fully trust you, but the Syndics are enemies to both of us." Michael gestured vaguely with one hand. "As for the rest, call it a return on your investment. You saved our lives, you freed us—"

"Because we needed you."

"You've *honored* our deal—"

"Stop using that word when it involves me."

"And we have a mutual enemy," he repeated. "The Syndicate Worlds."

Aragon nodded, her expression serious. "That point I will give you." She extended her hand. "I wouldn't shake on a deal with an Alliance officer. Not before this. Too much bad history, right?

With you, I will. Maybe you'll introduce me to Black Jack himself someday. I'll tell him his scion is worthy of him. Despite what you say, this deal leaves me deeply in your debt, Captain Michael Geary."

"You can work off that debt by making things as difficult as possible for the Syndicate Worlds, Executive Aragon," he replied, reaching to grasp the offered hand. "Deal?"

"Deal." She smiled. "For the people."

He nodded. "And to the honor of our ancestors."

Maybe he wasn't Black Jack, and never would be. But, for the first time in his life, he truly wanted to live up to the Geary name.

What happened at Kane? Find out in
The Lost Fleet: Outlands – Boundless

SHORE PATROL

CAPTAIN Anne Spruance commanded the Alliance heavy cruiser *Redoubt*, currently in orbit about a planet in Augeas Star System. Ensign John Geary, in charge of the hell-lance weapons division onboard the *Redoubt*, was currently standing at attention in Captain Spruance's stateroom.

If there was one thing Geary had learned during his so far brief career in the Alliance fleet, it was the importance of keeping the captain of whatever ship he was on happy. Unhappy captains had ways of expressing their unhappiness which made for very unhappy junior officers.

At the moment, Captain Spruance .did not look happy or sound happy. "Ensign Geary, last night you were in command of the shore patrol detachment sent down to the planet. Last night you also ended up in the local jail, along with about forty members of the crew, including all four members of the shore patrol."

"Yes, Captain," Geary said.

Standing up from the seat at her desk, the captain leaned her face close to Geary's. "Just what was it you thought your job was as commander of the shore patrol?"

"To preserve order among members of the crew and other Alliance military personnel who are on leave or liberty status," Geary recited from fleet regulations.

"Really?" Captain Spruance turned back to her desk and tapped a virtual window. "Let's see what the local law enforcement authorities think you were doing last night. Riot. Assault. Battery. Resisting arrest. Refusal to comply with orders of local police Disrespect for local government. Improper public behavior. What the hell happened, Ensign Geary? I can't wait to hear your explanation."

SIXTEEN hours earlier.

"Geary! Get out here!"

Twisting to get through the access shaft to the power supply for the number two hell lance battery, John Geary worked his way out and into the passageway where Lieutenant Sam 'Suck Up' Booth waited impatiently. "What's the problem?"

"You've got shore patrol duty tonight," Booth said. "The shuttle leaves in half an hour."

"Shore patrol? Setlie's supposed to be doing that."

"Setlie can't. You're doing it. Get going." Booth shoved into Geary's hands an armband with "SHORE PATROL" embossed on it in big letters before turning away and walking off of at a leisurely pace.

Geary stood and counted to five inside before turning to call into the access shaft. "Chief, I've been tapped for shore patrol."

"Good luck, sir," the reply came back in tones that suggested luck would be badly needed.

Getting back to the cramped stateroom he shared with three other junior officers and changing into his dress uniform took nearly fifteen minutes.

"Shore patrol members muster in dress uniform on the quarterdeck."

Geary breathed a sigh of relief as the announcement was made, realizing that he had forgotten to take care of that. Dashing out into the passageway again, he found Ensign Daria Rosen waiting.

"I heard you got stuck, so I had the watch pass the word for the shore patrol to muster," she told him. "That okay?"

"You're a life-saver," Geary replied. "What happened to Setlie?"

"He's skating again. Complained to Suck Up Sam that he had too much work to do, so to oblige his little protégé Sam shoved the work onto someone else."

"Figures. Thanks, Dar." Geary waved a farewell and raced to the quarterdeck where the four members of his shore patrol waited.

He braked abruptly as he saw the four sailors waiting in dress uniforms. The heavy cruiser *Redoubt* only had about three hundred crew members, so Geary knew them all at least in passing. He recognized Petty Officer Third Class Demore, who until a few weeks ago had been Petty Officer Second Class Demore before being busted down in rate on various charges, as well as Seaman Alvarez, who was three years into a four year enlistment and seemed determined to prove that for some people the simplest tasks were too difficult. The other two sailors were Chadra and Riley, both of whom had apparently decided within hours of enlisting that they had made a mistake. Every supervisor either one had worked for had quickly decided they were right about that, but the two continued to use up oxygen, food, water, and space that would have been put to better use by just about any other living object.

Geary turned about, walking just outside the quarterdeck as he tapped his comm pad. "Lieutenant Booth," he said, trying to speak diplomatically and respectfully, "are you aware of the individuals assigned to shore patrol?"

Booth sounded annoyed at the question. "Don't you think I can do my job, *Ensign*?"

"Those four sailors are not good choices," Geary said.

"You'll have to talk to the executive officer about that. It's his idea. If the worst performers are on shore patrol, they'll have to do a decent job, and they won't be able to get into trouble. I'm not going to argue with the XO. Are you?"

"Yes," Geary said, aware that he was unlikely to get any positive result from the argument but not willing to give in without trying.

"Unfortunately for you, the XO is off the ship, and I'm not going to bother him about your problems. So get the job done!"

Mumbling curses aimed at the ancestors of Lieutenant Booth, Geary went back onto the quarterdeck, where the sympathetic chief petty officer on watch called him aside. "Sir, they haven't been issued shockers yet."

"Of course not," Geary said, wondering what else could go wrong. "How long until the last shuttle drops?"

"Ten minutes. If you're not back I'll hold it, but the pilot won't like it."

"Thanks, Chief. Have the duty gunner meet me at the armory."

The four members of the shore patrol stiffened to various interpretations of attention as Geary addressed them. "We're going to the armory to get shockers. I don't want any nonsense tonight. No screw ups. Come on."

At the reinforced hatch to the armory where individual weapons were stored, the duty gunner frowned at the issue order in *Redoubt*'s data base. "Sir? This calls for shockers with no charges."

"What?" Geary read through the brief order, then hit his comm pad again. "Lieutenant, the issue order for my shore patrol specifies shockers without charges."

"That's right," Booth replied, sounding even more peeved. "The XO doesn't trust that bunch with loaded shockers. You'll be fine. Nobody with a shocker pointed at them is going to want to find out if it's charged."

"How am I supposed to impose discipline without any means to impose discipline?" Geary demanded.

"Use your command presence! Do I have to tell you everything?"

Mentally vowing to "accidentally" shoot Lieutenant Booth if he ever got his hands on a charged shocker, Geary made it back to the quarterdeck with one minute to spare. He led the way onto the crowded shuttle after making sure every sailor in his group had their Shore Patrol armbands on. They had barely strapped in to their seats when the shuttle dropped away from the *Redoubt* and headed down from orbit for the city officially named Barcara but known to sailors throughout space as BarCrawl.

Virtual screens inside the shuttle lit up with the port briefing, alternating views of the natural wonders of the planet below with stern warnings. "Barcara is the second largest city on the primary world of the Augeas Star System. Augeas is part of the Callas Republic, not the Alliance. As representatives of the Alliance and the fleet, you will be expected to maintain the highest standards of personal behavior. While many of the citizens you encounter in Barcara will be extremely friendly, do not forget that even if the services they offer are legal in Barcara you can still be prosecuted within the Alliance for any actions which are illegal under Alliance law…"

Geary noticed none of the sailors were paying attention to the port briefing. All of the ones he could hear were discussing the sort of "natural wonders" that would be hanging out in the bars of Barcara.

As the shuttle dropped down through atmosphere to the landing field, Geary hauled out his comm pad and quickly reviewed the captain's standing orders for the shore patrol. *Maintain good*

*order and discipline. Refrain from use of force unless absolutely nec-
essary. Identify the bar where most of the sailors of* Redoubt *are on
liberty and station half the shore patrol there while patrolling with
the other half...*

There went his plan to keep all four sailors with him at all
times so he could keep his eye on the shore patrol that were supposed to be keeping their eyes on everyone else.

After landing, Geary let the other passengers on the shuttle
leave the field while he held back with his shore patrol. "Demore,
I hear you've been to Barcara a lot."

"Yes, sir!" Demore agreed, grinning. "Four times! Barcrawl is
a great liberty port. You see that exit over there? Once you go
through, all you have to do is turn right and in no time you'll be
in among the bars and the rave huts and the girls and the boys
and whatever else you want!"

"Where do you end up if you go left at the dock exit?" Geary
asked.

Demore's grin faded into puzzlement. "I dunno, sir. I've always
turned right."

"Listen up," Geary told his four patrollers. "There are two
rules for tonight. One, do what I tell you to do. Two, don't do
anything I didn't tell you to do. Any questions?"

"What's our job?" Alvarez asked.

"To keep fights from breaking out, to make sure no one does
anything stupid, and to make sure no local laws are broken."

"Oh. Sir, I don't think four of us are going to be able to handle
that."

"There's five of us," Demore pointed out.

"Oh, yeah. Okay."

"Follow me," Geary ordered, leading his patrol toward the
exit. At least they all looked like shore patrol with their dress

uniforms, arm bands, and holstered shockers.

Just outside the exit, he found four local police officers waiting, one of them a woman with a chief's star on each collar, and
whose no-nonsense look promised trouble for anyone making
trouble. "Shore patrol," she said. "Where are the rest?"

"This is it," Geary said.

"What about the Marines?"

"Marines? What Marines?"

The chief eyed Geary as if suspicious that he was a trouble-
maker. "A unit of Alliance Marines has been working with Callas
Republic ships. They're on liberty in Barcara tonight."

"Marines?" Geary repeated. "On liberty? Here?"

"That's right. In the same place as your sailors. I don't want
any trouble!"

"Neither do I."

"And I don't want any trouble with the sailors from the two
Callas Republic warships who are also on liberty here tonight!
Keep your Marines and your sailors quiet!"

Geary rubbed his forehead, trying to imagine how this could
get any worse. The chief's next words answered that unspoken
question.

"And there's a squadron of aerospace pilots having some sort
of celebration downtown. I want them kept under control, too.
No street strafing!"

"Street strafing?"

"*No* street strafing! Give me your contact info!"

Geary heard Petty Officer Demore chuckle as they left the
local police, turning right and walking toward the lights and raucous sounds coming from the Entertainment District. "Contact
info. Like that'll do any good in there."

"Why wouldn't comms work in there?" Geary asked.

"Bar owners are always dropping off disposable jammers on the streets so anyone wanting to use comms has to go into one of the bars," Demore explained. "They also jam calls between bars, so anyone wanting to talk to anyone else has to go to the bar someone else is in to do it."

Geary checked his comm pad, seeing it already reporting degraded conditions. "We'll have to pass information face to face? Why do the authorities in Barcara allow that?"

"The way it was told me, sir, was that the more money the bar owners make because of doing stuff like that, the more money they have to pay off the authorities and the police. So it's sorta a win-win."

"This just keeps getting better and better," Geary grumbled. As his shore patrol walked past the border of Barcara's proper-sounding Entertainment District, Geary watched the last bar on his comm pad disappear to be replaced by an out-of-contact notice. "Where are our people going to be hanging out? Any ideas?"

"I heard meet up at the Brooklyn Bar," Chadra offered.

"There's a Brooklyn Bar here, too?" Riley asked in amazement..

"Every port's got a Brooklyn Bar," Demore said with the authority of years of service. "It's like the Forbidden Palace bar, and the Bolivar Bar, and the Jungle Bar. There's one in every port."

"The same people don't own them everywhere, do they?" Riley asked.

"Nah. I don't think so."

"You ever been to Brooklyn, Ensign Geary?"

Don't get too familiar with the enlisted. That was the advice officers like Lieutenant Booth gave. But at the moment Geary wasn't too impressed by the advice of Lieutenant Booth. And it wasn't like he was sharing private information. "My family left

Old Earth a long time ago. I don't know the last time anyone I'm related to went back there, if anyone ever has."

"We could be the ship sent for the celebration, right?" Alvarez said. "That's only a few years away, isn't it?"

"Every ten years," Geary said. "So the next trip back to Old Earth will be two years from now. It's a long haul, but *Redoubt* won't be the ship chosen. It's always a battleship or a battle cruiser. If you want a chance at going, you'll have to transfer to one of them. And you have to do it before the ship is chosen, taking your chances that the one you go to will be the one that goes, because my mother said when she was in the fleet as soon as the ship got selected everybody wanted to transfer to it."

"How could I make that happen, sir?" Chadra asked, surprising Geary with the question. As far as he knew, it was the first time Chadra had expressed interest in anything related to his work. Then again, Seaman Chadra was in Ensign "Skater" Setlie's division, so maybe his lack of motivation wasn't entirely Chadra's fault.

"You have to do a good job," Geary said. "Our captain has to recommend you for the transfer."

"And then maybe I could get to Old Earth?" Chadra grinned. "I'm gonna try that."

"Yeah, sure," Seaman Riley scoffed, rolling her eyes.

"Don't start," Geary warned them both. He'd noticed that Chadra and Riley were staying as far away from each other as they could while still staying close to him. But as long as they didn't let personal dislike get in the way of their work, he wouldn't make a big deal of it.

Barcara's main drag was even more garish than he had expected, virtual neon signs and images filling the street above head level, the sidewalks next to the bars and rave huts filled with a wide variety of local men and women dressed in clothing that varied from suggestive to borderline obscene. "Hey, sailor!" one called as she caught Geary's eye. "Special deal tonight! Just for you!"

"No, thanks," Geary called back, trying to spot the sign for the Brooklyn Bar amid the other bright advertisements floating overhead.

"There it is!" Demore called out, pointing to a sign featuring a smiling sailor waving in welcome against a backdrop of archaic skyscrapers.

Inside, the Brooklyn Bar was crowded, chairs filled around closely-packed tables and the bar elbow-to-elbow. Aside from a couple of big virtual pictures cycling through scenes that might or might not show the actual Brooklyn, the decoration was made up of bottles behind the bar and a scattering of plaques from various ships on one wall. "Real wait-staff?" Geary asked, startled to see the men and women weaving among the tables to deliver drinks.

"Yes, sir," Demore said, grinning as he looked around. "Real wait-staff can, uh, interact with the customers, you know?"

"Oh." He was supposed to post half his shore patrol here. Geary looked them over, trying to decide. Demore was not only the most senior among them, but also likely the most reliable, which was a pretty sad commentary on the other three. Alvarez was at least trying to look professional, and she was a fairly experienced sailor. "I need to post two of you in this bar to keep an eye on our sailors. That'll be you, Demore, and Alvarez. You'll be here on your own while I patrol with Chadra and Riley. Can I count on you?"

Demore smiled and nodded so quickly that Geary immediately distrusted him, but that still left him no other options. Alvarez brightened, though, as if being pleasantly startled by being given the responsibility.

"Stay here," Geary said, pointing to the end of the bar nearest the door and speaking loudly enough to be heard over the noise filling the place. "Keep an eye on everything. If you see trouble developing, try to call me. If you can't, send Alvarez to find me."

"What if a fight breaks out?" Alvarez asked.

"Find me." Geary led Chadra and Riley outside again, dodging come-ons for a variety of entertainments. Spotting a pair of local cops strolling by as if oblivious to the raucous offers, he hailed them. "Excuse me. Have you seen which bar the Marines are in?"

"Jungle Bar," one replied, looking Geary over. "Shore patrol? Don't go in there."

"Thanks for the advice." Chadra and Riley followed as Geary walked down the street, studying signs while weaving between packs of sailors who had obviously already consumed copious amounts of alcohol and other recreational substances. Finally spotting a bright display which showed lions, tigers, and elephants hoisting drinks under palm trees, he went to the door of the Jungle Bar. Looking inside, he could see the place was packed with Marines. "You two stay right with me," he told the sailors.

Eyes and heads swung to watch as Geary entered the bar, Chadra and Riley nervously staying so close that they kept treading on the backs of his feet. "Good evening," Geary said to the nearest Marines as he fought off the uncomfortable sensation of being a target on a firing range. "How are you Marines doing?"

Wary looks changed to smiles when it became obvious that Geary didn't intend trying to throw his weight around. "Just fine, sir. What can we do for you?"

"Where are your senior people in here?"

"Right this way, sir!" one Marine announced. Geary followed until they reached a small table with only two occupants, seated facing each other. One, a master sergeant, turned his stern visage toward Geary, while the other, a gunnery sergeant, watched with a polite but unyielding look on her face.

"Yes...sir?" the master sergeant asked.

"I'm in charge of the shore patrol for the *Redoubt*," Geary said.

"I guessed that, sir."

"I just wanted to make sure there weren't any problems tonight between my sailors and your Marines. I'd appreciate your advice on how to keep our people out of trouble."

"If we keep them away from each other there shouldn't be no trouble at all, sir," the master sergeant assured him, mollified by Geary's request for advice. A waitress brought by two full shot glasses, setting one down before the master sergeant and the other before the gunnery sergeant. "If you will excuse me a moment, sir." The two sergeants toasted each other before downing their shots. "Where are your people at, sir?"

"Most of them are in the Brooklyn Bar," Geary said.

"Hey!" the master sergeant yelled, producing instant silence in the crowded Jungle Bar. "Stay out of the Brooklyn Bar, you apes! And nobody go looking for space squids to fight! You all got that?"

"Yes, Master Sergeant!" Marine voices chorused, followed by a babble as individual conversations resumed.

"I can't ask for better than that," Geary told the master sergeant.

"You could," the gunnery sergeant said, grinning. "You being an officer and all."

"Yeah, I may be an ensign, but I'm not that dumb. I appreciate your help. Let me know in the unlikely event that you need my assistance with anything."

"We'll do that, sir," the master sergeant said as two more full shots arrived at the table. "Thank you for the offer. If I might offer you some more advice?"

"Please do."

"There's a bunch of pilots at the Lux. I might've heard something about street strafing."

Street strafing. Unwilling to admit his ignorance, Geary nodded. "Where's that at?"

"Down the street that way. You'll probably hear them before you see them." The master sergeant spotted Seaman Chadra watching him, and sized up Chadra with a single look. "Straighten up, you boot! You're on duty!"

"Yes, sir!" Chadra replied, coming to such a rigid form of attention that he seemed in danger of falling over.

"Don't call me sir! I work for a living!" The master sergeant paused, turning his attention back to Geary. "No offense meant, sir."

"None taken," Geary said. He wondered how long enlisted had been making that joke about officers. Probably for as long as there had been enlisted and officers. "Thank you, master sergeant, gunny." He nodded farewell to the two Marines before leading Chadra and Riley back out of the bar.

Once on the street, Chadra exhaled so loudly that Geary gave him a worried look. "Are you okay?"

"That sergeant!" Chadra said. "I was afraid to breathe!"

"Mr. Geary wasn't scared of him," Riley said, smiling proudly.

"You just have to treat people with the respect they deserve," Geary explained.

"What's that mean, sir?"

"It means...don't be a jerk. Even if you think you could get away with it. Let's find the Lux."

As the master sergeant had predicted, the whoops and shouts carrying into the street advertised the location of the Lux before they reached it. Somebody was having a really good time.

They passed a group of Callas Republic sailors huddled

together. "Shore patrol!" one of them shouted, and the entire group took off down the street.

"What do you suppose they were doing?" Riley wondered.

"Not our problem," Geary said. "They're not doing it any more."

Reaching the door to the Lux, where several citizens of Barcara were lounging as if awaiting any calls for their particular trades, Geary found his passage blocked by a local police officer. "No enlisted sailors in there," the cop said. "Officers only."

"They're on shore patrol," Geary said, trying to sound assertive but knowing he had no authority over local police.

The cop plainly also knew that Geary had no authority over her. "Officers only."

Geary looked at Chadra and Riley. "Can you two just stand there and do nothing until I get back?"

Riley nodded. "We're good at doing nothing."

"Right. I have to go inside. I'll be right back out. Don't. Do. Anything."

The police officer let Geary pass. Once inside, he found a large room with all the furniture pushed up against the walls. More than a dozen pilots were leaping from one piece of furniture to the next while several others cheered them on.

"Excuse me, Lieutenant," Geary asked the nearest one. "What's going on?"

"Touch and goes," the lieutenant replied, taking a drink from the bottle in his hand. "They drink a round, then they go around the edge of the room without touching the floor, then they remove some of the furniture and do it again. Repeat until a winner is declared or any survivors are incapable of continuing. Who are you? Shore patrol? Really?"

"Yes, sir," Geary said.

"You going to bust us, Ensign? Hey, the Shore Patrol's here!"

Another lieutenant came up, eyeing Geary as she grabbed the bottle from the male lieutenant and took a drink. "Where are you from?"

"The *Redoubt*," Geary said.

"Whoa! Deep spacer! You're not jump happy, are you?"

"No, I'm just trying to make sure things don't get out of hand tonight." On the heels of his words a crash announced the failure of one of the pilots to negotiate a safe landing on a piece of furniture.

"Have no fear," the male lieutenant assured Geary. "As you can see, we are professionals."

"Are you wearing an eject assist harness?" Geary asked, pointing to the device strapped to the pilot.

"He knows what an eject assist harness is!" the woman lieutenant commented. "You ever done any street strafing, Ensign?"

"No. I don't even know what it is."

"Say someone wanted to try flying down a street at low altitude with an eject assist harness. That would be called street strafing."

"You guys do that?" Geary asked. "I thought those belts had limited maneuvering capability."

"That makes it a challenge," the male lieutenant advised cheerfully. "Or so I've heard. Never done it."

"Me, neither," the female lieutenant said. "I don't know anybody who has."

"Why do you have a phrase like street strafing for something no one ever does?" Geary asked.

"That is a very good question! Want a drink?"

"I'm on duty. Could you guys please not make things any worse out there? I've got three ships worth of sailors and a bunch of Marines all drinking heavily."

"Seriously? Why don't you give up now?"

"I'm stubborn," Geary said.

The lieutenants grinned at him. "We will take your request under advisement," the man said. "Good luck, Ensign!"

Outside again, Geary broke through a ring of locals offering "services" to Chadra and Riley, who were back to back and looking around in confusion. "Follow me," Geary said, worried about what Demore and Alvarez might be up to back at Brooklyn Bar.

Their path was blocked by a group of Callas sailors moving like a herd across the street. Once past that obstacle, Geary stopped again as Riley called out. "Sir? Is that Petty Officer Frink?"

Looking that way, Geary saw Frink weaving alone down the sidewalk. Ambling along behind him were several citizens of Barcara, reminding Geary of predators waiting for a wounded prey to collapse. As eager as he was to rush back to check on Demore and Alvarez, Geary couldn't let this situation pass. "Hey, Petty Officer Frink, why don't you come along with us?"

Frink glowered at Geary. "I don't haveta. On liberty."

"Actually, yeah, you do have to," Geary said. "We're heading back to the Brooklyn Bar."

"Come on, man," Chadra urged.

With Chadra on one side and Riley on the other, they got Frink back inside the Brooklyn Bar. "Park him with some friends who'll look after him," Geary ordered his two sailors. "Make sure they know I'll be expecting them to get Frink back to ship in one piece. They shouldn't have let him wander off on his own in his condition."

He went to the bar, looking for Demore and Alvarez.

Neither was in sight.

But another sailor was standing at the near end of the bar, wearing the shore patrol armband, the shocker belt and holster at her waist. "Yerevan? What are you doing? You're not on shore patrol duty."

Petty Officer Yerevan squinted at Geary, then opened her eyes wider as if trying to identify him. Grinning, she saluted. "Oh, hi, Ensign Geary!"

It didn't take the smell of alcohol on her breath to let Geary know this sailor was loaded. "Where are Demore and Alvarez?" he repeated.

"Demore? Uh, I got no idea. Alvarez. That I know. She had to go to the bathroom really bad, so she asked me to take over for a few, because she said Ensign Geary told her someone had to be here," Yerevan explained. "She was being real responsible!"

"You can't—"

"Don't you worry, sir! I am fully funckal—functional!" Yerevan's eyes went past Geary, gazing down the bar, and lit with sudden fury. Before he realized what was happening, she had pulled out the shocker and was leveling it. "Get away from my glass, you beer-stealing bitch!"

"No!" Geary grabbed the sailor's gun hand, wrestling it down. "*Alvarez!*"

Alvarez came running up, hastily sealing her uniform. "Everything okay, sir?"

"No. Everything is not okay. Put back on the shore patrol armband, take back the shocker, and then stay here until I say otherwise!"

"You gonna report me, sir?" Alvarez asked, looking downcast.

"I don't see what purpose that would serve," Geary said, surprised to realize that Alvarez had been trying and simply hadn't done a very good job of it. Besides, if he reported Alvarez he'd also have to report Yerevan, who when not drunk was a decent sailor. "Just do your best from here on."

"Yes, sir!"

"Where's Petty Officer Demore?"

"He's at the other end of the bar. So's we can see everything that's going on," Alvarez said with a proud smile. "That was his idea."

"I bet it was." Geary headed along the crowded bar, finally spotting Demore at the far end.

Apparently tipped off that Geary was approaching, the petty officer spun about to face away from the bar. Demore stood at attention and saluted, a performance spoiled only by the bleariness in his eyes. "All is under control, sir!"

"Have you been drinking, Demore?"

The petty officer gaped at Geary with a wounded expression. "Drinking? Sir, drinking on duty would be a violation of fleet regulations." He looked around as if gravely concerned. "Sir, I have been observing the activity in this bar, and I have to tell you that many of the personnel from the *Redoubt* are drinking to excess."

"You've noticed that, huh?"

"Yes, sir. And so are some of the sailors from those Callas ships. I think we should keep a close eye on that."

"You do? Demore—" Geary broke off as a sudden burst of noise drew his attention. He saw sailors leaping to their feet and racing out the door of the bar. "What the hell is going on?"

"I do not know, sir," Demore said, pronouncing each word with exaggerated care. "I will investigate and—"

"No. You will stay here. Get back down to the other end of the bar with Alvarez so you can keep an eye on each other! And if I catch you with a drink in your hand you'll be busted back to seaman!"

Joining the tail end of the rush out of the bar, Geary found Chadra and Riley standing to one side, watching the stream of passing sailors as if vaguely aware that they probably ought to do something but unable to figure out just what that was. "Come on!"

They caught up with the rest of the sailors from the *Redoubt* at an open area intended for large gatherings. At the moment, the center of it was filled with Alliance sailors grappling with sailors in the uniforms of the Callas Republic. Geary heard yells and shouts that sounded oddly happy given the battle apparently under way. As he ran toward the central mass of struggling sailors, he encountered two sailors limping toward him as they supported each other. "Stop!" he yelled, then halted, staring. One of the sailors was Alliance, the other Callas, and they were grinning. "What's going on?"

The sailor from the *Redoubt,* Petty Officer Yamada, saluted with his free hand. "My left leg ain't working so well, sir, and his right leg is kinda messed up, so we figured together we had two good legs."

"Brilliant thinking," the Callas sailor agreed, also saluting Geary.

"What is this fight about?"

"Fight?" The sailors exchanged baffled looks. "There ain't no fight, sir," Yamada assured Geary. "These ex-cell-ent sailors are teaching us one of their tra-di-tion-al games."

"Rugby!" the Callas sailor added. "Nothing like it in on any world under any star!"

"*That* is a game?" Geary demanded, pointing at the clawing mass of humanity.

"I know it don't look like much," the sailor from Callas apologized, "because we're all sort of tired, but sometimes it gets really wild, you know? Arms and legs and noses and heads getting broken right and left and all about! Great fun!"

Geary heard a sound like a stick snapping followed by a whoop of pain. "Somebody just broke an arm or leg."

"It's getting good, then! Let's get back in!" The two sailors began turning about while still supporting each other.

"No! Everyone—!"

"Hey, shore patrol!"

Geary turned at the hail, seeing several local police officers approaching.

The officers paused by Geary to eye the mass of sailors. "Riot or rugby?" one asked the others.

"Kinda hard to tell," another replied. "I think it's rugby this time, though."

The first officer turned to Geary. "Do you want to handle this?"

Geary looked at his available personnel, Chadra and Riley staring back at him with very worried expressions, remembered that their shockers had no charges, and shook his head as he watched another sailor being carried off the field. "Be my guest."

The officers pulled fist-sized spheres from their belts, tapped some settings, then tossed them into the mass of sailors. Geary caught the edges of the subsonics being put off by the spheres, vibrations that were unpleasant at this range and unbearable closer in. The swarm of sailors scattered into individuals and small groups racing past Geary and the police. From what he could hear of their conversations most of them were headed back to the bar.

About a dozen bodies were left behind. "Any of them hurt bad?" a cop called as two others strolled among the fallen, protected from the vibrations by their vests.

"Nah. Looks like they're all just too drunk to stand on their own. Except for this one. Broken leg."

"Only one broken bone? They must have just started. We're going to take these guys in," the cop told Geary, making it clear that the statement was not negotiable.

"Fine," he said, looking around, "Chadra, Riley—" Geary

looked around some more, but neither were anywhere in sight. They must have joined the stream of sailors back to the bar, thinking that Geary would also do so.

"Lose something?" the cop asked.

"Someone. Excuse me." Geary checked his comm pad in the vain hope that the locater function would be working, seeing that it was jammed, too. He ran back toward the bars, seeing that most of the sailors had already rushed inside the Brooklyn Bar as quickly as they had recently dashed out. "Where are Chadra and Riley?" he called to Demore and Alvarez.

"We have not seen them, sir!" Demore called back.

He'd lost half his shore patrol. Geary ran back out to the street just in time to duck as someone shot past just over his head, trailed by the rumble of an eject assist harness and excited whoops.

More pilots followed the first, caroming off the upper stories of the buildings as they tried to control their flight and racing unscathed through the virtual signs and advertisements filling the air above the street. Sailors boiled out of the bars to cheer the pilots on.

Geary struggled through the crowds, looking for his two missing sailors, and finally spotted what he thought was Chadra and Riley. The two were close together, apparently either making out or trying to strangle each other. "Hey!"

The two broke apart with panicked expressions, bobbed in place for a moment like frightened squirrels, then dashed inside the nearest bar.

Which happened to be the Jungle Bar where the Marines were forted up.

Geary was a few several meters from the entrance to the bar when Chadra came flying out the door as if he had been launched by a catapult. A moment later Riley followed, her body tracing a similar arc before landing in the street near Chadra. Both sailors groaned, proving that neither was dead. "What happened?"

He received a couple of bewildered looks in reply. "We weren't doing anything!" Riley protested.

"You were supposed to stay with me. Why did you run when I called you?"

"We thought we were in trouble!"

"So you ran into a bar full of Marines?" Geary rubbed his mouth as he looked at the door to the Jungle Bar. No matter what Chadra and Riley had done earlier, there was no doubt that while members of the shore patrol they had been assaulted. Which meant he had to do something.

Chadra and Riley had gotten back on their feet, their expressions changing to alarm as Geary took a step toward the door of the Jungle Bar.

"Don't go in there, sir!" Riley called. "It's full of crazy rah-heads."

"I'll be fine," Geary assured her, aware of the many drunken sailors in the street watching him, clearly wondering how the officer would handle this. About all he could be sure of was that failing to do anything would destroy what little ability he still had to try to control things.

"But they said they'd kill the next space squid who came in there!"

Geary hesitated, remembering some of the stories he had heard about Marines on liberty, but also thinking of all the eyes on him, waiting to see if he would back down, or stand up for his sailors. "I've got a job to do. Wait out here this time." Taking a deep breath, he went into the bar. "Who did that?" he asked of the nearest Marines.

One of the Marines squinted at him, trying to focus. "Did what, sir?"

"Assaulted those two sailors."

"This young officer wants to know if anybody has seen any sailors in here," the Marine shouted to his comrades.

A loud chorus of "No, Sir!" echoed off the walls of the bar.

Geary exhaled slowly, trying to remain calm. He threaded his way to the table where the Master Sergeant and Gunnery Sergeant had been sitting.

Both were still there, face down on the table, its surface now littered with empty shot glasses. One was snoring.

A nearby Marine spoke mournfully, her eyes brimming with tears. "If only you'd seen it, sir. A mighty battle. A heroic struggle. Look at all the ordnance expended!" she added, pointing to the shot glasses. "Neither one would surrender. Both fought to the end, not yielding a centimeter. Heroic, I tell you, sir!"

"They're dead drunk," Geary said.

"Yes, sir. That's what I said, sir."

"Who's in charge in here now that they're both out?"

The Marine pondered the question, looking at her nearby comrades. "Corporal Windsock!" one cried.

"Corporal Windsock!" the cry went up.

A Marine corporal was shoved up to the table, saluting Geary with a grin as she wavered on her feet. "Corporal Wysocki, sir. What may I help you with, sir?"

"I need—" Geary's next words were cut off by an eruption of sound near the door.

"Save Mr. Geary!"

"We're coming, sir!"

Drunken sailors from the *Redoubt* began pouring into the bar, led by Geary's shore patrol, their sheer mass shoving aside startled Marines. "Space squids!" the Marines shouted, rallying and charging to reclaim the lost ground. Within moments the bar was full of individuals packed together, struggling to fight even though they were having trouble getting enough space to move their arms and legs.

"We're here for you, sir!" Seaman Alvarez cried as she somehow wriggled through the mess until she was close to Geary. "No rah-heads are going to get—"

A wave of bodies slammed into them. Geary lost sight of Alvarez as he fell. Forcing his way up again to a sitting position, he saw a Marine next to him on the floor choking Demore. "Stop!" Geary yelled, but the Marine either didn't hear over the noise or was too focused on his task to pay attention. Geary's fist bounced off the Marine's shoulder with no apparent effect.

His other hand, still on the floor, closed on a strip of leather. One end of the strip had a weight sewn inside.

Demore's face was going slack.

Swinging the weapon against the Marine's head, Geary heard a thunk. The Marine went limp. Geary pried his hands off of Demore's neck just before several more furiously entangled sailors and Marines fell on both of them.

"I think it was about then that the police arrived," Geary told the captain.

"You think?" Captain Spruance asked.

"I was a little dazed, sir."

"So I understand. The ship's doctor diagnosed you with a borderline concussion." She leaned back in her chair, eyeing Geary. "You certainly put a lot of effort into failing in your duty."

"I was doing my best not to fail, captain."

Captain Spruance dropped a dark leather object onto her desk, one end clunking from the weight sewn into it. "Does this look familiar?" She didn't wait for an answer. "The police report said it was among your possessions."

"It isn't mine, Captain! I…I picked that up, as I said, because Petty Officer Demore was being choked and—"

"Do you know what it is? They come with a variety of names, but this kind is usually called a blackjack. It's not yours?"

"No, Captain!"

"That's good, because it's illegal to possess a blackjack on an Alliance fleet ship." Spruance leaned back in her chair again as she looked at Geary. "What should I do with you, Ensign Black Jack? These charges normally call for some fairly serious punishments. But before you answer, it's only fair that I tell you a few things. Every sailor on liberty last night as well as your four shore patrol have been interviewed, and none of them can recall you doing anything even remotely contrary to regulations. Apparently, you were a paragon of proper behavior and an inspiring leader.

"The Marines involved in last night's incident say that you demonstrated great resolve in trying to prevent trouble," the captain continued. "The Master Sergeant was not yet awake when they were interviewed, but the Gunnery Sergeant insisted that it was good liberty and a by-the-book and per regulations good time was had by all. She had no explanation for the arrests of so many sailors and Marines, saying it was an over-reaction on the part of the local police."

Spruance paused, tapping her desk again to bring up another document. "The aerospace pilots who were also involved in the events of last night all claim that no drinking and no street strafing took place. They credit you with offering a 'good example.' Based on these testimonials, if you and a good part of the crew hadn't been arrested I'd probably be putting you in for a commendation."

Geary stared at the captain. "I…have no idea what to say."

"Maybe saying nothing else would be a good idea. The only

real evidence I have against you is what you've just told me," Captain Spruance concluded. "And I'm not really allowed to use your own testimony against you unless I first warn you about that."

How had the captain made that mistake? Geary wondered.

Had it been deliberate?

Spruance shook her head. "You do realize last night was a no-win situation for you, right?"

"Yes, Captain, I did get that impression pretty quickly."

"But you appear to have done everything you could, anyway. You didn't give up just because the situation was hopeless from the start. And you tried to succeed in a manner that earned the collective silence of the sailors who could have tossed you out the airlock with their testimony if they'd wanted to. Even the Marines and pilots who could have helped hang you were willing to keep quiet. For whatever reason, they all respect you, and that's important. You did *something* right. So here's what I'm going to do, Ensign Black Jack. I'm going to forget that last night happened. Officially, there's not going to be any record. I'm also going to tell you that it would be a very good idea for you to not leave the ship again while we are orbiting this planet. I'm sure that you have plenty to do aboard ship."

"Yes, Captain," Geary said, unable to believe his luck. "Thank you, Captain."

"Get back to work."

Geary left the captain's stateroom, still dazed, to find Ensign Daria Rosen waiting, worried. "How bad is it?" she asked. "Court-martial?"

"No. I'm just confined to the ship for the rest of the port call. Nothing official, though. Nothing on the record."

Before she could reply, the captain stuck her head out of the hatch to her stateroom. "Hey, Ensign Black Jack, the supply officer's locater is off again. See if he's in the wardroom and tell him I need to see him right away."

"Yes, Captain!"

"Ensign Black Jack?" Daria asked, grinning. "It looks like you did pick up a nickname."

"I hope not," Geary said. "I'd hate to go through my life with a nickname like Black Jack following me around." In years to come, as Black Jack came to be part of his official identity, he would sometimes recall those words and wonder just how loudly his ancestors were laughing as he said them.

"I've got shore patrol duty tonight," Daria said. "Any advice?"

"Hide somewhere on the ship until we leave orbit."

"I'm serious! You ended up in jail and still came out on the captain's good side. What can I do?"

John Geary thought about it, finally shrugging. "Don't give up. And look after the crew and the others on liberty in Barcara as best you can. If you do, they might look after you when you need it."

"Uh huh," Daria said. "Got that. Anything else?"

He tried to remember everything that had happened last night. "One other thing. Don't be a jerk."

"Thanks, Black Jack!"

"Don't call me that!"

GRENDEL

"**GRENDEL.** A star system where nothing is happening, nothing ever has happened, and nothing ever will happen."

Lieutenant Commander Decala, the executive officer of the Alliance heavy cruiser *Merlon*, turned a wry smile on Commander John Geary, the commanding officer. "Be careful you don't jinx us, captain."

"Advice noted and logged." Geary leaned back in his command seat on the bridge of *Merlon*, his eyes on the display floating before him. Six hours ago they had arrived at Grendel using the jump point from the star Beowulf. From Grendel they would jump to T'shima, where the fleet's main base for this region of space was located. The drives which allowed faster-than-light travel could only jump between points in space created by the mass of stars, and then only if the destination star was close enough. That made Grendel a necessary waypoint, and that's all it had ever been. No one went to Grendel because they wanted to go to Grendel.

At the moment, *Merlon* was the flagship for a convoy, with Geary also controlling the light cruiser *Pommel* and three destroyers as well as an even dozen massive cargo transports hauling military supplies. Against the vast reaches of Grendel star system, the convoy he commanded formed a very tiny human presence indeed. Still, in the human scheme of things it was both significant and something of which to be proud. The Alliance had been at least technically at peace for several decades, and the limited number of warships in the fleet reflected the casual attitude of a people who had not had much active need of defenses. Nonetheless, Geary had managed after long years of service to not only achieve the rank of commander with his pride and his self-respect mostly intact, but had also gained the command of a heavy cruiser.

Measured against that accomplishment was the reality that no one expected the Alliance would anytime soon require its heavy cruisers, or its few battleships and battle cruisers, to protect its people and its planets. Nor as far as anyone knew did the convoy actually need an escort to protect it. Regulations called for practicing convoy escort duties, and for convoys transiting border star systems to have escorts, so a few ships were temporarily assigned to that task and required to run various drills so that they would be prepared if someday, somehow, convoys really did need escorts.

Decala squinted at her own display. "We are lucky, though. We could be stationed on the emergency facility here and have to stay for years. At least it's only three days to the jump point for T'shima and then we get to leave."

"That is indeed a blessing." The orbital base at Grendel had a minimal crew, and only existed because every now and then ships passing through this star system enroute other stars needed repair assistance for their equipment or medical assistance for somebody aboard. If not for that requirement, the several barren planets which were either too hot or too cold and the mass of asteroids in the star system would have held no reason for any humans to linger at Grendel. The star system wasn't as bad as the gray nothingness of jump space, but that wasn't saying much.

Geary pulled out the scale on his display so that it showed the entire neighborhood of stars in this region. Grendel rested next to the border between the Alliance and the Syndicate Worlds, an imaginary wall with many a curve and bulge drawn through nothingness by the two greatest political powers in human space. In the dozen centuries since humanity had left Sol star system and the Earth of its oldest ancestors, most inhabited worlds had become part of either the Alliance or the Syndicate Worlds, though much smaller groupings such as the Callas Republic and the Rift Federation also existed on the Alliance side of the border.

The nearest star to Grendel on the Syndic side of the border was Shannin, but the two stars might as well have been a million light years apart since ships never jumped between them. On this side of the border, most of the stars belonged to the Alliance by the choice of the inhabitants of their planets. On the other side of the border, every star system belonged to the Syndicate Worlds whether the people living on the planets liked it or not. The leaders of the Syndics liked to proclaim their avowed love of freedom, but the outcomes of allegedly free votes in the Syndicate World either were never in doubt or made little difference since local authorities were given little real power compared to the corporate-dominated power structure.

Decala must have noticed what Geary was looking at. "What do you suppose the Syndics are doing? It's been almost six months since they announced that no more Alliance merchant shipping would be allowed in Syndic space."

He shrugged in reply. "You've seen the intelligence assessments. No one on this side of the border seems to know, and our embassies and other diplomatic posts inside the Syndicate Worlds haven't been able to find out what's going on. The best guess is that it was a protectionist trade measure, to seal out competition from the Alliance."

"It's not like we ever had that much trade with them. They never encouraged it."

"No. Not much tourism, either. But whatever the Syndics are thinking it hasn't ramped up tensions beyond the usual level. They seem to be behaving themselves and respecting the border agreements." Geary checked his daily agenda. "Only two drills scheduled over the next twelve hours, and those are just simulated maneuvers."

"We have to conserve fuel cells," Decala reminded Geary dryly. "Remember what Admiral Kindera said. Fleet budgets won't support racing around star systems."

"Or support carrying out necessary training," Geary agreed. "Keep the ship on a routine schedule today, but make sure the junior officers most in need of training are on hand for those simulated maneuvers this afternoon. I'll be there to supervise and make sure the other ships are taking the drill seriously."

He stood up. "Let me know if anything changes," Geary informed the bridge watch standers, then headed toward his stateroom to get some paper work done.

"CAPTAIN to the bridge!" Halfway through his regular walk-through of the ship, Geary's feet were moving toward the bridge before his mind fully absorbed the urgent summons. Rather than pause to call the bridge on the nearest comm panel he simply kept up a quick pace, any crew members in the passageways of *Merlon* jumping aside when they saw him coming so he would have a clear path. He was sliding into his command seat on the bridge when Lieutenant Commander Decala arrived on his heels. "What's going on?" Geary asked.

"A Syndic flotilla has arrived via the jump point from Shannin, sir," the operations watch reported.

"What?" The news was not only unexpected but also inexplicable. Geary activated his own display, seeing the data which *Merlon*'s sensors had already collected. Coming in-system from the jump point were not just a few Syndic warships, but a substantial flotilla.

"Four heavy cruisers?" Decala asked.

"Plus four light cruisers, six Hunter-Killers and ten corvettes," the operations watch confirmed.

Geary frowned at his display. Military attaches and other sources within the Syndicate Worlds had a pretty good handle on Syndic military capabilities, and he was certain that the Syndics had the same sort of knowledge of Alliance warships. The Syndic heavy cruisers each pretty much matched *Merlon* in maneuverability and protection, but the Syndic armament was slightly better even though the Syndic missiles weren't quite as good as the Alliance's wraith missiles. The light cruisers were significantly smaller, both more lightly armed and armored than heavy cruisers but faster because of greater propulsion capability relative to their mass. In a one-on-one match up, *Pommel* would have had a slim advantage against any one of them. The Hunter-Killers were smaller and less capable than the Alliance destroyers, but the HuKs were a little faster. The Syndic corvettes were smaller yet, singly not a match for any Alliance warship, and could just keep up with their heavy cruisers. Still, it was a very strong force relative to *Merlon* and the other Alliance warships at Grendel.

The Syndics had come in from a jump point to one side of the current track of the Alliance convoy, barely two light hours distant. Which meant the Syndic warships had already been in this star system for two hours before the light from their arrival reached the Alliance convoy. He wondered what they had been doing in those two hours. "I need an assessment of their track as soon as possible."

"Yes, sir. The Syndics have accelerated and come around to port." Space had no directions as humans understood them, of course, so humans imposed their own, arbitrarily designating an exact plane for any star system and defining one side of that plane as up, the other side as down, any direction away from the star as port and directions toward the star as starboard or starward. It wasn't the only possible means by which ships could orient themselves to each other in space, but it was the one which humans had adopted. Without an external reference and such conventions, no human ship could possibly understand what any other ship meant when it gave directions.

Rubbing his neck, Geary tapped a request into the maneuvering system and saw the result pop up. "I don't like this. They seem to be moving onto an intercept with this convoy."

"They could just be heading onto a converging vector," Decala noted, "if they were also aiming for the jump point for T'shima."

"Why the hell would a Syndic flotilla of that size be going to T'shima? For that matter, what the hell are they doing in Alliance space at all?" Protocol dictated that a foreign ship arriving in a star system announce its intentions, but any such message from the Syndics should have shown up right about the same time as the light revealing their appearance at Grendel. "There's nothing from the Syndics on any channel?"

"No, sir," the communications watch confirmed.

Geary pulled up the current version of the rules of engagement. This wasn't the first time that he had read them, of course, but he hadn't seriously expected to need the ROE on this trip. "We are supposed to defend Alliance space, Alliance citizens and Alliance property, we are required to be firm and resolute, but we are not allowed to explicitly threaten military action or open fire unless first fired upon. I wish the idiots who wrote these instructions were here now." He pounded one fist softly on the arm of his seat. "I'll send a challenge, but it'll be two hours before they get it, and even if they reply that will take almost another two hours."

"They're still a long ways off," Decala said. "We have time to figure out how to deal with this."

"Do we?" Geary's display updated, showing the Syndic flotilla had steadied out on a course and speed two hours ago, the now-converging paths of the Syndic flotilla and the Alliance convoy arcing across the expanse of Grendel star system. "There are heading for the jump point for T'shima, and they're going to get to it before we do." The jump point was only about two and half light hours distant now, but with the convoy loafing along at point zero four light speed that translated to about sixty hours of travel time. The Syndics, at about three light hours distance from the jump point for T'shima, were traveling at point zero eight light speed and would get there in a less than thirty-eight hours.

"We can accelerate," Decala suggested. "Fleet will raise hell with us for using extra fuel cells, but it's justified."

He hesitated before answering, then ran some quick checks using the maneuvering system. "That's not good enough. The transports are too slow. We could all beat the Syndic heavy cruisers and the corvettes to the jump point, but the Syndic light cruisers and HuKs could intercept us before the jump point if they separated from the rest and used their best acceleration. It wouldn't take much damage to the transports to leave them unable to outrun the heavy cruisers and HuKs."

Decala was now staring at Geary. "Sir, you're talking as if this was a combat situation."

"Maybe it is. Don't we have to plan as if it is?" He wished he had days to think about this, or at least a few more hours, but he had to act quickly or not at all. The slow, cumbersome transports needed all the lead time they could get if this was indeed a threat. *Think of it as a combat exercise. A drill. They're presenting me with this situation. What do I do? Hold off acting until my options are gone? Or do something knowing it might be wrong, and might get me laughed at for over-reacting and disciplined for 'wasting fleet resources?'* He'd probably even get that annoying "Black Jack" nickname thrown into his face again. But…"They didn't make me commanding officer of a cruiser because they expected me to do nothing."

"Sir?"

"I'm just lecturing myself." Geary punched his controls, calling up an image of Lieutenant Commander Lagemann on the *Pommel*. "I'm splitting the convoy," Geary announced without any preamble. "You are to take *Pommel*, all three destroyers and all of the transports, accelerating at the best pace the transports can achieve so as to reach the jump point for T'shima as soon as possible." The transports would accelerate slowly, but could eventually manage point zero eight light speed themselves. After factoring in how long it would take the transports to reach their maximum velocity if they started accelerating now, it would be thirty four hours before they reached the jump point. Time enough to beat the Syndics there, as long as none of the Syndics accelerated. But time delays worked both ways. It would take the Syndics two hours to see what the Alliance ships had done, two hours before the Syndics could react in any way.

Pommel's commanding officer didn't quite manage to conceal his surprise at the orders. "Sir, if you think those Syndics might be a threat, we should keep our forces concentrated," Lagemann objected.

Geary shook his head. "Our job is to get those transports safely to T'shima. That's the overriding priority. I will take *Merlon* and use her to block the movement of the Syndic light cruisers and HuKs if they are detached to try to intercept the transports. *Pommel* and the destroyers will be responsible for defending the transports and stopping any Syndics that get past *Merlon*."

Lagemann gave him the same look which Decala had earlier. "You really think this might turn into a combat situation, sir? If so, we shouldn't split our combat capabilities," he urged again.

"If that entire Syndic flotilla catches us, our entire combat capability won't stand a snowball's chance in a star's photosphere. You can see that as well as I can. If we weren't encumbered by the transports we might be able to wear the Syndics down until they had to withdraw, but we are responsible for those transports. We have to keep the Syndics from getting enough of their forces within range of the transports, and this is the only way to do it."

Pommel's commanding officer looked away, clearly unhappy. "Sir, you're asking us to leave *Merlon* to face the Syndics alone, to fight alone if necessary."

"I realize that and I appreciate your loyalty to your comrades." Geary smiled in what he hoped was a reassuring and confident manner. "This is our best course of action. Most likely, they'll stay clear of us and then leave after making whatever point they're trying to make. But if the Syndics do prove to be hostile, and if any of them get past *Merlon*, those transports will need *Pommel* and the destroyers. That's where your duty lies."

"I understand, sir." Lagemann saluted. "When do we detach?"

"Immediately. I'll send the message notifying everyone. Get those transports moving."

"Yes, sir."

That done, Geary called the Syndics. "This is Commander John Geary of the Alliance heavy cruiser *Merlon* calling the Syndicate

Worlds' warships which have entered the Alliance star system of Grendel. You are to immediately identify yourselves and your purpose for being in Grendel."

"Firm *and* resolute," Decala observed.

"Yeah." In another four hours or so, he would know if the Syndics were going to answer him. "Get the crew some rest while we can," he told Decala. Any executive officer's instincts were to keep a crew working, but at the moment Geary felt he should override those instincts. "We might need to come to full readiness and stay there for a while."

"Yes, sir."

He had either already made a major fool of himself by over-reacting, or had set up a situation where *Merlon* might have to actually trade shots with the Syndics. He wasn't sure which one of those things would be worse for his career.

"WE finally have a reply from the Syndics."

Geary accepted the transmission in his stateroom, where he had retired for a little while to avoid driving his bridge crew crazy out of his own frustration as the hours had gone by without any answer from the Syndics. His comm panel lit, showing a female Syndic CEO with the usual perfectly done hair, perfectly fitted uniform and perfectly insincere smile. "Greetings to Commander Geary from CEO Third Rank Fredericka Nalis on the Syndicate Worlds' heavy cruiser C-195. Our flotilla is on a peaceful diplomatic visit to Alliance space, arranged through your own fleet headquarters. It seems you were not informed of our impending arrival, but I trust there will be no incidents which might imperil a visit designed to reduce tensions between our peoples."

It sounded plausible enough, especially given fleet headquarters' tendency to forget to tell operational units what was supposed to be happening. "Commander Decala, have you seen the Syndic response?"

Decala's image appeared on his panel and nodded. "Yes, sir. I don't like it, sir."

"Fleet *has* screwed up in the past about notifying us."

"Yes, but not about something this big. A large Syndic flotilla entering Alliance space? Sir, they'd have been assigned an Alliance escort, wouldn't they?"

"That's the proper procedure." Geary tapped another command as an alert sounded. "Damn. The Syndic light cruisers and HuKs are accelerating away from the slower warships."

The image of Decala nodded again. "On an intercept aimed at *Pommel* and the transports, or maybe just the jump point. Same difference. Sir, this stinks."

"It surely does, Cara. Work up a direct intercept for us, bringing *Merlon* in toward those Syndic light cruisers and HuKs. I'll be on the bridge in a minute."

By the time he arrived the maneuver had been calculated. Geary studied it for a moment, thinking things through. Relative to *Merlon*, the Syndic heavy cruisers and corvettes were just abaft the port beam and just above, their course slowly converging on *Merlon* and their distance slowly decreasing. The accelerating Syndic light cruisers and HuKs would be creeping forward of *Merlon*'s port beam, their paths aimed ahead of *Merlon* and toward the rest of the Alliance convoy which now was off the starboard bow of *Merlon* and slightly below, drawing steadily away as the lumbering transports burned through fuel cells at a rate that would probably make the budget geeks at fleet headquarters faint from distress. If the maneuvering system estimates proved right, the Syndic light cruisers and HuKs could intercept the transports in less than eight and a half hours, half an hour before the transports reached the jump point for T'shima. There wasn't any time to waste. "All right. Let's go."

Merlon's thrusters pitched her bow around and slightly down, then the main propulsion units lit off and accelerated the heavy cruiser onto a vector which would cross just ahead of the path the Syndic light cruisers and HuKs were on.

As *Merlon* steadied out, Geary checked the time to intercept. The Alliance heavy cruiser would cross the path of the Syndic light cruisers and HuKs in seven and a half hours. He took a calming breath, then transmitted another message to the Syndics. "Syndic CEO Nalis, this is Commander Geary. We have no notification or clearance for your ships to transit Alliance space. Your light cruisers and Hunter-Killers are to rejoin your main formation at the earliest possible time, and you are requested to assume an orbit about Grendel until we receive confirmation that your visit has been approved."

Decala was shaking her head again. "If the brass try to nail you for causing a diplomatic incident, I'll back you up, sir."

"Thanks." Geary tried to ignore an increasing sense of disquiet as he watched the movements of the Syndics. "Let's hope a diplomatic incident is the worst that can come of this." He indicated the latest updates on the maneuvering display. "If those Syndic light cruisers and HuKs don't turn back, either we stop them or they'll get to the transports before the transports can jump out of this star system."

"Surely they wouldn't—Captain, I've reviewed the latest intelligence and news we have. It's just as we thought. There's nothing going on that should have triggered Syndic hostile actions. Things are tense, certainly, but they've often been tense." Decala made a baffled gesture. "I don't trust that Syndic CEO at all, but her story is the only explanation that makes sense for what's happening."

"The only explanation that makes sense to us, you mean." Geary rubbed his face with both hands. "Before the convoy jumps, I'll tell Lagemann to ask the brass at T'shima for guidance once he gets there. If there was a Syndic flotilla coming through a region of space that T'shima was responsible for, even fleet headquarters wouldn't forget to notify them. The commodore at T'shima can send instructions back with one of the destroyers telling us what to do with the Syndics."

"Assuming the Syndics do as you directed and maintain an orbit here until we get those instructions."

"Yeah. Assuming that." Geary looked at the course vectors curving through space on his display, shaking his head.

THE eventual reply from the Syndic CEO, once again hours later than it should have taken to arrive, was accompanied by the same artificial smile but a chiding tone. "We have been ordered to meet with certain Alliance officials and Syndicate Worlds diplomatic representatives at T'shima, Commander Geary. You're asking us to violate our orders and the Alliance's own agreement to our passage. My flotilla was delayed earlier by propulsion problems, so my light cruisers and Hunter-Killers are going on ahead to arrive at T'shima on time and bring word of the imminent arrival of the rest of the flotilla." The Syndic CEO's expression grew a little stern. "I hope you will not take any further steps to attempt to impede this important diplomatic initiative, Commander Geary."

"She's definitely pressuring us," Decala said. "It is possible they had propulsion problems. Those nickel corvettes are nothing for the Syndics to brag about."

Geary nodded. The Alliance fleet had nicknamed the Syndic corvettes "nickels" because they were small, cheap and would be easily expended in combat. "If they didn't have four heavy cruisers backing them up, I wouldn't waste sleep worrying about the nickels. But otherwise, I feel like you do. That Syndic CEO is trying to push us into letting them pass, and she's dragging her feet in dealing with us all that she can while she does keep pushing. Why?"

After a long moment, Decala replied. "It's what I'd do if I was up to something I wasn't supposed to be doing. If T'shima really expects them, then why hasn't a ship arrived here from T'shima by now to escort them?"

"And if the Syndics were delayed," Geary added, "it makes it all the odder that no one from T'shima has come here yet. None of that is proof the Syndics are planning anything hostile. But if they are… Cara, I have the distinct feeling that no matter what we do, we're going to be screwed."

"Join the fleet and service the Alliance," Decala agreed in the sailors' usual sardonic twist on the actual recruitment slogan to 'serve' the Alliance.

"We're two hours from intercepting the light cruisers and HuKs. I want the ship at maximum combat readiness one hour prior to intercept, just in case the Syndics try something else."

Decala nodded. "Yes, sir. But…combat readiness. Captain, if you're wrong—"

"Unfortunately, there's a lot of different ways for me to be wrong," Geary said. "We're going to stick to our most fundamental mission. Defend Alliance space, citizens and property." And hope that there hadn't been an unusually monumental screw-up by fleet staff which had left him at Grendel facing what was supposed to be a diplomatic situation but was fast spiraling out of control.

ALL systems at maximum combat readiness," Decala reported. "All personnel at combat stations."

"Very well," Geary acknowledged. He, Decala, and everyone else in the crew were in survival suits, ready in case the hull was breached and atmosphere within parts of the ship lost. "Charge hell lance batteries, load grapeshot launchers and prep wraith missiles."

A moment later, as his commands were being executed, a virtual image popped up on Geary's display. The avatar of Captain Erabus Booth, the current aide to the assistant to the deputy to the fleet chief of staff, gave Geary a stern look. "Charging and preparing weapons is not authorized by current guidance for routine encounters with Syndicate Worlds warships. You are directed to review regulations and instructions governing the current situation and to ensure that your every action conforms with those regulations and instructions. Failure to comply fully with existing guidance will result in appropriate reprimand or disciplinary action should investigation reveal failures or lapses in judgments—"

Geary closed his eyes. "Commander Decala, please instruct the combat systems officer to kill Captain Booth."

"Disable his avatar in the combat system alert routine, you mean, sir?"

"That's all we have within reach at the moment, so it'll have to do. Cara, if everything does go to hell here and I don't make it back, please do your best to get those damned staff avatar alert routines removed from fleet warship operating systems. Tell everybody it was my last wish." Not that he expected anyone would care what his last wishes had been if it came to that.

"Yes, sir." Decala didn't argue, since she and every other officer on the *Merlon* felt the same way about the automated staff alerts embedded in the programming of the ship's systems, and which ship officers usually referred to as headquarters viruses or staff infections.

Geary took another long breath, blowing it out slowly before he transmitted his next message. The Syndic light cruisers and HuKs were close now, only five light minutes distant, and coming on fast, the swift HuKs well ahead of the light cruisers. With *Merlon* approaching on an intercept from one side, the combined closing velocity was about point one two light speed, enough to stress the abilities of the combat systems to score hits during the very brief moments when the ships would be within range of each other. "Syndicate Worlds warships operating in the Grendel star system, this is Commander Geary on the Alliance heavy cruiser *Merlon*. Your ships are operating in an Alliance star system without authorization or clearance. You will not be allowed to jump for T'shima until such time as appropriate authorization is received. You must alter your vectors immediately. You will not be permitted to cross the current track of *Merlon*. You are ordered to veer off *now*."

He had done everything but threaten to open fire. Would it be enough? As the minutes went by with no reply from the Syndics and no variation in their course and speed, the answer increasingly seemed to be "no."

"We'll be within wraith range of the HuKs in fifteen minutes," Decala reported.

Fifteen minutes. Geary checked the missile engagement parameters. He could fire as early as fifteen minutes or as late as twenty five minutes from now. After that, *Merlon* would be too close to the Syndic warships for the missiles to acquire targets before they shot past each other.

Decala wasn't pressing him for a decision. He imagined she was grateful that the decision wasn't up to her. He would have been grateful in her place. "This would be a good time for my ancestors to give me a sign."

"I'll let you know if mine tell me anything. Why do they just keep coming? Are the Syndics trying to provoke us into firing at them?" Decala wondered. "Putting the blame on us? But we're in an Alliance star system. They're disregarding our warnings. Any fault for what happens will clearly be theirs."

Geary managed a crooked smile. "Do your best to get assigned to my court-martial as one of the voting members."

She swallowed and spoke with exaggerated calm. "Have you ever actually been in combat before?"

"Some minor incidents. Nothing like this."

"Me, either."

Ten minutes until they reached the engagement envelope for the wraiths. Geary made his voice as stern as he could. "Syndicate Worlds warships approaching the Alliance cruiser *Merlon*, you are ordered to change your vectors immediately to cease closing on any Alliance shipping or the jump point for T'shima. You will *not* be permitted to cross the track of this cruiser. This is your *final* warning."

Nothing changed, the Syndic warships approaching without the slightest sign of altering their courses or speeds. "Lieutenant Commander Decala, work up an engagement plan for the wraiths. I want the first wave targeted on the propulsion systems of the Syndic HuKs."

"Yes, sir." With the help of the automated systems, the solutions popped up almost instantly. "Engagement plan prepared."

Geary felt outside himself for a moment, as if were he watching himself giving orders. "Assign the plan to the first wave of wraiths."

"Plan assigned. Wraiths ready to fire. Awaiting command authorization."

A red marker glowed before Geary now. All he had to do was

tap that marker, call out "fire" for a verbal confirmation, and the missiles would fly.

Geary activated an internal circuit letting him speak to his entire crew. "As you are all aware, we are close to contact with Syndicate Worlds' warships. There is a real possibility that we may find ourselves forced into combat within a short time. You are an outstanding crew, well-trained, motivated and steadfast, and I know that you will face whatever challenge arises in a manner that will make our ancestors proud of us all." As Geary ended the internal transmission, he wondered if he had overdone the pep talk, but it was how he honestly felt at the moment. "It's up to the Syndics now," he commented to his executive officer.

"They must be planning something," Decala insisted. "Why else keep coming? They're counting on us not doing anything."

"We can't afford not to do anything. They must know that." Though the uncertainties made the temptation to not act very powerful. He didn't *know* the Syndics were planning to attack. But he did know that if the light cruisers and HuKs got past *Merlon* unmolested, they would easily overhaul the transports, and could overwhelm *Pommel* and the three destroyers. The entire convoy could be wiped out, *would* be wiped out if the Syndics staged a surprise attack, and the Syndics would arrive at T'shima with no warning.

Which had been the plan, Geary suddenly realized. "They didn't know we'd be here. Their target is T'shima, but once they saw us they knew they had to prevent any of our ships from jumping first and warning T'shima the Syndic flotilla was coming."

Five minutes to missile engagement envelope.

Decala nodded. "That explains what they're doing. Keep stringing us along as long as possible. Get as close as they can before they attack to ensure none of us get away. It all fits."

It fit perhaps too neatly. Geary clenched his jaw tight enough to hurt as he thought about what firing first might mean, how many people might die here and afterwards before the resulting conflict was resolved.

But a final piece of the puzzle came to him as *Merlon* entered the wraith engagement envelope. "No battleship. No battle cruiser. Why would a major diplomatic mission not be accompanied by a capital ship?"

"Because the Syndic battleships and battle cruisers must be engaged elsewhere," Decala answered, her voice momentarily faltering. "May the living stars preserve us. The Syndics must have flotillas entering Alliance space in many places. They're attacking all along the border, without any warning. They must be. That's why the Syndics here didn't call off the attack when they saw us. This is just of one of dozens of coordinated strikes."

Geary's finger hovered near the red firing marker. The Syndic HuKs were very close now, only a light minute distant, less than five minutes before intercept. He made up his mind, but as his finger moved alerts blared from the combat system. "The Syndic light cruisers are firing missiles!" the operations watch cried.

His finger finished moving, the red marker flashing green. "Fire," Geary said in a voice that sounded to him like that of a stranger. "Alter course up zero three degrees, come starboard zero four zero degrees. Hell lance batteries and grapeshot launchers engage when the HuKs enter firing envelopes." The charged particle beams of the hell lances had much shorter ranges than the missiles, and the solid metal ball bearings of the grapeshot were only effective at very close range where their patterns were tight enough for the kinetic impacts to overwhelm a ship's defenses. "Activate full counter-measures against Syndic missiles."

Merlon shuddered slightly as a wave of wraiths erupted from her, the missiles accelerating onto intercepts with the sterns of the oncoming Syndic HuKs. The Alliance cruiser was already turning, thrusters and main propulsion units pushing her onto a course close to parallel with that of the Syndics as the HuKs and *Merlon* rushed into contact. The final maneuver cut the closing rate slightly, but the two forces were still approaching each other at close to point one light speed, or about 30,000 kilometers per second.

The moment of closest approach came and went, the remaining distance dwindling too fast for human minds to grasp, weapons firing under automated control since humans couldn't react quickly enough, Geary barking out more commands the instant it was over. "Come starboard zero one two degrees, accelerate to point one one light speed." *Merlon's* structure groaned as the inertial dampers fought to compensate for maneuvering stresses which would have otherwise torn apart both ship and crew.

"Nice run!" Decala exulted.

Geary checked the results popping up on his display. Of the six HuKs, four had lost all or almost all propulsion as the wraith missiles slammed into their sterns. Two other HuKs were still able to maneuver, but one of them had been battered severely by *Merlon's* hell lances and grapeshot and was falling off to one side, most of its weapons assessed out of action. The sixth HuK had only taken a couple of hits, but *Pommel* and the three Alliance destroyers could easily handle a single HuK which had already taken some damage. "We've still got four light cruisers to deal with."

"Syndic missiles inbound on final," the combat systems watch called. "Hell lance batteries engaging."

Caught in a stern chase by *Merlon's* maneuvers, the Syndic missiles were relatively easy targets, but there were a lot of them against the defenses which the heavy cruiser could bring to bear as thrusters pivoted her to face the attack bow on. *Merlon* shuddered again as a missile tore into her shields, weakening them, then bucked as a second missile rammed through the weak area and exploded against the cruiser's armor. "Hell lance battery one alpha out of commission. No estimated time to repair. Armor breached forward. Damage control is sealing breached compartments," Decala reported, her voice steady.

"Target the next wave of wraiths on the propulsion systems of the light cruisers, then fire the final wave at the same targets."

"Yes, sir."

He had a few moments to make another transmission, one to which he didn't expect to have time to receive any reply. "*Pommel*, you are ordered to jump the convoy to T'shima as soon as you are in position to do so. All units are to jump. You are to warn T'shima that a Syndic flotilla is enroute and that they have initiated combat action against the Alliance. *Merlon* will follow if possible." He had to take a second then to ensure his voice remained steady. "If *Merlon* cannot follow, you must assume her destruction at the hands of the Syndics and request that the Alliance fleet undertake action to drive the Syndics from Grendel and rescue *Merlon*'s crew as well as the crew of the emergency station. Good luck and may your ancestors watch over you. Geary out."

He was bringing *Merlon* around again as more warnings erupted. "Another wave of Syndic missiles inbound. Syndic light cruisers four minutes from contact."

The red marker glowed and Geary fired his wraiths again. "I'm giving you release authority for the third wave," he told Decala. "Punch them out as soon as they're ready to fly."

"Yes, sir. Captain, if we continue around like this we'll be heading right into the teeth of the Syndic missile barrage, and we'll be hit by all four light cruisers as we pass through their formation."

"I know. We have to stop those light cruisers and we only have a small window of time to do it in, so we have to ram straight through them." Geary shook his head. "It's going to cost us, but it's the only way so we're going to do it."

Decala nodded. "Yes, sir."

Two more missile hits staggered *Merlon*. "We lost the port wraith launchers," Decala reported. "Firing remaining wraiths."

The light cruisers and *Merlon* tore past each other, the heavy cruiser hurling out hell lance fire and grapeshot to all sides as she went between the Syndic light cruisers at a slight down angle and a sharp side angle. At the same time, fire from the Syndics lashed at *Merlon*, the heavy cruiser wobbling in her course from the impacts of three more missiles as well as hell lances and grapeshot hitting from every direction.

It took Merlon's battered sensors a few more moments than usual to evaluate damage to the enemy this time. Three of the light cruisers were out of the fight, their propulsion systems too badly damaged to allow them to catch the convoy now. The fourth light cruiser was in fairly good shape, but Geary was bringing *Merlon* back again on a long curve, aiming to get in a firing run.

"Forward and amidships shields have failed, hull armor is breached in multiple locations. All wraith launchers out of action," Decala reported. "Hell lance batteries two bravo, three bravo and four alpha out of action. Grapeshot launchers three, five and six are out of action. Heavy damage amidships. Propulsion capability reduced to fifty percent. Seventeen dead confirmed, wounded total unknown."

Geary felt that curious detachment again as he stared at the display where the damage to *Merlon* showed as growing patches of red, then to the three disabled Syndic light cruisers still throwing out long range fire at *Merlon*, to the operational light cruiser firing missiles again, and then to the track of the Syndic heavy cruisers and corvettes coming on, steadily closing the distance. Doctrine called for pulling clear now, gaining distance and time for shields to rebuild, for damage to be repaired, to get up velocity shed by the turns. But if he did that, that last Syndic light cruiser would make it to the transports before they jumped, and *Pommel* and the destroyers wouldn't be able to stop it before it crippled a bunch of the transports. Which left him only one option. "All nonessential personal abandon ship."

"What?" Decala shook her head, then focused on Geary again.

"All nonessential personnel abandon ship," Geary repeated. "Get them moving."

"Yes, sir."

He concentrated on the remaining light cruiser as *Merlon* bore down on it. The Syndic light cruiser was beginning to draw away, but Geary brought *Merlon* across her stern at close enough range to blow apart the enemy's main propulsion and leave her out of the battle.

Merlon had saved the convoy, but the price for that victory was about to go a lot higher.

A moment later two more missiles hit *Merlon* and the lights dimmed as circuits fought to automatically reroute themselves. "Propulsion down to ten percent." Decala's voice had grown mechanical, as if she were walling off emotion. "Only hell lance battery one bravo remains in action. All shields have failed. Engineering requests permission to retain all personnel aboard for damage control."

"Negative. Get them out. Get everyone out." Decala stared at him again. "Not just nonessential personnel. Everyone. Abandon ship. Now! Those heavy cruisers are going to tear this ship apart and I don't want my crew dying when they can't fight back!"

She passed on the orders and then shouted "get out of here!" at the remaining personnel on the bridge. As the others left at a run, Decala faced him, pale but determined. "I'm staying. I can handle the remaining working systems on the ship from the bridge." Another Syndic missile hit rocked *Merlon*, and both Decala and Geary had to grab for support as more damage alerts blared urgently.

"No, you're not," Geary insisted. "I'm the commanding officer. It's my responsibility to stay. I'll keep her fighting as long as I can. You don't need to be here."

"I won't leave you alone, captain! *Merlon* is my ship, too!"

He reached out and grabbed her shoulder. "Cara, if this is really the start of a major war, the Alliance is going to need every experienced officer it's got. My duty requires me to stay here and keep *Merlon* fighting as long as possible so the convoy and you and the rest of the crew can get clear. When the last combat systems go dead I'll set the power core for self-destruct and I'll abandon ship, too. I promise. But if I don't survive this then you have to. Because you're going to be needed. The rest of the crew needs you at this moment. Thank you for being an excellent officer and a friend. Now get out of here!"

She wiped an angry tear from one eye, then saluted. "Yes, sir." Decala appeared about to say something else, then turned and ran.

He sat down, then carefully checked the seals on his survival suit. The well-protected bridge in the heart of the ship still had atmosphere, but according to the readouts which continued to function on *Merlon* most of the rest of the ship was in vacuum.

A flock of escape pods was accelerating away from the heavy cruiser, carrying those of her crew who hadn't died already, a few more escape pods following at irregular intervals.

He hadn't had time to be scared before this, caught up in the fighting and responding to events, but now he was alone on the bridge, there was a brief interval before the rest of the Syndic warships got within range, and Geary had to fight down a wave of dread as he faced the reality that he and *Merlon* might die together.

But he still had a job to do. He had to keep the Syndics focused on *Merlon*, and not on the escape pods carrying most of her crew. He wouldn't let his crew be captured, to be made prisoners or even hostages on the Syndic warships heading to attack T'shima. The Syndic heavy cruisers and corvettes were ten minutes from firing range as Geary entered maneuvering orders. *Merlon* staggered in a wide, slow loop, trying to come onto a course facing the enemy.

He checked on the convoy. Almost to the jump point. The lone operational Syndic HuK had veered off, and Geary realized that it was trying to lure the convoy ships into chasing it. But Commander Lagemann could be trusted to use his head and follow orders.

More alerts, warning of the oncoming Syndic heavy cruisers. Geary targeted *Merlon*'s last functioning hell lance on the leading cruiser, setting it to fire automatically as the Syndics raced past. Outnumbered four to one, with his cruiser's shields down, almost all of her weapons knocked out and her armor already breached in many places, Geary had no illusions about his chances.

Syndic hell lance fire tore through *Merlon*, riddling the cruiser from one end to the other. Every remaining combat, life-support and maneuvering system was knocked out, atmosphere rushed out of the bridge where holes had been punched through consoles and bulkheads, and the stricken Alliance warship began an uncontrolled tumble off to the side. The final hell lance battery was dead, but Geary felt *Merlon* tremble as more Syndic fire ripped through her. It must be the nickel corvettes making firing runs now, the scorned nickels able to pound the stricken Alliance cruiser with impunity.

He pulled open a special panel on his command seat, accessing the emergency self-destruct system. Geary punched in the authorization code with trembling hands. As far as he could tell, *Merlon*'s power core still had enough left to blow the ship apart. The Syndics wouldn't capture her intact. Though whether he needed to blow the heavy cruiser to pieces was a good question with the Syndics continuing to pound the Alliance warship into fragments. Why not just take her apart with a volley of missiles? But the Syndics probably wanted to save those missiles for the attack at T'shima, and perhaps hoped that prolonging *Merlon*'s death throes might entice the convoy to try a despairing rescue.

Code in and acknowledged. Enter confirmation code. Confirm again. Accepted. He had only ten minutes before the power core overloaded and *Merlon* exploded. More Syndic hell lance fire and grapeshot pummeled *Merlon*, and the local backup systems for bridge functions failed, the last virtual displays fading into the darkness.

He had no time to lose, but Geary hesitated before he left the bridge, gazing around at the deserted, ruined compartment. His ship. His command. *Merlon* had died fighting, but now he had to leave her and he hated it, cursing the Syndics who had reduced his beautiful ship to a hulk which would soon destroy itself.

Moving through the ship was a nightmare of another kind, the uncontrolled tumble making the bulkheads, decks and overheads rotate erratically and seem to swing in and out as Geary propelled himself through passageways choked with wreckage and in some cases the heartrending remains of those of his crew who hadn't lived long enough to abandon ship.

But it got worse, as he found every escape pod access showing either a pod already ejected or the red glow of a status light indicating the pod had been too badly damaged to launch.

Finally he found a pod with a yellow status light over its access. It was damaged, but with less than five minutes before core overload Geary couldn't be picky even if he had known whether or not any other functional escape pods remained aboard. He pulled himself inside, sealed the hatch, strapped in as fast as he could, then slapped the ejection control.

Acceleration pinned him to his seat as the pod raced clear of *Merlon*. The pod lurched wildly, more damage lights blazing to life on its control panel, and Geary realized it had been caught in the edges of the blast from *Merlon*'s core overload.

The pod's propulsion cut off abruptly in the wake of the additional damage. It should have kept going a lot longer. Geary, feeling numb, tried to read the status display. He had ample power reserves still functional, but no maneuvering controls. Communications were out. The life-support systems on the pod were damaged, too, and while still working wouldn't hold out long.

Maybe he hadn't escaped after all.

Then his seat began reclining and Geary realized the pod was activating the emergency survival sleep system. He'd be frozen, kept in a state where his body needed only the tiniest amount of life support.

The panel which should have displayed an image of the outside was dark, not that he could have physically seen any of the ships already far distant from his pod. Surely the convoy had jumped by now. Lieutenant Commander Decala would be assembling the other escape pods from *Merlon*, keeping them together, heading for the emergency station orbiting Grendel. His crew, those who had survived to abandon ship, should be safe.

The lights on the panels above Geary were going out one by one or dimming into dormant status. He hadn't noticed the injections preparing his body for survival sleep, but felt lethargy stealing over him as his metabolism began slowing down.

He hated being cold. The idea of being frozen was far worse. But it would only be for a little while. *Pommel* would bring to T'shima the news of the Syndic attack here. The Alliance would counter-attack, resecure Grendel star system and rescue everyone from *Merlon*.

A war had begun, though he had no idea what had led the Syndics to launch surprise attacks. How long would it last? His last conscious thoughts as the cold took him were that surely it couldn't last too long. Sanity or the firepower of the Alliance fleet would prevail. Maybe by the time he was picked up the war would already be over.

Geary's body slipped into survival sleep, his damaged pod drifting amid the wreckage of battle, its beacon dead, its power usage levels too low to stand out among the other debris.

He slept, while more battles raged in Grendel, one side then the other prevailing, the emergency station long since destroyed, larger and larger fleets clashing, then for a long time no ships at all. Around Grendel nothing orbited but the wreckage of earlier battles and one badly damaged survival pod, its power sources slowly draining.

Until one day another fleet came, the largest of all, and a destroyer spotted a suspicious object amid the leavings of battles.

Electing to investigate rather than simply obliterate the object, the destroyer picked up the pod and delivered it to the fleet's flagship.

Geary's mind drifted back to partial awareness. His body felt like a block of ice and he couldn't see. Perhaps his eyelids were still frozen shut. Vague noises around him resolved into a few words. "Alive," "miracle," "Black Jack," and "war." He struggled to make sense of the words, finally feeling some emotion as aggravation at the nickname came to the surface.

"He'll save us!" That sentence came through clearly just before Geary began passing out again. He caught one more word; "*Dauntless.*"

Was *Dauntless* a ship? He had never heard of an Alliance warship by that name. And who was this man they were talking about saving them? The war must still be going on. How long had he been asleep? Geary drifted back into unconsciousness.

Soon enough he would be fully awakened and learn the answers to those questions.

ISHIGAKI

THE former cruise liner, which stripped of its fine furnishings now served as a military transport, had crossed the gulf between stars to arrive at a gas giant planet orbited by half a dozen massive construction yards. Sailors, many of them fresh from their first training, barely noticed the majestic view on displays as they were packed into shuttles and distributed to the new warships being built as fast as humans and their devices could do the job. A few of those sailors, probably on their first journey to another star, might have been thinking of the bitter irony that the discovery of a practical means for interstellar travel had also made interstellar war practical, but even they would have insisted that this was not a war of their choosing. Their homes, their families, their freedom, had to be defended against those who threatened all three. Though humanity had found new battlefields, it still fought the same wars.

"Chief Gunners Mate Diana Magoro reporting for duty."

"Welcome aboard the *Ishigaki*," the nearly-overwhelmed-by-work officer of the deck said, his eyes scanning her data on his pad rather than looking at her face. "Durgan! Take the chief to Ensign Rodriquez."

A tired-looking sailor gestured to Magoro before heading into the interior of the ship.

She followed past a ship's crest painted on one bulkhead, a

stone tower looming in the center of the crest and the words "Stone Wall of the Alliance" along the bottom. Apparently the name *Ishigaki* had something to do with that. It wasn't surprising that a heavy cruiser had such a name, as they were usually called after defensive fortifications or parts of armor. But this was the first time she'd encountered a cruiser named *Ishigaki*. Traditionally, Alliance ships had tended to pass down the same names as old ships were stricken and new ships constructed. These days, with the Alliance Fleet adding warships as fast as they could be built, new names were being revived from the history of humanity far away on Old Earth and the cultures that people had brought with them to the stars.

Along with war. People had brought that, too, of course.

Magoro followed her guide down passageways that were never quite wide enough for all of the personnel moving through them. Cables, conduits and ducts along the sides and the overhead further constricted the passages. Everything about *Ishigaki* felt new, something Magoro still had trouble getting used to. In the pre-war fleet, nearly every ship had been at least a decade old, sometimes much more than that. Now, nearly every ship felt new.

The old ones were gone. Destroyed in battle, fighting desperately until new ships could be built.

They passed a lot of other sailors, faces and names that were unfamiliar to her but would become well-known before long. Those other sailors glanced at her face, followed by a glance at the ribbons on the left breast of her uniform. Everybody did that. She did it to them. Do I know this person? And what has she done? The face told one story, the service ribbons and medals another.

She hoped no one would notice one of her ribbons. Regulations required her to wear it, but it tended to gather way too much attention.

The sailor left her at a compartment with Weapons Department stenciled on the hatch. Inside, several desks fastened to the deck were covered with scattered parts and equipment, many tagged as faulty. A female ensign with a harried expression on a face that seemed too young for an officer looked up as she entered. "Yeah?"

Diana offered her comm pad to the ensign. "Chief Gunners Mate Magoro, sir."

"You're mine?" The ensign stared at her orders. "You're mine! Welcome aboard, Chief! Have a seat! I'm Ensign Rodriquez. Gunnery Officer. Just a moment while I check your record…"

She jerked with almost comical surprise. "You've been in the fleet for ten years?"

"Yes, ma'am."

"You've got ten years of experience as a gunners mate?"

"Yes, ma'am."

"Ten…years?"

"Yes, ma'am."

"My ancestors must be smiling on me!" Ensign Rodriquez grinned at her. "An old fleet sailor! With pre-war experience!"

Magoro nodded in reply. Everything today seemed to be measured that way. Not yesterday and today and tomorrow, but pre-war and war and after-the-war, though she'd noticed that after six years of fighting people weren't mentioning after-the-war as much lately. "I've been working on weapons for a while," she said. Ensign Rodriquez's reaction to her wasn't surprising. Many of the old, experienced sailors of the pre-war fleet had died in the first desperate year of the war, and the survivors were now spread thin in the much larger fleet. She felt a bit like a ghost at times, part of a dwindling remnant of what had once been.

"You actually made chief?"

The voice, tinged with what sounded like mock-surprise, was

vaguely familiar. As Ensign Rodriquez scrambled hastily to her feet, Magoro stood and turned to see a face she remembered better than the voice. "I see you made commander, sir."

Ensign Rodriquez, startled by their exchange, took a moment to speak. "Chief, this is Commander Weiss, captain of the *Ishigaki*. You know Chief Magoro, sir?"

Commander Weiss smiled slightly as he looked at Magoro, but his eyes stayed hard, questioning. "We served together on another ship about six years ago, when I was an ensign."

"Six years—" Ensign Rodriguez's voice cut off as she stared at Weiss and then Magoro, her eyes going to the dark ribbon with a bright gold star centered on it. "You were on *Merlon*, too, Chief? With Black Jack himself?"

Black Jack? "Um…with Commander Geary, yes, ma'am."

"At his last stand," Rodriguez said, looking at her in awe that exceeded the previous wonderment at her experience. "Ancestors save me. *Ishigaki* has two veterans of Black Jack's last battle aboard!"

Magoro, uncomfortable, looked back at Commander Weiss, who this time gave her the polite smile of a shared past. But the eyes of *Ishigaki*'s captain remained challenging.

"I'll talk to you later, Chief," Weiss said, nodding in farewell to Ensign Rodriquez. It sounded like a simple, polite, statement, but to Magoro it carried more than a whiff of a grim promise.

Great. Her past had really caught up with her this time. Magoro listened to Ensign Rodriquez continue her welcome speech and description of the challenges facing the Weapons Division on the *Ishigaki*, familiar challenges involving new equipment hastily churned out to meet demands and new sailors who had passed technical training but lacked much actual experience. Through it all, half of her mind stayed on Commander Weiss.

She wasn't looking forward to that talk with the captain.

ABOUT four very long hours later, after meeting the sailors who'd be working for her, a blur of new faces and names that would gradually become familiar, and making initial inspections of the hell lance batteries, which were in better shape than she had feared but still needed work, Diana Magoro ducked into the chief's mess to grab some coffee. Despite everything else that had changed since the war began, that one thing remained the same. There was always coffee available. It was usually bad coffee that sometimes looked and tasted like tar, but that was also traditional. She shuddered as she took a drink, grateful that it was so hot it helped mask the flavor.

"Diana, right?" Another chief extended his hand to her. "I'm Vlad Darkar. Engineering. Welcome aboard."

"Hey, Vlad." She followed the other chief to the small table with chairs fixed around it, grateful for the chance to relax for a moment with another chief who'd give her straight information. "What exactly happened to the guy I'm replacing?"

Vlad shook his head, looking down at his coffee. "He cracked during our work-ups. Couldn't handle the pressure." Darkar shifted his gaze to look at her. "Part of that was because he didn't know the job well enough. You know how that is."

She nodded. Officially, no one got promoted unless they had the necessary skills. Unofficially, everyone knew that the demand for senior enlisted personnel far exceeded the qualified supply. Some of the "old hands" in a chief mess probably had only three years of service under their belts.

"I hear you're old fleet, though," Darkar continued. His eyes flicked across her ribbons, pausing in their movement as he focused on one in particular. "Damn. You were at Grendel?"

"Yeah." She took another drink of the coffee to avoid having to say more.

"With Black Jack himself, huh?"

She managed not to frown in puzzlement at Darkar's use of the nickname. First the ensign and now a chief? "Commander Geary was my captain, yeah."

Vlad Darkar sat back, his eyes admiring. "What was that like?"

"Grendel, or Commander Geary?"

He grinned. "Both."

Magoro shrugged. "Grendel was a battle. I was on a hell lance crew. Battery 2 Bravo. We knew the odds we were facing, but you do your job, right? We felt the ship accelerating and braking, changing course, and sometimes our gun fired." Some people in a fight saw the big picture, knew what was happening, but many others saw only their small part of it. She knew it disappointed those who wanted her to describe Geary issuing heroic orders, but she hadn't been on the bridge. "Then we got hit bad a few times. We took some hell lances right through the battery. They killed some of the guys in the crew, and the hell lance got torn up too bad to fix, so I was sent to another gun crew trying to get their battery back on line. We were still working it when word was passed to abandon ship and we headed for the escape pods."

She paused, remembering fear and haste amid the minimal light cast by the emergency lights on the badly hurt cruiser, sailors a bit clumsy in their survival suits scrambling past damage, the harsh sound of her breathing inside the suit and the unnatural sharpness of everything she could see with the ship's atmosphere vented through holes in the hull. "It wasn't until we boosted clear that most of us on the pod I was in heard that Commander Geary had stayed behind to keep the *Merlon* fighting a little longer, so we could get away and so the Syndics wouldn't be able to catch any of the convoy we were escorting." Guilt lingered whenever she thought about that. But it had been the captain's decision to stay behind a little longer, and disobeying his orders wouldn't have been right.

Darkar shook his head in admiration, as if she'd just told some story of her own heroism. "They say that if Black Jack hadn't stopped that attack force at Grendel it would've allowed the Syndicate Worlds surprise attack to do a lot more damage. Maybe enough to have knocked out the Alliance before we could react in time."

"We just delayed that Syndic flotilla at Grendel," she said. "And made sure our convoy jumped clear so they could warn about the attacks on the way."

"But that made all the difference! Black Jack saved the Alliance!" Vlad Darkar leaned a little closer to her. "You talked to him when he was your captain, right?"

"Sure." Diana Magoro hoped she wouldn't wince at any of those memories as they flashed through her mind. Especially that one time, standing at attention, waiting for the hammer to fall, knowing she deserved whatever she got.

If she did flinch, the other chief didn't notice. She managed to redirect the conversation to the state of *Ishigaki* and her crew, picking up some new information before heading back out to try to catch up with work that should've been completed weeks ago.

DIANA Magoro was half-inside the bulk of a hell-lance particle beam projector when the ship's interior lights dimmed to mark the official beginning of "night" aboard. Space didn't care about day and night, but humans needed it. They clung to things from the past, she thought, like the way gunners mates called the hell lances "guns" instead of using some more technically accurate name.

She checked the connection on the part she'd finished replacing before pulling herself out of the weapon's interior and yawning as she stood up.

"Working late?"

She tensed, looking to see Commander Weiss watching her. "Yes, sir. I've been personally checking over each hell lance projector."

"That doesn't sound like the Diana Magoro I knew on the *Merlon*," Weiss said.

"I've changed a bit," Magoro said.

"Hmmm." Commander Weiss switched his gaze to the hulking hell lance, whose shape tended to remind people of an ancient troll kneeling as it prepared to leap at an opponent. "How are you fitting in?"

"Okay, sir." Magoro shrugged. "Lots of questions about *Merlon* and the captain. Commander Geary, I mean."

"I understand." Weiss smiled crookedly. "Even though I'm commanding officer of this ship, I know who you'll be talking about when you say 'the captain.' I do the same thing."

"I guess we all do," she said. "No disrespect to you intended, sir."

"Really? You used to skate as close to disrespect as you could." Weiss paused, his expression growing colder. "Have you told anyone that one of your personal encounters with Commander Geary involved him busting you down two paygrades?"

"No, sir." Magoro grimaced at the memory. She noticed Weiss waiting for more and realized why. "I deserved it. I admitted it at the time. You were there. And I haven't done that since, sir. Nothing like that."

Commander Weiss made a face. "Falsifying maintenance records. Hacking system records to hide it. You know why I'm worried."

"Because now I'm responsible for making sure the hell lances on this ship work. Your ship. I haven't done it since, sir. Commander Geary gave me a second chance. I was stupid back then, but not too stupid to realize how lucky I was."

"Lieutenant Commander Decala wanted to court-martial you and kick you out of the fleet," Weiss said.

"So I heard."

Weiss sighed. "We really need an experienced chief gunner on this ship." He gestured around the ship surrounding them. "You know what we're facing. The crew's been rushed through training. Actual experience is rare. They know the theory, but they haven't got the time working with the gear."

"Yes, sir. It's a familiar problem these days."

Commander Weiss studied her again while Magoro waited. "Chief, if you pull anything on *Ishigaki* like you did on *Merlon*, I won't court-martial you. Instead I'll let the fleet commander have you shot for malfeasance in the face of the enemy."

"Then I have nothing to worry about," Magoro said, feeling her stomach knot and hoping it didn't show. "Because I'm going to do my best, sir. And I know this job." To emphasize her words she stood straight and offered Weiss the best salute she could manage.

Weiss cocked one eyebrow at her. "Maybe you'll be okay. You're certainly not the same. The Diana Magoro I remember was always getting chewed out for sloppy saluting and sloppy bearing and sloppy uniforms. Now, on a ship full of new sailors who can barely wear the uniform right and have trouble saluting without hurting themselves, I'm seeing you in a flawless uniform and rendering salutes so sharp I could shave with one of them."

Magoro grinned despite her nervousness. "I have to be a good example now, sir."

"I'm glad that you realize that. You were my biggest problem child when I was an ensign." Commander Weiss nodded at her. "Don't be a problem now. I've got a lot to deal with. Six years from ensign to commander of a heavy cruiser is a fast leap."

"Six years from being busted back to the lowest grade of sailor to Chief is pretty fast, too, sir."

"They need our experience, limited as it is," Weiss said. "And we have to make sure we don't let down those depending on us. Especially you and me. People look at us differently because we were on the *Merlon* at Grendel."

"I've noticed," Magoro said, drawing a real smile from Commander Weiss this time. "Sir? How many of us who got off the *Merlon* are left? Does anyone know?"

The smile faded. "I think there're about fifty survivors who haven't joined their ancestors yet. Probably less than that now. We lose some with every battle."

Magoro grimaced. "It feels wrong. To die, I mean. Because Commander Geary gave his life to make sure the rest of us got off the ship. Dying seems like betraying what he gave his life for. That sounds kind of stupid, doesn't it?"

"No, it doesn't," Weiss said. "I know exactly what you mean."

"Sir, can I ask you something about Commander Geary? What's with this Black Jack stuff? I try not to get too involved in talk about that, but it's getting kind of weird, isn't it? I mean, Commander Geary was a good commanding officer. I owe him a lot, not even counting him saving our lives at Grendel. But I think back on *Merlon* I heard somebody whisper that Black Jack nickname once and everybody said don't ever do that again he hates that name. And now people who never knew him are calling him Black Jack like they're old shipmates and talking like he was a living star come to save us."

Weiss looked to the side, his expression troubled. "You're right that he hated that nickname. Just like you hated being called Gundeck Magoro."

She winced. "Yes, sir. But that nickname didn't follow me."

"Hopefully that's for a good reason. As for Black Jack, even ensigns like me knew better than to say it anywhere Commander Geary might hear us. But it's part of the way the fleet is treating his memory. The new people are being told stories about Commander Geary, about how amazing he was. I can't really talk to them because if I say he was just human they look…betrayed or something. I guess the Alliance needs a hero, he got the job, and using the Black Jack nickname makes him feel like one of us even though he was supposedly more than us."

"I guess it can't hurt him," Magoro said. "Him being dead at Grendel and all, but it doesn't seem right. I mean, it's good to remember the best things about people who're dead, but making up stuff seems wrong. I figure that has to bother his spirit."

Commander Weiss shrugged. "Commander Geary's spirit can probably handle anything thrown at it. I'd rather you worried about the guns on this ship. Your record since Grendel looks good, so I'll give you the same chance Geary did. Don't make me sorry I did that, Chief."

"You won't be, sir."

DID everybody get that?" Diana Magoro said, looking at the rank of gunners mates who'd just watched her demonstrate a complex maintenance task. "You have to get this right. Hell lances use a big burst of energy when they fire. That energy has to be handled right and built up to the right level at the right rate of increase. You do not get slack with any step of this."

"Ma'am?" one of the younger looking sailors asked.

"Do not call me or any other chief ma'am, or sir," Magoro said. "We work for a living."

"I'm sorry! Chief, what if we're asked to power up the weapons faster than the procedures call for?"

Somebody always asked that. The answer was always the same. "You tell the bridge that they're being powered up as fast as they can be."

"But what if it's an emergency? Can't we shave even a little time off by pushing against the safety parameters?"

That called for a Chief's Glare at Maximum Intensity. "No. Everybody! What happens if you try to power up a hell lance too quickly?"

A gunners mate named Bandera raised a tentative hand. "Um...doesn't that cause a Catastrophic Energy Containment Failure, Chief?"

"Very good. Take an extra cookie tonight at dinner." Magoro kept her glare fixed as she swept it across the sailors before her. "For those who like small words, another way of saying Catastrophic Energy Containment Failure is *explosion*. If you somehow survived that explosion, the fleet would bend every effort to keep you alive just long enough for a firing squad to be collected so they could kill you legal and proper. Don't mess with the safety parameters on the gear! Because if you do and the gear doesn't kill you, and the fleet doesn't kill you, *I'll* kill you. Got it?"

"Yes, Chief!" they chorused.

After the others left, Bandera stayed behind. "Chief? Can I ask you something?"

He was a hard worker, and enthusiastic in a naïve way that both pleased her and pained her. Life in the fleet would wear down that enthusiasm in time, but for now she liked him. "Sure. What?"

"That stuff about powering up the hell lances faster," he said, looking hesitant. "When we graduated from tech school, some of the older gunners mates took us out to celebrate and while we were all drinking some of them started talking about ways to power up faster." The sailor swallowed nervously as he saw Magoro's reaction to his words. "I just…Chief, why'd they talk about doing that if it's so dangerous?"

She sighed, looking over at the bulk of the nearest hell lance. "It's a challenge. That's why. We're gunners. We want to play with the guns. Tweak them, test them, try new stuff. I'll bet you the very first gunner who was shown the very first hell lance immediately started trying to think of ways to make it power up faster. It's natural for us to wonder about that. But it's stupid."

Magoro looked back at the sailor, who she was pleased to see was watching her with an appropriately sober expression. "Before the war, when all we had were drills and maintenance to keep us busy, some gunners mates on a lot of different ships decided to spice things up by having a secret competition. They tried to see who could power up a hell lance faster, shaving tens of seconds or even hundredths of seconds off the process so their ship would have bragging rights. What do you think eventually happened?"

The sailor winced. "An explosion?"

"Yeah. Somebody shaved off just a little too much time, energy containment failed, an entire gun crew died, and the investigation into the accident found out about the competition. That was peacetime, so nobody was shot, but a lot of people ended up wishing they'd been in the gun crew that did die."

"I understand, Chief. Thank you!" Bandera hustled away.

Magoro heard someone clear their throat and looked to see that Ensign Rodriquez had been listening. "That was great, Chief," she said. "I couldn't help listening, and…that's just what they needed to hear. Follow the rules."

"Thank you, ma'am." Magoro eyed the ensign. "Ma'am, you know that there are circumstances when you shouldn't follow the rules, right? That's one reason why we're here instead of letting 'bots do the job, because the 'bots always follow the rules even when that'd be stupid. But the thing is, those new guys don't know what those circumstances are. It's our job to know when we need to do things a little different."

Ensign Rodriguez hesitated. "Chief, were you…?"

"Part of the competition before the war? No, ma'am. I joined the fleet a couple of years after that came to light. Lots of people were still talking about it, of course."

"Of course." Ensign Rodriguez hesitated again. "Uh, Chief, when it comes to deciding when not to follow the rules…"

She tried to look reliable and reassuring. "I understand, ma'am. I won't use any initiative without asking permission beforehand."

"Good! Good!" Rodriguez hustled out, on her way to do some more of whatever it was officers did.

Diana Magoro stood alone for a while in the hell lance battery compartment, thinking about the mistakes she had made. It wasn't about being perfect, she told herself. It was about learning and not doing that sort of stupid thing again.

"I think you're smart enough to learn from this," Commander Geary had told her more than six years ago as she nearly shook with fright. *"I think you can be a good gunners mate. Prove me right."*

She still didn't know whether the captain had been right. But she wasn't ready to stop trying.

A week later the *Ishigaki* joined up with a group of other warships taking on supplies. When they headed out afterwards, even the dumbest sailor knew the cruiser was headed for her first fight.

A long, high-pitched, wavering whistle sounded over the ship's general announcing system. Conversation in the chief's mess halted as they waited for whatever announcement followed.

"All hands, this is the Captain. We're part of a task force headed for Kairos Star System," Commander Weiss said. "That's a Syndicate Worlds held star near the border region of space. The fleet is preparing a major attack on Atalia Star System, so our job is to carry out a successful diversion to draw Syndicate warships to the defense of Kairos, leaving Atalia weakened when our main force hits it. Be prepared to hit the Syndics hard and fast, then live up to *Ishigaki*'s name as we fight a delaying action against Syndicate reinforcements. To the honor of our ancestors!"

Diana Magoro looked upward, puzzled. "That's a new one. Why tell us where the real attack is going in? What if some of us get captured?"

"Did the captain tell us where the real attack is going in?" Chief Drakar asked. "Or is it really going to be someplace other than Atalia?"

"A double diversion?" Chief Kantor from fire control looked worried. "Send the Syndics scrambling to Atalia if some of our people crack under interrogation? But that'd mean the brass are hoping some of us get captured and spill our guts about what we heard."

"Yeah," Magoro agreed. "I hope you're wrong, Vlad. I'd rather believe the fleet brass didn't think things through. Based on experience, that's not too hard to believe."

"You're the old sailor," Chief Darkar said with a laugh.

"Anyway," Kantor added, "I heard the Syndics aren't always taking prisoners any more. Unless they think we have some special information, they'd probably just shoot us."

"Aren't you the cheerful one," Darkar said, no longer laughing.

"I'm just a realist," Kantor said. "The war's stalemated, isn't it? Who knows how long it could go on? And I know my history. The longer a war goes on, the worse it gets."

JUMP drives made interstellar travel routine, allowing ships to use jump points that existed only near objects as massive as stars to enter a gray nothingness called jump space that shrank distances so that another star was only a week or two travel time away. Diana Magoro had long ago decided that traveling through jump space was like being in an apparently endless fall. You could do things, work, eat, sleep, but hanging over it all was the realization that you weren't really anywhere and that at some point the whole thing would abruptly end. And it was then, that moment when your ship lurched back into normal space, that things could really get bad.

Since they were arriving at an enemy star system, everyone was at battle stations when the drop out of jump space occurred. Magoro was in charge of the port hell lance batteries, while Ensign Rodriguez was with one of the starboard batteries. She'd chosen to post herself at battery two bravo, forward of amidships but not at the bow. Two linked hell lance projectors sat facing the firing ports, their energy cells maxed, ready to fire on command. Magoro and the three members of this battery's gun crew were all in survival suits, ready in case enemy fire put a hole in the hull and the atmosphere in the compartment vanished into space.

As a chief, Magoro had the benefit of being able to link her survival suit's internal display to the fire control status, so she was able to see what was happening outside the ship.

The entire task force had dropped into normal space. A battle cruiser, four heavy cruisers of which *Ishigaki* was one, two light cruisers, and a dozen destroyers. They were in a spherical formation, the battle cruiser in the center, the heavy cruisers space around, above, and below it, and the light cruisers and destroyers making up the outer portion of the sphere. She gazed at the image, thinking that before the war that "small" task force would've represented a substantial fraction of the entire Alliance fleet.

The jump point they'd arrived at was a good four light hours from the star Kairos. The sole inhabited world in this star system orbited about three and half light hours from here. No enemy forces were near the jump point, but Magoro saw a Syndic flotilla only a light hour distant. It seemed to be about the size of the Alliance force.

It'd be an hour before the Syndicate forces saw the arrival of the attacking warships, but the Alliance task force wasn't going to wait for that. Magoro felt the force of *Ishigaki's* main propulsion cut in as it and the other Alliance ships accelerated toward an intercept with the enemy formation.

DAMN. Damn. Damn.

At point one light it had taken more than half a day to cover the distance between the opposing forces, the Syndics only accelerating in the last hour before contact.

Magoro wasn't an officer, wasn't trained in the skills of fighting in a three dimensional battlefield with no limits, no up or down, and distances so immense that light itself, and messages sent at the speed of light, took seconds, minutes, and even hours to bridge the gap.

But she'd seen a few battles since Grendel, and as the two forces closed to engage this one had felt wrong. Clumsy. Unimaginative. She couldn't have said why, but maybe it was just because the admiral in charge of the Alliance force was charging straight in without trying any fancy maneuvers. How much experience did that admiral have? Six years ago, today's admiral could have been a lieutenant. If that.

The first pass had been a brutal exchange of fire that rocked *Ishigaki*. Magoro monitored the performance of the starboard hell lance batteries as they hurled streams of charged particles during those moments when enemy ships were close enough to target. The second pass was better as the enemy concentrated fire on other Alliance warships, and *Ishigaki*'s own fire helped knock out a Syndic cruiser. Unfortunately, two Alliance heavy cruisers had been taken out, one of the light cruisers had exploded, and six destroyers were gone. The Syndics hadn't been hurt as badly, but at least the Alliance battle cruiser was still in decent shape.

On the third pass, *Ishigaki* took two enemy missiles followed immediately by a barrage of hell lances and grapeshot. The heavy cruiser's shields collapsed, the enemy fire lashing the hull. Hell lances punched holes through everything in their way, while the solid metal ball bearings that made up grapeshot either tore their own holes or gave up their energy in flashes of heat that shattered anything they hit.

Two enemy hell lance shots went through the compartment that Magoro was in. She didn't see them, only the holes bigger than her fist that suddenly appeared on the outer hull, on the casings of one of *Ishigaki*'s hell lance batteries, and on the inner bulkhead and deck as the enemy particle beams tore through anything in their path.

Which also included two of the gun crew. One of them didn't move, a large hole completely through one side of his chest, his body lax in death. The other stared at the thin strip still holding her upper arm to her body, the rest of that part of the arm gone.

As atmosphere rushed out of the ship, Magoro slapped an

auto-tourniquet on the sailor's arm above the injury, the device latching on, slicing cleanly through her survival suit and the arm beneath to seal off the wound. Magoro punched the first aid controls on the sailor's suit to have it slam sedative and anti-shock drugs into her. "Bandera, take her to sick bay."

The remaining member of the gun crew stared at her. "Chief? But…but…the guns."

"They took hits. They're off line. I'll see if they can be repaired. Get 'Ski to the sick bay so they can save her and then get back here."

"Yes, Chief."

Magoro glanced at the status of the other starboard hell lance batteries, shocked to see that all of them were out of action. "I need status reports on batteries Two Alpha and Two Charlie!" she called over the internal comm circuit for the guns.

"This is Richards in Two Alpha," a quavering voice answered her. "Both of our guns are gone."

"Gone doesn't tell me status, Richards! How much damage did the guns take?"

"They're *gone*, Chief! Grapeshot blew open this part of the hull and tore off half the deck in here, along with most of both guns. We found ourselves staring into space on the edge of what was left!"

"Ancestors save us. Two Charlie, what's your status? Two Charlie!" No reply. That lack of response served as an ugly answer to what kind of damage Two Charlie had probably sustained. "Richards, can you get back here to help me at Two Bravo?"

"We'll try, Chief. There's a lot of damage between us and you."

"Get out of that compartment and try to get to another battery on the starboard side if you can't reach this one," Magoro ordered. She wondered why she was able to handle all this without panicking at the amount of damage *Ishigaki* had sustained and the number of sailors who'd already been killed and wounded, realizing that it was just experience working, her mind automatically doing the things it had trained to do over and over again.

She finally checked the hell lances in this battery, yanking open access panels to see sections that she couldn't get outside readings on. Both guns were down hard, probably unrepairable in the time available. "Ensign Rodriguez, we've lost all hell lances on this side of the ship."

Rodriquez's reply sounded breathless. Almost overwhelmed. "Very…very well. Chief, they're coming in for another run at us. The ship's lost maneuvering control. I think—"

Ishigaki jolted as if dozens of hammers had slammed into her in a discordant salvo. Magoro grabbed onto the nearest grip to hold herself steady. "Ma'am? Ensign Rodriguez? Anybody on this circuit?"

Silence.

She fought a rising sense of fear, wondering how badly the cruiser had been hurt.

Where was Bandera? Had he made it to sick bay with 'Ski? Was he blocked by damage from getting back here?

She tried checking the status of the grapeshot launchers, but the links were down.

Ishigaki jerked again as something hit her hard.

Magoro closed her eyes, trying to control her breathing, remembering the near-panic when the crew had abandoned *Merlon*. They'd never taken abandon ship drills seriously in the pre-war fleet. Why would they ever have to abandon ship? The memory of fighting her way through the damaged ship, trying to find an undamaged escape pod, had haunted her ever since.

I think you can be a good gunners mate.

Who'd said that?

Commander Geary, pronouncing sentence on her, or rather showing mercy when she had no reason to expect any.

All right. Maybe she could handle this.

Diana Magoro opened her eyes and tried to find out the status of the rest of the ship, but most of those links were dead as well. She couldn't feel any thrusters firing, though, or the main propulsion cutting in. The only good thing was that the power supply running into this compartment to feed the hell lances was still up. The power core must be okay, so *Ishigaki* wasn't close to blowing up.

She tried checking fire control to find out what was happening outside the ship, but fire control was completely down. What else might work? Magoro went to a comm panel on the bulkhead and cycled through anything that was still working on basic systems. Not much. Wait. Navigation. That'd give her a view of the outside.

The other surviving Alliance and Syndic ships were tangling a few light seconds away where the battle had drifted since *Ishigaki* was knocked out. But one Syndic had broken free of that fight and was swooping up toward an intercept with the helplessly drifting *Ishigaki*. A light cruiser. No, one of the Syndic hybrids, an assault cruiser, loaded with extra special forces troops. No wonder it was heading for *Ishigaki*. They'd seen that the heavy cruiser was helpless and meant to board this ship to see what intelligence they could gather.

I heard the Syndics aren't always taking prisoners anymore.

Diana Magoro bent her head so the helmet of her survival suit rested against the bulkhead. She could feel vibrations and jars through the contact, the movements of equipment and sailors aboard *Ishigaki*. This ship, *her* ship, wasn't dead yet. But *Ishigaki* was in serious trouble.

"All hands draw weapons and stand by to repel boarders! I say again, all hands..." The announcement trailed off as the comm circuit failed.

Magoro tried to yank open the hatch and found it was jammed. One of the last enemy blows that had hit *Ishigaki* had damaged this part of her hull enough to seal this hatch until someone could cut it open.

She couldn't get to where she needed to be to repel boarders and she was stuck here with a useless hell lance battery. She glared at one of the holes in the hull that gave a view of space, wondering if she'd be able to see that Syndic cruiser on its approach, watching helplessly.

Wait a minute.

Magoro tapped the navigation menu again, getting a zoom of the projected approach of the Syndic warship. If that cruiser meant to board, and it was coming along that vector, it'd come in...here. She would see the enemy ship as it made its final approach, coming very close to *Ishigaki*, their vectors matched, so the enemy troops could board.

She looked at the hell lance projectors.

No.

Crazy.

They were knocked out. Impossible to fix in the time she had even if the spares had been right here.

Could she fire them anyway?

One of the big advantages of really knowing how something worked, what all the parts did and why, meant it was sometimes possible to figure out how to make it do things even without some of those parts. And Diana Magoro had been working on hell lances for ten years.

She started ripping open any access panels that were still closed, checking damage to the hell lances. Yeah. Number one's power regulator was gone, and the backup regulator had failed, which meant number two couldn't fire either since they drew on a common power storage. There was other damage, but that was the main thing. That and there was no way to aim them with fire control dead.

But the *Ishigaki* still had power. If she could power up the hell lances in time...

She'd die. The incoming Syndic warship would detect this hell lance battery powering up. They'd target it, and this little piece of *Ishigaki* would become a little piece of hell. Diana Magoro shook her head, knowing that she'd never have time to get a shot off.

Unless...

Containment would fail if it tried to hold energy pumped into it too quickly. But what if she didn't try to hold the energy? What if she overrode safety and control settings on the hell lances so they'd fire as soon as containment registered enough energy for a shot? There'd be a tiny delay in which containment had to hold. But maybe tiny enough to hold.

Normally, that sort of thing wouldn't make sense. Hell lances had to be prepped to fire during the vanishingly short moments when the enemy got within range. They had to hold a charge until that moment came. But this time she'd be looking at a ship coming in close. She could fire the moment she had power up.

If she was wrong, either the Syndics would target this battery and kill her, or the hell lances would explode and kill her. There didn't seem to be a *this didn't work so I'll try something else* option.

But if she could make this happen...

How fast can I power up a hell lance? Maybe I'll set a record that no other gunner can ever beat.

She tried comms to the bridge or the weapons officer or fire control again, but they were all still out.

This was her decision.

Oh, hell, why not? If she was going to die along with what remained of *Ishigaki*'s crew, why not go down trying to get in one last shot?

The power distribution panel was half gone. She ran physical links between gaps, turning a sophisticated piece of control equipment into a web of hard-wired connections. One big span stymied her for a moment, until she jammed a heavy metal tool into the gap, spot welding it into place. Electricians tended to joke that any piece of solid metal was a gunners mate's circuit breaker, but even they probably never expected someone to do this.

She checked the circuits, and found power blocked. The power regulator on number two couldn't talk to the power regulator on number one, because there was a hole where that had once been, so it was blocking power. She tried disabling, by-passing, or powering down the power regulator on number two, but the designers had been fiendishly clever when it came to this safety feature. Nothing worked.

An electrical tech or a code monkey couldn't have solved the problem. But she was a gunners mate. Magoro picked up her heaviest tool and slammed it repeatedly into the number two power regulator.

Sparks and pieces flew.

The regulator powered off.

She worked as fast as she could to reroute everything, bypassing the sophisticated controls and regulators that still existed and would never let the weapons work under these circumstances. She hard-wired power bridges and couplings so they'd keep working long after they should've tripped. The aiming systems were out, too, so Magoro hastily cut out the control circuits, replacing them with a simple switch which when triggered would slowly pivot the aim of the hell lances. By the time Magoro stood back, breathing heavily from exertion, the hell lances had been turned into manually controlled particle beam projectors.

She had two switches. One to aim the hell lances, and another that when pressed would let power flow all out into the energy containment unit. With the firing commands shorted out and the discharge set to automatic, the hell lances should fire the moment enough energy registered in the containment unit.

Should.

Her work done, Diana Magoro leaned against the nearest bulkhead, unhappy that she had time to think.

Why was she doing this? Wouldn't it make a lot more sense to try to cut that hatch open and join the rest of the crew to repel boarders?

Not that they'd have much chance against Syndic special forces in the numbers that light cruiser would be carrying.

This wasn't about heroism. No way. She wasn't a hero. Despite the chief's uniform she was a screw up. She knew it. And it wasn't about the honor of the fleet. It wasn't about her being some shining example of a sailor. That was the sort of thing a guy like Commander Geary would've worried about.

Commander Geary. Maybe it was just about repaying a favor. A second chance that a young sailor hadn't deserved. *I still owe you one, Captain. Now I can finally pay you back.*

But maybe also it was just because she was a gunners mate. *If I'm going to die, I'm going to go out trying to make a gun do something it shouldn't, just to see what happens. I'm going to set a record, or I'm gonna die. Because I'm a damned gunners mate and these are my guns.*

Holding one switch in each hand, Magoro went to one of the holes in the hull and stared out, looking for the spot of light among the stars that would mark the main propulsion of the Syndic light cruiser that was braking to match the vector of the *Ishigaki*.

So many stars. She stared out at them. Even though she'd spent years in space, like many sailors she didn't spend much time actually looking at space. If a ship wasn't near a planet, all there was to see were countless stars blazing against infinity. And after a while even countless stars blazing against infinity got to be a familiar, everyday view.

Humans had laboriously colonized the nearest stars, then burst out of the region near Earth when the jump drives were invented. Hundreds of star systems now had humans living there, some of them on welcoming, fertile worlds that hosted many millions of people, and others on too cold or too hot airless hellholes that might have only a few thousand inhabitants offering essential services to passing shipping.

But it was all still just the tiniest of a tiny portion of even this galaxy. Against the scale of the universe, did it even count at all? Diana Magoro stared at the immensity, wondering why even in the midst of innumerable stars and a universe with no limits humans had still found reasons for war.

Limits. That was the war was about, wasn't it? Because one thing people like the rulers of the Syndicate Worlds could limit was human freedom. The universe might go on endlessly, but people could be corralled, forced to live as others demanded. The Alliance, she'd been told, had been founded to ensure its member star systems could protect each other from such a fate. The Syndicate Worlds, though, had been founded by people who didn't like governments putting limits on them but thought they had the right to control others. Maybe this war with the Syndics had been inevitable, bound to happen sooner or later.

Her eyes fastened on an object among the stars, pulling her

mind out of its exhausted reverie. There. Below and to her left. It was getting brighter, but it didn't appear to be moving. Why not?

It wasn't until the Syndic ship was close enough for her to see its lean, deadly shape illuminated by the blast of its main propulsion that Magoro realized the enemy warship didn't seem to be moving because it was coming straight at the *Ishigaki* on a perfect intercept. This close, she could see the ship getting bigger, though.

She twisted the aiming switch, bringing the aim of the hell lances a little lower to where the Syndic ship should end up.

She was aiming manually. Crazy. A chief should know better.

The enemy light cruiser loomed closer and closer, thrusters firing on it now, coming in slower and slower as it prepared to perfectly match vectors with *Ishigaki*, right next to the stricken Alliance cruiser so that the enemy boarders could leap across the small remaining gap between the two warships. The enemy, facing a part of the Alliance heavy cruiser with no working weapons powered up, would be powering down their shields that would normally help block enemy fire so those shields wouldn't hinder the attack force from reaching the *Ishigaki*. A real close target, with its shields down. If Magoro's hell lances fired, each one would punch all the way through that enemy ship and out the other side, going through everything in the way.

How long did she dare wait? Even if this worked, how many shots could she get off before the hell lances overheated?

The light cruiser was maybe half a kilometer away, barely moving relative to the *Ishigaki*. She waited, trying to judge when it was close to a quarter kilometer away and almost completely stopped. Hatches began opening on the Syndic warship to let the boarders jump across the remaining gap. She couldn't afford to wait any longer.

Breathing a prayer to her ancestors, Diana Magoro pressed down hard on first the power switch and then the aiming switch.

She heard a shriek from the containment system transmitted through the soles of the boots on her survival suit as components protested the immense surge of energy hitting all at once, followed immediately by the shudder of the hell lances unleashing their invisible bolts. To her own amazement, she was still alive and the hell lances were firing. The shrieks kept coming, the shudders following in a nearly continuous series of pulses, the hell lances slowly pivoting their aim aft to walk their shots down the side of the enemy ship.

Bright light flared within the compartment and the weapons stopped firing and moving. Magoro looked into open access panels on the nearest hell lance to see that several power couplings had completely melted. The farther off hell lance seemed to be imploding as its innards shrank and slagged under heat that caused the weapon to visibly glow.

The side of her survival suit facing the hell lances felt really hot. She'd have some burns under there.

Realizing that she wasn't dead, Magoro looked out the hole in the hull again. The hatches on the enemy warship had frozen only partly open, no sign of motion around them, and its thrusters had stopped firing. The Syndic cruiser seemed to still be very slowly coming closer. Would it collide with *Ishigaki*?

Something blew up aboard the enemy ship, a bit aft of amidships and down toward the keel. The explosion jolted the Syndic cruiser, pitching it upwards and starting a slow pivot of stern over bow as it began drifting over the *Ishigaki*.

She watched the enemy warship ponderously spin until it vanished from her view.

"HEY, Chief."

Diana Magoro looked up from where she was sitting against a

bulkhead. She was still in the damaged hell lance compartment. Somebody must have forced the hatch open. How much time had passed? Who was this talking to her?

She recognized the voice and tried to get to her feet, but found it hard to move her arms or legs. "Captain. I'm sorry."

"At ease." Commander Weiss looked about him. "What'd you do? We were waiting for the boarding party to hit us when this battery lit off and laced shots down the side of that Syndic. He's still drifting with no maneuvering control."

"I broke a few rules," she admitted. "To get the hell lances to fire."

"How'd you aim your shots?"

"I looked through those holes in the hull."

"Ancestors save us." Weiss held out a hand. "Are you hurt? Can you stand? The side of your suit looks scorched."

"There was a lot of heat in here for a little while. But I'm not hurt much, sir. Just…having a little trouble."

"I imagine," he said, helping her get up. "What exactly did you do that enabled you to fire those hell lances?"

Magoro looked at the half-melted remains of the hell lance battery. "Captain, if you want me to be honest, you don't want to know."

"The fleet will want to know. It could be really useful."

"No, sir, I really don't think so. I don't think the fleet is going to want anyone knowing what I did and how to do it, because it was crazy, and it broke every rule, and by all rights those hell lances should've blown me to hell instead of hitting that Syndic."

"I see." He surprised her with a short laugh. "You still can't follow the rules, huh, Chief?"

"I broke them for the right reason this time, sir." She paused. "Sir? Can I ask you something I've been wondering for the last six years?"

"I think you've earned the right to a question," Weiss said.

"Back on the *Merlon*, I know you couldn't say if you disagreed with what the captain did. But did you agree with Commander Decala that I should've been court-martialed? Or with Commander Geary that I ought to have another chance?"

Commander Weiss didn't answer for a moment. "If you want the truth, I agreed with Decala. I didn't think you were salvageable. I did think getting you out of the fleet and in particular out of my gunnery division would make my life a lot easier. And it would've, right? My life would've been a little easier without you around, for a couple of months until the fight at Grendel, after which we went our separate ways."

"Okay," Magoro said. "I can understand that."

"I'm not done, Chief. If you'd been gone from the fleet in disgrace, forbidden from serving again because of a court-martial conviction, then today I probably would've died at the hands of that Syndic boarding party. So you know what? I was wrong. Commander Decala was wrong. Commander Geary was right."

Diana Magoro reached to wipe her eyes, her hand instead hitting the face plate of her survival suit. "That's, um, good to know."

"Can you function, Chief? You're acting Gunnery Officer now, and I need you on the job."

Magoro nodded. "I'm okay. What happened to Ensign Rodriguez, sir?"

"Dead. She was at hell lance battery One Alpha when some grapeshot hit it and vaporized most of the compartment. No survivors from the gun crew."

"Damn." She could see the eager, young faces of the sailors who'd died in that compartment. Faces she wouldn't see again in this life. Magoro looked about her, feeling stiff and old. "I need to burn a candle for their spirits as soon as I can, to let them know we won. And I guess I need to burn one for Commander Geary's spirit, too." No way would she call him Black Jack. He wouldn't have wanted that.

"You and me both," Commander Weiss said. "Commander Geary's decisions at Grendel saved us then, and his decision about you saved us both today. I guess he's still with us. I hope his spirit welcomes-" Commander Weiss's voice choked off. "We lost a lot of people, Chief."

"I know," Magoro said, thinking about the losses the gunnery division alone had sustained. "You gonna be all right, sir?"

"Yeah. You?"

"I guess. It's what the captain would want, for us to keep going."

"Then get going. And thanks, Chief."

"Yes, sir." She went to the hatch, only to encounter Bandera struggling through the damaged passageway beyond. One of his arms was fastened against his side by a quickcast. "What happened?"

"I got 'Ski to sick bay, Chief," Bandera said. "But just as I left we got hit near there and my arm got banged up so they gave me a temporary fix. It took me a while to sneak out and get through all the mess back to here."

"Sneak out? Why didn't you stay in sick bay?"

"Because you told me to get back here, Chief." He looked past her at the slumped wreckage of the hell lances and even through his face shield Magoro could see his eyes widen. "What the hell happened here, Chief?"

"I did something I told you never to do."

"Then why'd you do it?"

"Because I knew what I was doing." She stepped out into the passageway, beckoning to Bandera. "Come on. We need to see how many guns we can get working again. This war ain't over yet."

Bandera hesitated. "Chief, did we win the battle?"

"Yeah, we won the battle." Victory felt a little too much like defeat at the moment, but she couldn't confess that to the sailors looking to her for leadership. "Someday we'll win the war."

"How, Chief? How are we gonna win?"

"We've got better gunners." She led Bandera aft to find out what had happened to some of the other gun crews.

She'd finally proven Commander Geary right.

But instead of thinking about that, Diana Magoro was wondering if she'd ever forget the sight of all of those stars while she waited to spot the approaching enemy ship.

FLECHE

SOMETHING slammed into the Alliance light cruiser *Fleche*, jerking the warship's mass down and to one side. That brought a bulkhead swinging around to batter Lieutenant Tanya Desjani as she tried to make her way to the bridge.

Tanya bounced off the opposite bulkhead, momentary dizziness from the blow made worse by the way the passageway she was in rotated and wobbled as *Fleche* moved in the same uncontrolled fashion. The survival suit she wore had minimal armor and minimal padding, but it had kept her alive as repeated hits had torn the hull of *Fleche*, venting the ship's atmosphere into cold, empty space.

The lights flickered twice, then went out, replaced by the scattered radiance of emergency lighting running off batteries. Gravity had gone out, too. Something had happened to the power core. Not an overload. That would have produced a moment of intense heat and light in which both cruiser and Tanya would have been vaporized. But a shut down power core meant the ship was now totally helpless. If *Fleche* wasn't already dead, she soon would be.

The same was likely true of every member of her crew.

Tanya jerked in involuntary fright as the nearest body to her, lacking a left arm and shoulder and clearly dead, suddenly twitched into motion not related to the light cruiser's tumble.

"Lieutenant Desjani." *Fleche's* executive officer finished pushing aside the dead and hung for a moment before Tanya. She couldn't see his features through the survival suit's face shield, but he sounded oddly abrupt, his words coming out in brief bursts. "Weapons officer. Status."

Tanya swallowed on a raw throat before she could speak. "Weapons central control completely off line. No weapons left. All hell lances out. All grapeshot projectors destroyed. We expended the last missile half an hour ago. Weapons crews have suffered serious casualties." She felt her voice cracking and fought to hold on to her self-control as *Fleche* lurched from several more hits. Another Syndic warship must have made a firing run on this wreck which was still technically a light cruiser of the Alliance fleet. "Internal comms are out and all of the wreckage in the passageways is interfering with my suit comms, so I was heading for the bridge to get orders."

She would never know what the executive officer's response might have been. Tanya suddenly realized that, during the last Syndic barrage, matching holes the size of her fist had appeared in a star-shaped pattern around her and the exec, one set high up on one side of the passageway where Syndic hell lances had torn through Fleche's light armor and another set down near the deck on the other side where the particle beams had kept going through what were for them minor obstacles.

One of those pairs of holes bracketed the exec. He had jerked slightly as a hell lance instantly bored a hole through his torso from shoulder to opposite hip, a movement she hadn't understood at the time but did now as the body of the exec drifted lifelessly to bump into that of the dead sailor he had earlier shoved aside.

Feeling panic threaten, Tanya closed her eyes and strove to fight down fear and confusion. Promotions came fast in a fleet suffering brutal casualties. Less than two years ago she had been an ensign, quickly trained and naïve. The experience she had gained since then had not included anything this bad. *But I can do this. Black Jack faced this same situation when he fought his ship to the last at Grendel. He did his duty. We're all supposed to follow his example, to be like Black Jack when he stopped the first Syndic attack on the Alliance. He's been everyone's hero since then. I have to be like him now.* That helped. Every Alliance sailor was urged to be like Black Jack, who legend said wasn't dead and who would return some day to save the Alliance. He wasn't here now, though, and while she couldn't be Black Jack, she could do her job. *The bridge. I need to get to the bridge. The captain will give me orders, will tell me what to do when there doesn't seem to be anything anyone can do.*

Her mind steady, Tanya shoved off, pushing aside wreckage and bodies blocking her path until the hatch to the bridge loomed before her.

The bridge was located deep within the ship, as well protected as any compartment could be, but that did not mean much when a light cruiser was being pounded into scrap by heavier units. Tanya paused to gaze at the mess here, made up of drifting debris and torn portions of bodies. "Captain?"

A figure pulled himself over to her. "Lieutenant Desjani? I'm Master Chief Milam, from engineering. The captain's dead."

Her mind whirled in counterpoint to the wild motion of the ship, but Tanya gripped a railing with one hand and brought her senses back to stability by force of will. "Who's in command?"

"The executive officer. Before the captain died, the exec went out to—"

"No. He's dead, too. I saw it happen."

"Dead?" Master Chief Milam pointed at her. "Then you are in command, Lieutenant. I don't know of any other officer left alive."

In command. Of a light cruiser whose remaining existence might be measured in seconds. What should she do? Take charge. "What's our status?"

"All comms are out, internal and external. All we've got are survival suit comms and those are patchy. The chief engineer sent me up here to tell the captain that maneuvering controls were completely gone. We can't repair them with what we've got aboard. Most of the main propulsion units are gone, and with the power core down we can't use what's left. Life support, sensors and all other automated systems are out. I don't know about weapons."

"They're all gone, too." Her mind seized on one thing the Master Chief had said. "Why isn't the chief engineer in command?" Absurdly, the primary concern motivating her question was one of precedence and honor, which over decades of war had become of overriding importance among the officers of the fleet. The chief engineer would raise hell if a more junior officer stepped on his prerogatives, no matter how severe the emergency. Even with the ship wrecked and the captain dead, Tanya felt an irrational worry about impugning the honor of a superior officer.

But in reply to her question, Master Chief Milam indicated a sailor nearby. "Petty Officer Deladrier showed up two minutes after I got here to tell me that main engineering had been shot up and half the personnel there killed, including the chief engineer and the assistant engineering officer."

Deladrier nodded, expression unknowable behind his face shield. "We took several volleys. They must have aimed to avoid the power core area and hit the watch teams, but they tore up the power core controls, too. The survivors were trying to shut down the power core when I left to keep it from blowing us all to hell."

The assistant engineering officer dead, too. Her roommate, Lieutenant Mei Singh. *Don't think about her. Not now. Focus on the job. Why did the Syndics target the engineering crew and not the power core itself?* Tanya was doing her best to concentrate on that question when another sailor pushed forward. "Lieutenant, my acting section chief sent me up to see if we're supposed to abandon ship."

If only she had days to think this over, to get a full picture of the situation. "How many escape pods are still working?"

"I…don't know."

Training and experience finally offered a clear course of action for her. "Master Chief Milam, get an inventory of the escape pods. How many haven't been destroyed or disabled? I need to know if abandoning ship is even an option. I also need a muster. How many of the crew are still alive and how many of those are able to function?"

"Lieutenant, we may not have time…" His voice trailing off, Master Chief Milam looked around. "I'm not feeling any more hits. Maybe there's no Syndics coming in on us right now, or maybe they figure we're not worth any more attention."

"Or maybe we won." Tanya swung over to a status panel and swept junk away from it, avoiding looking at what she was pushing away. Only scattered status lights reporting systems failures answered her examination. "Is there anybody here who can get us a look outside?"

A petty officer with one arm cradled in the other kicked herself toward Tanya. "I can try, Lieutenant. We've still got some back-up battery power here. Our sensor systems are shot to hell, but if there's even one set of working back-up circuits I can route through I might be able to link to the fleet net and get a status picture."

"Do it." Was there any fleet left in this star system? Before *Fleche* had been overwhelmed Tanya had watched the status display in her weapons control station showing the Alliance battleships and battle cruisers with this force trading blows and being annihilated as they wiped out the Syndic battleships and battle cruisers opposing them. Were any left? Or had the Syndics triumphed here?

Master Chief Milam had sent runners off to find out the information Tanya had asked for, and now echoed her thoughts. "I hope we won. Otherwise the best we can hope for is getting captured and taken to one of those damned Syndic labor camps for the rest of our lives, however long that is."

He knew as well as she did that the odds heavily favored death instead of capture. Neither the Alliance nor the Syndicate Worlds took captives very often these days. Sometimes she wondered what her ancestors thought of that, but it wasn't as if she could change the ugly patterns that had developed over nearly a hundred years of war between the two main factions of humanity in space. "They may just leave us here to die aboard *Fleche* when our suits give out," Tanya said. "I don't know why they didn't target the power core on that last run."

The petty officer laboring over a status panel gave a gasp of satisfaction. "Here, Lieutenant! I hope it holds, but look fast just in case."

A grainy display had popped into existence above the panel, showing the situation in this star system. Tanya focused desperately, fighting down a gust of despair at how few ships were still active.

There were only two Alliance heavy cruisers left, both badly-damaged and both nearly ten light minutes from Fleche. The rest of the Alliance warships which had entered this star system were gone, blown into fragments either by enemy fire or when their own power cores overloaded. She could list them in her mind. Three battleships, four battle cruisers, five other heavy cruisers and eleven other light cruisers, and twenty-four destroyers. Swarms of escape pods drifted through the vast area of battle. Often a ship died too fast for anyone to escape, but other times many of the crew could get off and hope for rescue if their side won. If the other side won the outcome might only be a quick death when the winners used the losers' escape pods for target practice, or a slower death as life support gave out in pods the winners had not the resources or the motivation to bother recovering.

But the Syndics had taken losses almost as bad. All of their battleships and battle cruisers were gone, too, along with all of their light cruisers and Hunter-Killers. They had three heavy cruisers left, but two of those were in at least as bad a shape as the surviving Alliance heavies. The last Syndic heavy cruiser, though, was nearly untouched. Given the state of the surviving Alliance forces that one ship provided the Syndics with overwhelming superiority.

But it wasn't going for the kill on the two surviving Alliance heavy cruisers. Not yet. The sputtering display showed the operational Syndic heavy cruiser on a curving intercept path ending where it met the staggering path of *Fleche*. Why bother with a firing run on what was obviously a dead ship when those two Alliance heavy cruisers were still threats?

Because it wasn't a firing run. That was the only explanation. "Damn. They didn't destroy us because they want this ship. They tried to kill a lot of the crew but avoid causing a core overload. They can tell we've had to shut down our power core so we can't deliberately overload it and take them with us if they board us."

Master Chief Milam didn't answer for a moment, then looked around meaningfully at the wreckage surrounding them. "Why do they want the ship?"

"They must have a reason. Something they—Ancestors preserve us. Master Chief, they think, or hope, we've got an Alliance hypernet key aboard. If the Syndics could capture one of those it would give them access to the Alliance hypernet."

"We don't have one," Master Chief Milam objected. "But they'll come aboard and kill us all while finding that out, won't they?"

"Yes." Her voice stayed amazingly steady as it pronounced a death sentence on them all. "I need that muster, Chief. I need to know how many sailors on this ship can still fight."

So much needed to be done and yet she could do so little. Suit comms remained erratic except at close range, so Tanya waited, trying to sound and look calm, as runners came to the bridge with reports. "Only four escape pods in working condition, Lieutenant," one said. "There's a fifth that might work, if we're really desperate."

Master Chief Milam looked up from where he was tabulating muster reports. "We've got one hundred and two sailors still able to fight. That includes the lightly wounded. There's another thirty-six too badly injured to move or fight, including Ensign Ybarra. The rest are dead."

Fleche had gone into battle with two hundred thirty five crew aboard. Ninety-seven were dead, nearly as many as were still effective. "May the living stars receive their souls," Tanya muttered. Would they ever receive proper burial, cast into the nearest star? She couldn't worry about that, or about how many of her friends and comrades were dead. What she faced now was a simple math problem. An undamaged escape pod could carry twelve sailors. She could get as many as forty-eight survivors off of this ship, to face an uncertain future as best. Or keep as many able sailors aboard as she could to fight the Syndics.

A simple math problem, involving lives to be subtracted from the universe. *I'm in command. I have to decide.* "Get the badly-wounded into the working escape pods and eject them," Tanya said. "They'll at least have a chance that way. Divide the thirty-six evenly among the four working pods and add one light-ly-wounded sailor in each pod to look after the badly-wounded. All other personnel are to break out small arms and be prepared to repel boarders."

The sailors around her stood, not reacting, as frozen by events as she had almost been earlier. "Were my orders unclear?" Tanya said in a voice that made them all jerk to attention.

"No, Lieutenant," Master Chief Milam said. "Get going!" he told the others.

Only after the runners had scattered to pass on Tanya's orders did Milam speak to her again on a the private command circuit. "What are we going to do, Lieutenant Desjani? We've got less than a hundred effectives left, and whoever comes aboard is probably going to have heavier weapons and a lot more bodies."

"If we're going to die, Master Chief, we might as well go down swinging." She thought she had accepted that. Maybe somewhere deep inside a remnant of sanity was screaming in terror, but everywhere else a dull calm filled her.

"Yeah," he agreed. "Might as well."

"How many do they carry on Syndic heavy cruisers?" Tanya asked him. "It's about three hundred in the crew, right?"

"Roughly. They carry fewer per ship than we do, which is the main reason they can't repair battle damage like we can. But if they've picked up anyone from the other ships the Syndics have lost, they'll have more."

At least three to one odds, then. Maybe worse.

Hopeless. Hopeless.

Tanya realized that she was looking toward the command seat which the captain had occupied. The captain's body was still there, most of it, anyway, surrounded by controls which no longer worked. *We can't save this ship, can't keep the Syndics from taking Fleche. But we can't retreat, even if the Alliance fleet did retreat instead of standing its ground. What does that leave?*

Attack.

"Once they finish with us," she said to Master Chief Milam, "they'll finish off those two heavy cruisers."

He nodded wordlessly in agreement.

"But if we hurt that ship badly enough, our cruisers might have the time to repair enough systems to defend themselves and maybe even take out the remaining Syndics."

He took a moment to reply. "How do we do that? What have we got left?"

She was maybe half his age. Remarkable, really, that Milam had managed to survive this bloody war for this long. And now he was looking to her for orders, while she could turn to no one else to ask what to do. "We've got nothing to lose, Master Chief. That gives us something. What can we do to take out that heavy cruiser?"

"With a hundred sailors out-numbered three to one? We can't take that Syndic ship, Lieutenant, even if we don't care what happens to us. We'd have to seize the bridge and engineering and we'd have to do it fast."

"I know," Tanya said. "Syndic ships have their control compartments inside armored citadels that can be sealed and defended for some time. We'd have to get inside those citadels before they could be sealed."

"And we can't do that. No way. We don't have the firepower or the numbers. The Syndics will seal their citadels and bring their boarding parties back and wipe us out."

"How do we make our deaths count, Master Chief? What *can* we do?"

Master Chief Milam took a long moment to reply. "There's something we could try, as long as we're going to die anyway."

Tanya felt a dull ache inside as she spoke her next words. "Let's hear it."

SHE had known one thing, that the Syndics would aim the majority of their boarding party toward the part of *Fleche* where a hypernet key would be located, and that they would aim their suppressing fire ahead of that boarding party at the areas around those compartments to help knock down any resistance between them and their goal.

She had guessed another thing, from the records she had seen of other Syndic boarding operations. "Since they don't know whether or not our captain is still alive they will send a force toward our bridge to capture the captain for intelligence purposes."

Master Chief Milam nodded. He was packed in next to her, here in the main forward passageway where any Syndic boarding party heading for the bridge of *Fleche* would come. Here where every surviving member of *Fleche's* crew was also packed in, a solid mass of defenders. "If they fire in this area, they'll wipe us out easy, Lieutenant."

"We have to risk it, Master Chief. The launches of the four working escape pods twenty minutes ago might convince them that none of the living crew of Fleche has remained aboard."

"They'll still shoot us up a little more, but if I were them I wouldn't waste time and energy slamming shots through the whole ship," Milam agreed.

"Let's hope we're both right. I doubt there will be time to talk much after we start fighting. Remember your objective, Master Chief."

"I got it, Lieutenant. Just keep them off my back as best you can."

Calm voices. Rational voices. Discussing an insane course of action.

A single sailor who had been posted near the riddled outer hull came back toward them at a rush. "I saw them. They're matching our motion now."

The Syndic heavy cruiser had met their path, had matched their speed, and now was maneuvering to match the tumble of *Fleche* so that boarding parties could easily reach the Alliance light cruiser. How long would it take the Syndics to match movement? It was an article of faith in the Alliance fleet that the Syndics were not equal to Alliance sailors when it came to driving ships, but Tanya knew the Syndics were at least competent, and even if they hadn't been competent then automated systems could do the predictable job of matching movement well enough though without any imagination or special skill.

It felt so strange, waiting here in the dim glow of the emergency lighting, on a ship which was dead in all but name. In Tanya's mind she could see *Fleche* alive, her passageways and compartments filled with men and women Tanya knew, power flowing through her hull, main propulsion hurling her through space, weapons ready to wreak havoc among any targets. But around her was only silence, the light cruiser bereft of any life except that among her surviving crew members.

As Weapons Officer, Tanya had controlled two hell lance batteries and one specter missile launcher. Awesome weapons, really. She had gloried in the damage they could do. Now she grasped tightly a simple slug thrower. An anti-boarding weapon little different from the hand-weapons humans had carried centuries ago. She would have to ensure she was braced whenever she fired it in zero gravity or the recoil would cast her helplessly backward.

The crew members around her held a wide assortment of other hand weapons. Some pulse rifles, but not nearly enough. A lot more slug-throwers. A few sailors carried hand tools, the only weapons available until either friend or enemy died and relinquished their weapons to those who had none. Against soldiers or Marines, wearing full battle armor and carrying heavier weapons, Tanya and her crew wouldn't stand a ghost of a chance. Against Syndic crew members equipped little better than themselves, they might survive long enough to make a difference.

Fleche shuddered as if someone were beating a rhythm on her hull. "Aft of us," Desjani told the others. "They're shooting up the area around the navigation compartments."

A long pause, then *Fleche* shuddered again, this time throughout her length, as if spasmodically attempting to return to life.

"Zombie ship," someone muttered nervously, earning a scattering of edgy laughter.

"Grapples," Master Chief Milam told everyone. "They're going to dampen the motion of this ship so they can send boarding tubes across."

Fleche jerked, fighting the Syndic tethers, but her twisting movements eased, smoothing out.

A close-set series of heavy thuds caused *Fleche* to quiver. "They've attached the boarding tubes," Master Chief Milam said. "My guess is two of them aft of us, but I could feel another one hitting near here. You called it right, Lieutenant. Any minute now."

The passageway flared white with brilliance as Syndic breaching charges dissolved a big square of hull material. Tanya's face shield automatically darkened to protect her vision, then just as swiftly cleared to show figures in suits not too different from her own bursting out of the breach.

"Fire!" she yelled, pulling the trigger on her slug thrower and feeling it jam her backwards against those with her.

The Syndics boarding the light cruiser here had expected to meet some defenders. They had not expected to meet a solid plug of defenders, all firing down the passageway at those storming aboard.

The first wave of boarders died under that concentrated storm of fire, the Alliance volley going onward to tear into those behind them.

"Go!" Tanya cried again, a wild elation swamping her fear as the mass of Alliance sailors surged forward. "Go! Go! Go!"

She had meant to lead the charge, as she had been told an officer should, but as the welter of bodies stampeded forward Tanya found herself falling behind the leaders, those in front firing wildly as they swamped the rest of the Syndics boarding here. Some Alliance sailors fell, but not enough to slow the charge. Then the counter-attack was in the three meter wide tube the Syndics had attached to the *Fleche* at this point and was rushing onward toward the opening at the other end.

As it turned out, not being one of the first sailors to reach the Syndic ship saved Tanya's life.

Syndic standard procedure called for sentries to be posted at the entrances to their own ship offered by boarding tubes, and if the Syndics could do nothing else they excelled at following standard procedures. Surprised and off-balance as the counter-attack hit them, the sentries nonetheless held their ground, firing at and killing the Alliance sailors in the front of the charge. The Syndics kept shooting until literally overrun and wiped out by the Alliance sailors.

Tanya slumped against a bulkhead inside the Syndic heavy cruiser, gasping for breath and staring at the dead sailors from both sides. On this living ship she had gravity under her feet again, something which helped steady her emotionally as well as physically. "We have to keep moving. We need to hit them while they're still reacting to our attack so we can take as many of them with us as we can. Master Chief, good luck."

Milam paused to bring the fingertips of one hand to his brow, and she realized he had saluted her, a gesture almost lost to the fleet though still followed by the Marines. She awkwardly returned the mark of respect, but Master Chief Milam was already racing out of the compartment with about half of the surviving Alliance sailors in his wake.

They could not take this ship, but enough Alliance sailors heading for engineering might be able to get access to the heavy cruiser's power core, might be able to damage it, before the Syndics could stop them by bringing the boarding parties back from *Fleche* to reinforce the Syndic defenders of this heavy cruiser.

That required a two-pronged assault. Milam was leading half the Alliance counter-attack toward the power core where he had the knowledge to do the most damage in the shortest time, while Desjani would lead the rest of the sailors to block as much as possible the return of the Syndic boarding parties, protecting Master Chief Milam's flank and rear. The odds of success were impossibly long, but trying it beat dying without attempting anything.

Or so it had seemed amid the wreckage of *Fleche*. Now, as Tanya looked at those remaining with her, many clutching weapons taken from dead Syndics, she had to struggle to keep her fears from overwhelming her.

She told off a dozen sailors to hold this position. Names and faces Tanya knew. "Good luck," she said, knowing how meaningless the words were since the dozen would all soon be killed here. "Hold off the Syndics as long as you can when they try to reboard their own ship."

"We'll die with honor," a petty officer said in a tight voice, hands gripping a captured Syndic pulse rifle.

"You will." Not knowing what else to say, Tanya turned to the rest of her sailors, their numbers much diminished by those who had gone with the Master Chief and the twelve who would stay at this spot.

"Let's go," she managed to get out through a ragged throat, then led her group along the inside of the heavy cruiser near the outer hull. "Set your survival suit guidance displays to project the deck plans for a Syndic heavy cruiser. If you get separated from me and the others, keep heading aft toward where the next boarding tube is most likely to be."

She was in the lead this time, through a series of hatches and short passageways alongside the outer hull of the Syndic warship, some of her sailors peeling off to take slightly different routes.

The sentries guarding the next boarding tube over were startled to be hit by attackers coming from the side, above and below. But one of the Syndic boarding parties was already coming back in response to alarms from their ship, arriving seconds after the Alliance sailors, and the compartment rapidly clogged with bodies locked together as they fired point-blank at each other. Tanya found herself jammed next to a Syndic officer who was twisting to fire on her. Tanya fired first, her hasty shot clipping the front of the Syndic's face shield and shattering it.

For a moment, a bare instant, Tanya looked directly into the eyes of the Syndic woman. Eyes very much like her own, eyes reflecting confusion and determination and fear, eyes changing in that instant to fill with dread as the Syndic's mind grasped that she would surely die in the next second.

Tanya's weapon had automatically chambered another round. As she stared into the Syndic woman's eyes her finger twitched spasmodically on the trigger, the impact of the shot hurling the woman away from Tanya.

She became aware that the fighting had stopped and looked around. All of the Syndics were down. "How many do we have left? I see...eight?"

"Nine, Lieutenant," someone gasped. "And you."

They would never take another boarding tube with those few. How many tubes were left? One? Two? The Syndic boarding parties must be storming back aboard everywhere else, aiming to intercept Master Chief Milam's group as well as sweep up Tanya and her remaining sailors.

"Lieutenant!" The tone of voice was urgent but the volume over the suit comms was weak. "This is Cahalan at the first tube! They're hitting us! We're—"

Tanya waited a few seconds, then called back. "Petty Officer Cahalan. Reply. Petty Officer Cahalan."

Nothing. The small force left to hold the first Syndic boarding tube had died holding their ground.

She was trying to decide where she and the sailors still with her should die when her suit's comm circuit lit off again. "Lieutenant?" The voice was even weaker than Cahalan's had been, riddled with digital static, but recognizable.

"Master Chief Milam? Where are you?"

"We made it to the power core. Six of us."

She fought back tears. *Ancestors forgive me. Only sixteen left, and none of us for long.*

"Lieutenant," Milam was continuing, "I have enough time here to manage a partial core collapse. I'm setting it up as I talk to you. I have to override remote signals from the Syndics and local safeguards, which I can't do well enough to achieve a core overload. A partial power core collapse won't destroy this Syndic ship, but hopefully it will blow out the aft end."

"Do it and get back here!" If the Master Chief could get to this compartment before the core collapse, if they could fight their way back to *Fleche*—

"Can't do it, Lieutenant. Not a chance we'll make it out of here alive. Even if the Syndics weren't on top of us we'd have to stay to hold down the overrides and cause the collapse. This was always a one-way mission. We knew that. But the Syndics coming for us will catch the collapse, too. They'll make a nice honor guard for me when I meet my ancestors, huh?"

She couldn't say anything, could only stare sightlessly ahead. *I knew he wouldn't get out. I knew none of us would get out. But I didn't realize he would have to stand there physically holding down safety overrides until the core collapse killed him.* "Master Chief… may the living stars welcome you with every honor."

"You, too, Lieutenant. You did damned good. You've done all you can. Get back to *Fleche*. There's a chance she'll still be intact after we blow out this core. Maybe some of you will make it after all. If you do, please let my family know I died with honor."

"I will." From somewhere an odd thought emerged. "If you see Black Jack, tell him to get his ass back here. We need him."

"I'll do that. Goodbye, Lieutenant. They're knocking hard on the hatch and I'm setting the final collapse sequence. You got maybe one minute."

She wasted a couple of seconds of that minute pulling herself out of shock, then glared at her remaining sailors. "Back to *Fleche*! As fast as you can move!"

Gravity vanished again as they jumped into the Syndic boarding tube to return to *Fleche*. She had to fight down an irrational sense of abandoning Master Chief Milam and those with him. Staying, fighting, would make no difference at all. But still she felt sick at leaving him and the others behind, and repeatedly reached to check her motion. Each time, Tanya fought back the impulse. *Save the ones with me. Maybe I can still do that.*

Were there any Syndics still on the Alliance light cruiser's remains? They had surely had time to learn there was no hypernet key aboard. There would have been no reason for any Syndics to stay, and doubtless frantic orders to get back to their own ship to deal with the crazy Alliance counter-attack. But that was no guarantee no Syndics were waiting for them. Tanya held her weapon in a death grip as she shot out of the boarding tube back onto *Fleche* and looked around frantically for danger. Only wreckage and drifting bodies were visible. "To the far side of the ship! Away from the Syndic ship! Move!"

They were still going in that direction when a huge fist slugged the wreck that had been *Fleche*, hurling the light cruiser's broken carcass away from the Syndic heavy cruiser, breaking loose the boarding tubes, and bashing Tanya and the sailors with her against surfaces that had suddenly accelerated toward them.

One of those surfaces crashed into Tanya's survival suit helmet. She had an instant to wonder if she would see the light of the living stars beckoning to her through the dark as blackness filled her mind.

"LIEUTENANT Desjani?"

Tanya jerked into wakefulness, startled to see above her the tangled mass of conduits and cables that marked the overhead on an Alliance warship.

She looked over, seeing a chief with a physician's insignia on her breast. Tanya didn't recognize the chief, but from her surroundings Tanya was in a bunk in a crowded sick bay. The chief checked some read-outs, nodded and turned to speak to someone else. "She'll be fine."

A man wearing commander's insignia came into Tanya's field of vision. He extended a hand toward her, smiling. "Lieutenant Tanya Desjani. I'm captain of the *Hauberk*. May I shake your hand?"

"What?" Tanya tried to unravel her tangled thoughts. *Hauberk* had been one of the surviving heavy cruisers. "What happened?"

"What happened was that you took out that last operational Syndic heavy cruiser. Blew her butt off and left her helpless. After that, *Hauberk* and *Utap* had the time to get enough systems fixed for us to move in and wipe out the two Syndic ships disabled during the battle and what was left of the heavy cruiser you crippled. Thanks to *you*, Lieutenant."

"Me?" She had automatically extended her hand and the captain of *Hauberk* now pumped it enthusiastically.

"You. By my ancestors! Attacking under those circumstances! Black Jack himself must have been by your side."

"I didn't see him," Tanya said without thinking.

"Of course you didn't, Lieutenant Desjani, it was his spirit that was with you. I'm putting you in for the Alliance Fleet Cross. You deserve it if anyone ever did. If there was a higher award I'd put you in for that. You avenged *Fleche*, you saved *Hauberk* and *Utap*, and you enabled the Alliance to hold onto this star system. Of course, you also saved the rest of your crew. After we finished off the Syndics we checked the hulk of *Fleche* to see if anyone was still alive aboard her and brought you and the other nine off."

Nine. Out of two hundred thirty five. "Master Chief Milam—"

"He'll be put in for the Fleet Cross, too. The others from *Fleche* told us what happened, what the master chief did, what *you* did." *Hauberk's* captain grinned. "Black Jack himself couldn't have done better. Your ancestors must be very proud."

He shook her hand again and left, saying he had a lot of repair work and wounded crew members to check on. Tanya laid back, her eyes on the overhead, trying to feel something. Pride, relief, surprise. Anything. A darkness still seemed to fill her, a darkness in which familiar faces now never to be seen again in life appeared briefly before vanishing.

The chief she had seen before came up beside Tanya, slapping a med patch on her arm. "That'll help, Lieutenant."

"I thought you said I was fine."

"Your body is fine. Your head…that's going to take some work."

Feeling finally came. "They died. Everybody died. I was in command and they died."

The chief looked down at Tanya somberly. "From what I understand, they all would have died no matter what. As it was, they saved a lot of other lives with their sacrifice. And they're not all dead. You got nine of them out. And you. That's ten people who should have died, who by all rights should be among their ancestors now, and aren't. Because of you. And the escape pods you launched with your badly-wounded on them. We've been overwhelmed by the casualties. We couldn't save every one and not all of them lived until we managed pick ups of the pods. But sixteen of those will live, too. You know if the Syndics had won here they wouldn't have bothered to save your wounded."

Twenty-six, then. That ought to have helped. It didn't. "How many died here? On all of the ships?"

"I don't know, and if I did I wouldn't tell you. Lieutenant, it's what we do. It's what we have to do. They attacked us, a long time ago. They keep attacking. We have to fight."

"We have to fight," Tanya echoed. "Kill them. Just keep killing them." One vision filled her mind now, the memory of the eyes of the Syndic woman who had looked at Tanya and seen death. Tanya knew she would never forget those eyes. "It's all we can do. Kill them until they stop. Kill them until they stop making us kill them."

"I guess so. I wish there was some other plan, but I don't know of one."

Tanya thought of the captain's words. "We don't need another plan. We need Black Jack. Somebody like him. If he'd only come back…"

"Well…maybe. It's been almost a century now. If he was coming, he ought to have made it by now."

Tanya locked her eyes on those of the chief. "He'll come back. He'll hurt them badly enough that they'll finally give up."

The chief looked down at Tanya. "Wouldn't he try something else? If it's about nothing but killing, that would be like the Syndics, wouldn't it?"

"We're not like them! We're only killing because we have to!" But despite her insistence the chief's words still stung. "What else can we do?"

"I don't know, Lieutenant. I wish to hell I did. Maybe Black Jack will come back someday, maybe he'll know what else we can do. I sure don't. You get some sleep now. You'll get meds, you'll get therapy, and you'll be able to go back to fighting and help end this war."

Grief and despair forced the words from her. "I can't end this war. Maybe no one can end this war."

The chief hesitated, looking uncomfortable. "Maybe not. We do what we can. You did good. A real hero. You saved a lot of Alliance lives. Remember that."

Tanya felt sleep stealing over her as the meds took effect. The eyes of the Syndic woman looked back at her, not seeing a hero, not a saver of lives, but death. *If death is what I must be, I will be that. As long as I have to. Death to the Syndics. Until real heroes like Master Chief Milam don't have to die fighting them anymore. Is there another answer? Ancestors, please beg the living stars to tell us. Tell us if there is something to strive for besides being death.*

She fell into darkness again, this time the shadows of sleep.

Tanya dreamed of Black Jack. She saw him sleeping. She couldn't see his face clearly, but she knew it was him. Instead of basking in the glow of the living stars he lay surrounded by darkness and a sense of cold that struck at Tanya. Despite that, she knew that he was not dead. She yelled at him to wake up, to come back and save them. But Master Chief Milam shook his head at her, gesturing Tanya to be quiet, giving her the fleet hand sign that meant *wait*. She watched Black Jack and Master Chief Milam fade away, watched everything fade into the darkness, and could remember nothing else from her dreams when she finally awoke to once again face the reality of a war to which she could see no end.

ACKNOWLEDGMENTS

Special thanks to Christy Admiraal for all of her work putting this book together, as well as to Lisa Rodgers and Valentina Sainato for their constant support. Thanks also to my agent Joshua Bilmes, Robert Chase, Kelly Dwyer, Carolyn Ives Gilman, J.G. (Huck) Huckenpohler, Simcha Kuritzky, Michael LaViolette, the spirit of Aly Parsons, Bud Sparhawk, Mary Thompson, and Constance A. Warner for their suggestions, comments and recommendations on the various stories.

ABOUT THE AUTHOR

"Jack Campbell" is the pseudonym for John G. Hemry, a retired Naval officer who graduated from the U.S. Naval Academy in Annapolis before serving with the surface fleet and in a variety of other assignments. He is the author of *The Lost Fleet* military science fiction series, as well as the *Beyond the Frontier* continuation of *The Lost Fleet*, spin-off series *The Lost Stars*, the *Stark's War* series, and the *Paul Sinclair/"JAG in Space"* series. His short fiction appears frequently in *Analog* magazine, and many have been collected in the three Jack Campbell ebook anthologies, *Ad Astra*, *Borrowed Time*, and *Swords and Saddles*. He lives with his indomitable wife and three children in Maryland.

FOR NEWS ABOUT JABBERWOCKY BOOKS AND AUTHORS

Sign up for our newsletter*: http://eepurl.com/b84tDz
visit our website: awfulagent.com/ebooks
or follow us on twitter: @awfulagent

THANKS FOR READING!

*We will never sell or give away your email address, nor use it for nefarious purposes.